CLIMBING
THE
GOD
TREE

WINNER OF THE 1997 WILLA CATHER FICTION PRIZE

The Willa Cather Fiction Prize was established in 1991 by
Helicon Nine Editions, and is awarded annually to a
previously unpublished manuscript chosen by a distinguished
writer through an open nationwide competition.

The judge for 1997 was Dawn Raffel.

CLIMBING THE GOD TREE

A NOVEL IN STORIES

JAIMEE WRISTON COLBERT

Winner of the 1997 Willa Cather Fiction Prize

HELICON NINE EDITIONS
KANSAS CITY, MISSOURI

Grateful acknowledgment is made to the editors of the following magazines
and anthologies in which some of these stories first appeared:
New Letters, Potato Eyes, Tampa Review, F Magazine, and *Ohio Short Fiction.*

The author wishes especially to thank Wesley Brown, Shawn Shiflett,
Michael Steinberg, and Maud Warren for hours of editorial and emotional
support during the various incarnations of this book; also Barbara Hope
and the Stonecoast Writers' Conference for the friendships of other writers.

This book is a work of fiction. Although some of the episodes take place in a prison set
in Maine, it is a fictitious prison, in a fictitious Maine town, and is not representative of
the Maine State Prison. In her capacity as an educator the author has worked in several
different prisons, and has formed valued friendships at the Maine State Prison.

Cover photograph and book design: Tim Barnhart

Helicon Nine Editions is funded in part by
the National Endowment for the Arts, a federal agency, and by the
Missouri Arts Council and the Kansas Arts Commission, state agencies.

LIBRARY OF CONGRESS CATALOGING-IN-PUBLICATION DATA

Colbert, Jaimee Wriston
    Climbing the God tree : a novel in 24 stories / Jaimee Wriston Colbert.
1st ed.
    p.   cm.
    "Winner of the 1997 Willa Cather Fiction Prize."
    ISBN 1-884235-25-5 : (on acid-free paper)
    1. Maine--Social life and customs--Fiction. 2. City and town life--Maine--
Fiction 3. Violence--Maine--Fiction. 4. Crime--Maine Fiction.   I. Title.
PS3553.04384C58   1998
813'.54--dc21   98-40365
                                                                  CIP

Printed in the United States of America
FIRST EDITION
HELICON NINE EDITIONS

For Donald, Nathanael, Maile, and Ian

THE PANTHER IN THE JARDIN DES PLANTES, PARIS

His glance, worn by the passing of the bars,
has grown so weary it has lost its hold.
It seems to him, there are a thousand bars,
and then behind a thousand bars no world.

The soft gait of the supple, forceful paces,
revolving in a circle almost nil,
is like a dance of power that embraces
a core containing, dazed, a mighty will.

Rarely the pupil's curtain, soundlessly,
is raised—and then an image enters him,
goes through the silent tension of the limbs—
and in his heart ceases to be.

—Rainer Maria Rilke
(Translated by Walter Kaufmann)

CONTENTS

PART II

PART I

"Climb, climbed, climbing...to move up by using the feet, the hands...to ascend gradually...to move (down, over, along) using the hands and feet...to grow upward...a climbing...a place to be climbed."

— Webster's New World Dictionary

CLIMBING THE GOD TREE

HE'S LIKE AN ITCH IN A PRIVATE PLACE, can't get to him, can't make him stop. He's everything that sickens Eli Hyde in a man, belly erupting with surplus flesh, pendulous forearms, purple lips. Morton Salvitore. His lips leave the prison with her like she's pocketed them. They roll across her arms, shoulders, neck, howling nights, her own husband turned away in their bed. Eli despises Morton Salvitore but here's the remarkable thing: sometimes her heart aches when she thinks about him, that fake leather jacket he wears so carefully, only thing in the world that's his.

Dallas Hyde, Eli's handsome, stubborn husband, has moved them three times in as many years, each place colder than the last. Maine now, maybe next year Alaska; after that, where? Said, "Mecca's not what you think. You think you've arrived and what do you know, another road." Another U-Haul, thinks Eli.

Eli's husband is a carpenter. Says he can get work any place there's wood. So maybe that eliminates Saudi Arabia, she thinks. Though she doesn't tell him that. Lately they aren't in the habit of speaking much to each other. No one thing in particular caused it this time, just one of those silent seasons.

Eli teaches Art Therapy at Rock Harbor Adult Correctional, R.H.A.C. "The Rack" is what the inmates call it, maximum security. "Don't turn your back on them!" Dallas hissed. It's not the future she planned. She always figured she'd be a real artist by now. Eli is thirty-two. She missed the good generations, the ones with the names, Flower Children, Generation X. Sometimes her life feels like jello, no edges to it and she's quivering in the middle.

First day at R.H.A.C. was the hardest. Five metal doors banging shut, locking automatically behind, with each fierce clang Eli's stomach sank. A metallic world, bars, unadorned gray walls, concrete floors, cold. Two prisoners transported in manacles yelped when she walked past. "Shaddup!" the guard commanded. They grinned and Eli tried not to. Manacles rob a person of his humanity; howling at a woman, she figured, helps him remember. Eli followed the guard to the "studio." She noticed his fat waist and the thick belt of keys fastened around it. Well, didn't she already know about being trapped?

Turned out the studio was really the chapel. "We don't have much extra space," the Rehabilitation Coordinator confided, long face, body, angled and wiry as a stretched out slinky. His badge said Travis Hill—REHAB. "God darned warehouse in here, too many of 'em packed in like veal. Ever seen veal calves in them little crates? By the time they're taken up to slaughter they're too damn weak to moo about it. Not that it would make any difference if they did, I suppose," Travis said, setting up easels, a folding table with state-issued water color sets in plastic cases, paint names like Hallmark greeting cards: Yearning Yellow, Pleasingly Pink, Bucolic Beige; brushes, paper cups with water but no brush cleaner, on top. "Chemicals can be made into explosives," he said. "Sometimes, all else fails? They'll ball up paper, set fire to it, throw it out the cell block. Boredom's a plague in here. You know, the long nights."

Eli has known the long nights. What for chrissake was she doing here? Butterflies in her stomach flopped about like their wings were torn off. She stared up at a fresco, Jesus on the ceiling reaching down his hand. She stared at a cross on the metal barred window, giant gray prison wall beyond, gulls wheeling over it in the pink winter light, taunting their easy freedom; razor wire fence on top. She thought about her mother, just gave up and died last year with a broken back. "I can't move anymore," her mother cried, "what's the use? It's like my own bones are my prison and now old-ness's creeping in." Travis led in the inmates who lined up silently behind the easels, staring at Eli.

A month later they're painting a mural: rampaging camels, dam-aged stick-figure people in beards, U-shaped breasts, crumbling one-dimensional cities, God's giant finger like a lost cloud wafting down out of a bruise-colored sky. "I guess we don't have to be too Biblical," Eli tells them. She's never been completely comfortable with things of a Biblical nature. As children in their parents' house Eli and her sisters were made to say their prayers, say grace, but were seldom taken to any church. Sunday was housework day. The Bible was the biggest book on the shelves their mother made them dust. An ocular kid, she couldn't accept that God was invisible, or, more troublesome, that He was inside them all. Eli's own image of God was an ancient, towering tree that bent its branches down to you when you died, and your soul, which looked just like you when you were alive except it couldn't speak, stepped out of your body like a cartoon ghost, climbed up and kept on climbing. For some forgotten reason Eli was convinced she would die on her twelfth birthday and so avoided very large trees during her eleventh year.

Eli's students at The Rack treat her well. "Eli's guys," they joke. Like she's their little sister, little mother, a small composite of all their women, the taken-for-granted parts of their lives now lost. Nothing's taken for granted in R.H.A.C. Eli is fine-boned, skin clear as water, red-head skin, cream colored and soft as cooked pasta. They honor her by pretending not to notice. Except for Morton Salvitore. Mort is a lifer, different from the others. Older, late forties maybe, hair the color of the prison wall, eyes flat as a fish. He's disdainful of the mural, organized activities, other inmates. Wants to work on his own and Eli gladly set him up. But something about him has Eli glancing over her shoulder periodically, making sure he's not behind her. Something uncomfortable, ruinous, and terribly sad.

One day before the bugle blows and the inmates are escorted to lunch, Mort shows Eli his painting, reclining nude, swollen, out of proportion neck, a fountain of Roaring Red water-color flowing out of her stretched open mouth. He gazes up at the cross on the window and Eli feels the intense January cold pressing down on the glass like a fist.

"That Salvitore's a bad one," Travis says when the class is over, staring with disgust at Mort's painting. "Stuck a .357 down a girl's throat, no good reason. You can almost understand the ones who at least have a motive, you know? Like if she'd been married to him and going out on him, something like that."

Later, when Eli finally falls asleep, she wakes up immediately tasting the cold chunk of steel in her mouth. Heart hammering, sour smell from her husband's breath sleeping accidentally close to her, she slips out of bed quietly, checks the doors, then collapses down on the bare living room floor. She hears the sounds her weeping makes; she hears the sounds of an infant crying, though there is nobody in the house but her sleeping husband. The wind, she tells herself, only the wind.

During the next class Mort pushes a scrap of paper into Eli's hand, discreetly, walking close to her in the line of men moving out of the chapel. She reads it in her car: "Dear Eli, you're reading this in your 1987 off-white colored Ford Escort, registration 13279-AH, Ohio—The heart of it all. Yours Always, Mort." Dallas and Eli keep their cars registered to the state they last lived in, a monument of sorts to where they've been.

The next note, folded into quarters and dropped inside her L.L. Bean tote bag reads: "Happy Birthday on March 18th. Where will we celebrate? Consider wearing your abundant hair down around your shoulders. Your Humble Servant, Mort."

Eli wears her hair back in a clip. Once she fastened it up and the guard at the front desk, "Screws," her students call the guards, made her take out all the bobby pins. "Small metal objects?" he said accusingly, rolling his eyes at the obvious.

How does Mort know these things about her? Eli reads the note again, at home, at night, her husband someplace else. And again, chewing her fingernail, tugging her hand through her hair, yanking out the clip, hair down around her shoulders and red as his tongue.

Eli hears something behind her and her heart flops; only the whine of the furnace, only the whine of the wind, only the whining inside her head, over and over for a month now though she's tried to silence it: her husband is having an affair. Eli's seen her, works at the bank. The tall smug type. Eli's seen the way she looks at him. It's not like she is his first.

Another class, Mort tells Eli his still life is for her. "Well? Do you get it?"

She shrugs, cheeks burning. "A leaf and a pear."

"That's correct, a leaf folding around the pear. Do you understand now?"

She shrugs again, fakes nonchalance, but her stomach does that crunching sensation and she's sweating. She wanders nonchalantly over to a mural painter slapping Grateful Gray over one entire scene. "Smoke," he announces, "Bethlehem's burning up. I'm in for arson." He grins.

Dallas is having an affair. He offers no excuses, just doesn't come home much. Eli's L.L. Bean bag, discovered at an autumn lawn sale—front yard dickering as integral to Maine as the luau is to Hawaii—has become the venue for communications with Mort. She's written him back: "Please Stop!" Stuck it up like a folded paper airplane out of the corner of her bag in his direction. It's mid-February, utterly frozen, stark bony outlines of mountains the only contrast on the white-hardened land. She reads his notes at night, huddled beside the wood stove. Wind howls and sometimes she imagines footprints in the field of snow outside their rented house. She reminds herself that he's a murderer, a lifer, they won't let him out. She imagines her husband with the tall woman, taller than him, her legs curled around him like edges of a dried-up leaf. She imagines the dead woman, was she Mort's girlfriend? He's drawn her several more times, in several positions, always the swollen neck. A blond. Eli knows this because yesterday Mort asked her to help him mix the paint. I need a pale yellow, the color of the moon when it's just rising, when the sun's still on it, he said. She thought: can you almost forgive a man who sees the world in subtle shades of its primary colors? Her husband doesn't talk that way, the color of the

17

moon rising. Once, in a season when they were speaking, she asked him to describe the color of her eyes. "Big," Dallas said. Mort's recent note: "Your eyes are Cerulean Blue, the way I am without you. But I WON'T be without you. Yours Forever, Mort."

Eli knows she should probably tell. She asks Travis, "So what about Morton Salvitore?" Heart hammering and she's wet under her arms.

"What's to say? He's an asshole, college educated, a smart guy. Some sort of business man until one day he flips. Something dark in that one, a black hole where his conscience should be, you know? The others made mistakes, maybe. Salvitore doesn't make mistakes. He's just biding his time in my program. You can't rehabilitate something like that. He's an animal, worse. No animal would blow out some woman's insides, you know. No motive. If there's a Hell it's waiting for that one. Don't folks at least have reasons for the damage they do?"

Today's note's a poem, slipped into the sleeve of Eli's coat tossed on a chair near his easel. Says in verse that he knew her in a former life. Describes making love to her on a beach in Tahiti. For a moment Eli sees him, Captain Bligh! His flesh rolling down the length of her, a wave of it, his purple lips opening like sea anemones.

The next day Eli wears a sweater with pockets, shoving her hands inside so he can't press notes between her fingers. She leaves her tote bag and coat in Travis's office. Mort whispers to her at break, the others lined up around the water fountain in the smokers' hall outside the chapel, dragging on cigarettes: "I'm the color of your soul."

The thing is, Eli feels sorry for him. A monster, how not? But something so sad, so wrenchingly human the way he protects that jacket of his and it's not even real leather, no slinging it on the tops of chairs, tossing it in the corner like the others do. Tenderly he lays it over the back of a chair, she can almost feel the warmth from his body on the hard metal. There must be something innocent in him, a small place unformed that needs to be forgiven.

At night Mort haunts Eli's dreams, waking her in a cold terror as she reaches for her husband who is seldom there. She thinks about buying a gun. She thinks about lying under Mort, his outrageous body snuffing out the one thing she's been trying to forget, but more and more she simply can't do it: their son, hers and her husband's, their baby who died before he could live. "Don't talk to me about it!" Dallas commanded, "and if I were you I'd just forget it. It's over. Move on, for chrissake." The moves, Eli thinks, each place colder, as if a slow icing of his memory will eventually wipe it out; as if winter could cauterize the pain of it, freeze its advance like liquid nitrogen froze the skin cancer on her husband's forehead, all those years in the sun, building other peoples houses. "Zap!" he said, "Now I don't have to think about it."

Their son was their dream together, the thing that drew them together, Dallas's work-calloused hand moving carefully over Eli's swollen belly, feeling for his life. Secretly though she had imagined how he would love her, Benjamin, the name she's not allowed to speak, little Benjamin folded into her arms, squiggling the length of her lap like a puppy. Older, she'd pull him down on top of her, "Will you always sit on my lap?" Smell of new grass in his hair, perpetual summer.

Six and a half months drifting inside Eli, little boat in the bathtub of her belly, the doctor told them the baby wasn't growing properly and then the bloody truth of this between her thighs. But what's a right way to grow? she had wondered, legs open on the table, white light burning above, trying not to think the unthinkable. Eli imagined bread growing, rising, falling; breathing, rising, falling. Tried to breathe, in, out, in between the fierce spasms imprisoning her inside like a vice. At one point she begged Dallas to take her home. Then it was over. Benjamin torn away from her, stolen by a drug-induced darkness that came too quickly. But not so quickly that she didn't hear it, his one small cry.

In the gray hospital morning Eli lay on a bed, clean sheets, white, bloodless. "You won't be able to do this again," the doctor spoke, not looking at her. At her husband. "It's a miracle she even conceived." From the accident, Eli thought, her little sister died. Eli was sixteen and they were roaring down the Tantalus mountain road in their older sister's boyfriend's Corvette, Honolulu spread out below, a rain-slicked dream. The impact hurled Eli against the door as if she were already a ghost passing through. She thought: It would have been better if Benjamin never even tried to take a breath of this life.

Something in her husband shut down. "I could leave you, you sonofabitch!" Eli whispers now, thinking about the tall woman from the bank. Benjamin forged them somehow, Eli and Dallas, the unspoken yet irreparable mixing of their blood, their genes, their spirits. "I already loved him, Eli. How do these things happen? It's just not fair." That was the last time Dallas said their son's name to her, "Benjamin."

In the Maine spring there is mud, and tender, wet, new leaf-smelling days. Eli wears a raincoat to the prison just in case. Her students are restless, eyes eating up the yellow drag of light from the barred window, out to the blue space of sky. Morton Salvitore has been transferred to the "Supermax" prison for harassing a female guard. Eli feels strangely jealous, as though she should have been the only one he stalked.

Two weeks slide by and her class suddenly ends, she's not invited back. "Budget considerations," Travis sighs, "a warehouse is what we are. Taxpayers don't want to pay for art therapy when most of 'em can't afford therapy or art for that matter in their lives. Hate the thought of criminals getting something they don't, you know? Can't blame them, can you? Why should Salvitore get anything, for instance? What he should get is the chair, only, we're not a death penalty state." Sighs again.

Eli thinks about Mort's jacket, nobody to love it when he's gone. Says, "You know it's not therapy. Just art." She holds back tears saying good-bye to the others, the solemn way they each shake her hand, thanking her as if she did it only for them.

Then her husband's home again, nights, then days too. When Eli walks into the bank the tall woman disappears in the back. She walks out of the bank, air clean and hard, warming some but still clutching stubbornly to a recent freeze. Eli wonders if summer in Maine is a holding pattern, a waiting for winter. Terminal Green.

And her husband's sprawled on the sofa, something on TV, clicks the remote, now something else. He doesn't look at her, but Eli says it anyway, the lines she's rehearsed since her final time at the prison, five metal doors banging behind her, shutting her out. "I'm thinking about moving on. Somewhere else. Florida maybe. Maybe even back to Hawaii. No winter to speak of, no cold. I'm sick to death of the cold." He still doesn't look at her. And then Eli shouts it: "Benjamin! Benjamin, Benjamin, Benjamin! Just because you won't speak the name doesn't mean he didn't happen! He happened to us both. You can't just erase things because you won't name them. You can't run from memory like abandoning a used car. Three years, three states, and I still hear his cry in the night!"

Eli marches into the bedroom, rented, nothing permanent in their life, after all, and begins to pack. She knows packing. She has it down to quick, thorough, no loss throwing away the accessories of her life not used in a year. Dallas is behind her suddenly, her husband, remembered warmth of his hand on her shoulder. There was a time when his hands on her meant everything. "Eli, don't do this."

Eli lets herself fall against his chest, he pulls her down on top of him on the bed already stripped of its sheets. "Please Eli, I don't think I can live alone anymore. I don't even remember how."

"What drives a man to kill love?" she asks him, pressing her husband against herself, feeling his life flow through her own veins, fighting tears, the weight of their loss.

"I'm sorry," Dallas says. He thinks she means him. "It's just that I can't imagine feeling things again, Eli, not the same way as before. I keep remembering the sight of him, all shriveled and blue. He was already old. Like he lived his whole life inside that one breath and I never even got to know him. I felt cheated of something. I felt like somebody or something should be blamed but, goddamnit, who or what?" Dallas strokes Eli's neck and she jerks away, her handsome husband, face craggy and chiseled and cold as the Maine coast. It's the neck in Mort's paintings she's seeing, Roaring Red, the tragedy of Morton Salvitore.

Dallas unbuttons Eli's shirt, climbs on top of her, pushes his chest against hers. "Don't leave me, OK? I'll try harder, I promise. Look at my eyes and tell me you won't go." But Eli is gazing out the window, rented window over the bed that at least is theirs. She sees a white bar of light between the top of the window and the shadow the shade makes, somebody else's shades. She remembers the bar of light in the chapel's window, so strong now that it's spring you felt like you could walk on it, step outside into the Cerulean Blue color of freedom. She remembers Jesus's hand reaching down from the ceiling and her students, Eli's guys, their final try at painting the mural—sun over city buildings, neighborhoods with sidewalks, giant trees, grass, houses with porches, lounging people, guitars, cars, a well-traveled highway, and birds, gulls mostly, cream-colored strokes of freedom soaring permanently on the blue edges of the prison canvas. "Like it is in my heaven," one of them said.

Eli remembers when they first moved to Maine she and Dallas took a walk on the beach, cold October air, nobody but the gulls circling over something hopping about on the sand. Moving closer they could see it was another gull, impaled by a fish hook through its mouth and cheek, one leg bound tightly in the silvery line, sticking out at an awkward angle. "Must have tried to free itself using its foot," Dallas remarked. The gull hobbled weakly on its one good leg, wings fanning the sand. Eli wanted to save it, could almost feel the stream-lined feathers in her arms, carrying it home. "For chrissake no," Dallas said, "can't you see it's too late? And anyway," he said, "gulls are wild, they're scavengers. You think it would live caged up in our house?" Back at the parking lot Eli turned around and saw the cloud of birds descend, a wave of them, their ravenous cries, swooping down on one of their own.

Dallas is still moaning over and over like a chant or a prayer, "Don't go, Eli, promise me you won't." Eli reaches her hand up, latches it onto her husband's neck, drags his face down on top of hers, whispers the name in his ear like a breath that is his and hers at the same time, in and out: "Benjamin."

MOTHS

BUCKY AND MARNIE ARE STEAMING DOWN the Volcano Highway in Marnie's stepmother's Plymouth Fury, her small slippered foot plastered like a cement block to the accelerator, when they hear the siren wailing behind them. "Damn!" mutters Marnie. She sucks in a breath off her Camel unfiltered, her heavily glossed lower lip slipping over the upper into a startled pout, crushes the butt on the metal edge of the stuck-open ashtray then flicks the remains inside. "Damn, damn, double-damn!"

Bucky whips his head around, sees the flashing blue lights, hears the voice on the megaphone ordering them over to the side of the road. "Side-a-the-road!" bellows the voice. Soft shoulders, this road once had sliding volcanic soil. Pull over and half your car would immediately sink, like stepping into the giant tree ferns his mother nags him about, long hairy trunks disguising lava tubes shooting down to the center of the earth. "Watch out for the ferns!" his mother howls.

Marnie says, "Let me do the talk. I'm good at this kind of thing."

Bucky notices the legs first, impossibly large thighs crammed into his blues. The cop leans his head down, peers into Marnie's window. "You know how fast you were doing?" Fishy eyes glare at Bucky as if he's the one driving. He's a white cop, German, maybe, and very, very big. And maybe this won't go too good for them, thinks Bucky, the way this cop, flat eyes the color of Mel Gibson's eyes, leers at Marnie, giving her the up, the down, then back to her own yellowy-brown eyes. Last night they rented "Man Without A Face," watching it sprawled across Marnie's floor because her cats took up all the chairs. One half of Mel's face was like an avalanche hit it, but the other side proved he was still Mel Gibson, great looking guy. "To die for," said Marnie. From the waist down this cop appears a size too huge for his own uniform.

Bucky stares straight ahead at the Fury's windshield. A small white moth lights down on it, glass still damp from the rain forest drizzle. Drizzle, rain, the flowery Hawaiian air sucked up into everything. Like breathing into a skin lotion bottle, thinks Bucky. In Maine, where Bucky's from, the air gets so cold and hard you can bite it.

"Flew," the cop snarls, "you flew down this highway at eighty miles per! You're on the Big Island, for chrissake, did you think it was Indi?" He hooks a slab-sized thumb under his polished belt, grins into Marnie's face at his own cleverness exposing a row of perfectly sized teeth.

The moth sticks its proboscis into the moisture. Bucky understands the order Lepidoptera. This moth is thirsty for special chemicals, nutrients, salt. He knows a kind of moth that drinks tears from the eyes of cows. Flutters against the cow's eyes, using its long mouth parts to sweep across the eyeball making more tears flow which the moth then drinks. Moth is fed, cow's eyes are dried. Everybody gets something. But the moth's the clever one. If it wasn't batting its wings at the cow's big eyes like some bitchy flirt the cow wouldn't be crying.

Bucky's mother said his father was like that. "Had me convinced our survival depended on him," she said. "What do you know, here we are without him." At sixteen the two things Bucky likes most are entomology, and the idea of having sex with Marnie. What he likes least are his parents and his grandmother. Bucky and his mother live with Grandma Shirley. Sometimes his mother forgets about Bucky. She never forgets Grandma Shirley. "Grandma wakes up with a howling inside and she thinks it's hunger," his mother said. "But I think it's the person she used to be just falling away." His grandmother has Alzheimer's disease. Her mind dies a little each day.

"Well," Marnie sighs, her voice muffled and sweet, sticky as a doughnut. She peers up into the cop's looming face, rolling her yellowy-brown eyes, "The thing of it is, we got stuck behind a tour bus at Volcano. You know how that goes." She yawns, squiggles the top half of her body into a slight, slow stretch, runs her tongue across her lower lip and smiles.

The cop shoots up a wormy eyebrow, slides his gaze down. He narrows his eyes. "Are you playing with me, young lady? Because, you know, if you are I'd have to give you a ticket just on the principle of it." He grins.

Bucky groans, fakes a cough.

Marnie says, "Oh, no, I wouldn't do that. I'm just putting out something to consider here. See, what if I was speeding because I was just making up for having to go so slow before? In a way it evens out, don't you think?"

"Well, I don't know about that," the cop says. "That's a kind of nutty logic there. Is that female logic? You won't find much female logic in the laws of the highway, young lady. You're sure you'd never try to get out of a ticket? You got any idea how much speeding tickets are up to these days?"

The cop's posture has gone from rigid to lounging, his chin thrusting its way inside Marnie's window as if independent from the oversized face it's attached to. Must have to shave three times a day, thinks Bucky, surveying the blackened stubble. He tugs at his own shiny chin, watches Marnie ferret out a purple marker from her backpack, scribbling a number onto a gum wrapper. He feels that aching inside, that punished, helpless hurt. The moth wheels away in a gust of wind. He misses it like a lost friend. "We're on our way to the airport," Marnie informs this cop who probably doubles as a steroids poster-boy and looks only at her now, Bucky no longer exists. "First I'm going to Honolulu. Then I'm going to the mainland, to see my real mother."

"Well," the cop straightens, stretches his stuff, "I know how it is

25

catching a plane. So today I'm just calling this a warning. But you watch that speed, huh? Cause next time I'm going to give you something. A ticket." He winks and struts back to his cruiser, slips inside and peels off. Marnie buttons the button on her shirt that somehow worked its way open, displaying a shadow of cleavage. "What a geek," she says.

Bucky memorizes that cleavage. Takes a mental snap shot to drag out during his sleepless nights with his other imagined photos of her body parts, slipping them together like a jig-saw puzzle. "So why did you give him your phone number?" he asks her. "You told him your life story practically, isn't that enough?" Bucky hears a ringing in his ears. He has to be careful. When Marnie's mad she snubs him for days. The truth is she's his only real friend here. Besides, he thinks maybe he could love her.

Marnie aims the Fury back onto the highway. In minutes they're flying again, past ginger groves, fern forests, skinny waving papaya trees, palm trees, small houses with corrugated roofs and lava gardens, then further down the mountain toward the sea gleaming like a stretched out sheet of aluminum. Six months ago when his mother moved him from Maine to Hawaii she pointed at snow-capped Mauna Kea, "They can ski that mountain in bikinis," she announced. As if this would mean anything to Bucky. As if his life without his father in it could be any kind of a life. He thinks about his father now, picturing the way his father looked the last time Bucky saw him. He memorized what his father wore when he drove Bucky and his mother to Portland Jetport, silence of that ride, strips of fog hanging low over the road like old smoke, his father in his red flannel weekend-jacket. Once his father put that jacket around Bucky's shoulders, a Patriots game, light misty rain, Bucky shivering beside his father in the bleachers. So why couldn't they just live together, his mother and father, like roommates? They wouldn't have to be married. "Good-bye, Richard," his father said.

Bucky's real name is Richard, but Hitter Harrison, third grade Little League star, nicknamed him on account of his big teeth. The name stuck. He didn't mind. It wasn't like being called Lardass or Dork. It's just that his teeth were so big. Richard would sound moronic in Hawaii, where guys have names like Kimo and Duke and D.G., it would set him apart even more than he already is. His mother had wanted to put braces on his teeth, but his father said wait. His father was the warden for Rock Harbor Adult Correctional and his motto was, Wait and be ready. His father told Bucky, "Never question what you think you know. If you question things you lose the advantage of being right." So they yelled at each other, his mother, his father, about Bucky's teeth, and about how his father waited on things and always thought he was right. Their house was a cold house, as if it were always winter.

Bucky misses that house, an old house in a neighborhood of old Rock Harbor houses, predictable yards with trees that blossomed every spring. He misses the timelessness and permanence of his life in Maine, even though he knows now it was all a lie.

"Damn, Buck-o, what you don't get about life!" says Marnie. "Hell-o? You hear me tell that geek I'm going to the mainland, or what? Besides, did you actually think I'd give some cop my real number? He was so busy mouthing off and trying to look at what's under my shirt, no way did he think to look at the phone number on my license. And even if he did he'd call my house and get a date with The Sleaze!" Marnie tosses back her moon-colored hair and roars.

Bucky laughs too. The ringing in his ears stops. When he thinks about Marnie's breasts it makes him buzz all over, like he's plugged in, like he's electric, like he can turn on and shine. Marnie calls her stepmother The Sleaze. None of them live with their real parents, at least not both at the same time, not Bucky, not Marnie, or the others they hang with sometimes. Marnie said if people were meant to have mothers and fathers men would also get pregnant. "You can tell God's a man," she said. "Because, otherwise, don't you suppose guys would have to get periods too?"

Bucky tips his head back against the Fury's torn seat, closes his eyes. The motion of the car under him is like the spinning of the world around him, too fast to jump out, too late to turn back. Never mind that he stole money from Grandma Shirley's room so Marnie could fly to Honolulu. His grandmother can't know the difference.

Never mind that his father sends money from Rock Harbor in the prison's blue envelopes, not even a How are you? for Bucky. When his mother told Bucky about the divorce she stretched out her arms, "You'll want to live with me, won't you?" What was the thing he could have said?

Humid noon air pours into the Fury's open windows. Bucky swipes angrily at the tears in his eyes, slides his hand over the seat, fake leather upholstery, up and around Marnie's tight shoulders. There are moths that drink mud, blood, anything. Bucky imagines sinking his mouth parts into that sweaty place on Marnie's neck where her fine blond hairs wisp like curls of smoke. He'd attach himself there. He'd never let go.

JUST THINGS

THE MORNING AFTER ELI LOST THE BABY Dallas came home from
Queens Hospital, slipped into the baby's room, crumpled down onto
the wicker rocker Eli's mother gave them to rock the baby in before
putting him in the wicker bassinet, and cried. This was the first and
the last time Dallas cried about it. He's not a crier, but he was up all
night in the hospital, and he lost what had given him hope.

Dallas never understood that word before, bassinet. It's a kind of
half-formed baby bed, the way his son was not a fully formed baby.
The baby's brief existence was like a spark that ignited and blazed
open a whole new world for Dallas, a world with things in it like
bassinets. Even now, three years and eleven months later, he tells
himself to think of it this way; the baby wasn't complete so the loss
of him can't be a complete and utter tragedy, can it? It's just that he
always wanted a son. A son finishes a man somehow.

In the weeks after the burial, the mahogany urn Dallas had built
placed into the red earth of Nuuanu cemetery beside Eli's sister,
Dallas thought maybe if they didn't talk about it the whole thing
could just fade. He didn't want to talk about it, or anything, for that
matter. Eli's family didn't talk about her sister. Talking was just sylla-
bles expelled into the air, a breath full of words. Means nothing.

But in Dallas's silence he understood this one thing: his infant son at six and a half months gestation was a person, just very small. Too small to hold onto the life in his lungs. And he couldn't get any bigger, the doctor told Dallas, because of the massive scarring inside his wife, the same accident that killed her younger sister.

Not that Dallas blames Eli of course. He just wishes he could've somehow known. Presently he's in the living room of their rented house in Rock Harbor, Maine, sprawled out on the beige corduroy recliner they found at Salvation Army Surplus, perfect condition except for the burn marks on the arms. It's not a big room, and one corner is filled with stacks of unpacked boxes, mostly his stuff (Eli is a more deliberate packer), the same items that followed him through three states, each address a few more left unpacked so that now he's about forgotten what's inside some of them, things they clearly don't need but he's not ready to part with. If you get rid of your history who are you?

Eli's painting the porch. He sees her hand through the bay window swooping the brush back and forth, redwood stain spreading across the dull wooden railings, now almost the red color of her hair. When the owner of the house discovered Dallas was a carpenter he reduced their rent with the understanding they would participate in its "rejuvenation," he called it. They divide their labor the way they always have, nails and it's Dallas's task, a paint brush it's Eli's.

Dallas thinks back on that morning again, sitting in what should have been his son's bedroom, Kailua apartment, staring at the walls Eli painted Morning Glory Blue, shelves Dallas built already stocked with powders, ointments, thermometer, diapers, miniature articles of clothing that appeared so ridiculously tiny when they bought them, but in fact would have smothered the baby in their hugeness. Eli hung curtains with embroidered suns, moons, stars, and inside the bassinet was the first and only toy he bought his son, a lemon-colored Pooh in a red felt vest. Dallas has tried to stop picturing it, he even plays nasty little games with himself: every time you imagine that baby, see him blue on that table, pinch your neck until it burns. It just won't go away.

Outside the city of Kailua was steaming that morning, twentieth of August, the baby's birth, his death. Everything shone with a kind of taunting clarity, as if the world was normal. Outside the baby's bedroom window an ironwood tree's needles wove a deep green path against the glass, scratching like something that wanted to come in. Mynah birds chattered on grass that needed mowing, other people's kids splashed in the apartment pool, water the color of his son's skin when he couldn't manage that next breath, skin shrunken up and wizened like he was already old, too weak to flail about, just that sputtering sound, a soft rattle as the life came out. Eli was howling, "What is it? It's a boy, right? Let me see him, I can't see!"

"Get him out!" the doctor hissed, pointing at Dallas. Outside the delivery room a nurse handed him a paper cup filled with guava juice. "Here, honey," she said, as if this was a solution? Like Dallas could drink his own soul back down inside, the part of him that fell away when he saw his son die? They tried to revive the baby. It seemed an eternity Dallas waited in the long hall, a fluorescent light winking on and off in the distance, before the doctor came out, shaking her head.

Eli once accused Dallas of being the type who imagines the worst in life so that whatever happens seems better than what he thought. Well, so the worst happened. He understood he was supposed to be there for her, that the mother supposedly felt it more. Dallas let Eli clutch his arm during the burial service, but he had to force himself not to pull away from her icy fingers.

Eli's mother touched his shoulder, "I know what you're feeling," she said. He nodded, kept his head down. Because he knew she didn't. Because the fact was he wasn't feeling anything anymore, not a bloody damn thing. A numbness washed over him after he left his son's bedroom that morning and even now, almost four years later, it's like he's walking through the world asleep. He knew he wouldn't feel things again the same way as before. When things like this happen to people a permanent altering takes place. It's not like people are rubber and can just bounce back. Not hardly. Everything changes. Everything at his son's funeral was like going through the motions of it, pretending to support Eli, reciting what they wrote, something about the pain their child would never know that his spirit was free. Neither of them believed. It didn't matter about the child's feelings, he was gone. It was the rawness of their own pain that was left.

Now Dallas studies Eli's hand as it moves across the far wall of the porch, sweeping the brush down. A small hand shaped like a bud, her fingers uncurl graceful as petals. Sometimes it amazes him that Eli's art, its grating colors and fierce shapes, springs onto the canvas from this peripheral hand. It surprises him that he found anything in common with her, a painter creating her world when the very fabric of Dallas's seems cut from the same plain wood that pays their bills—the bland presence of his, unrestrained future of hers—how did they come together? Dallas had loved the surprise of Eli's art. He loved her stubbornness, her passion, the way she could move right down into the bones of things. He loved the way she cried out in bed with him, back when making love was the promise, his way of getting through the hours until he could be with her. He loved lying beside her afterwards, her skin sweat-warmed and funky, breathing in the scent of her, of him, dreaming about the parents they'd be, the child they would have. All this has changed.

Eli's listening to the radio, a jazz station and every once in a while he hears a crackle of static, they live too far from wherever the signal is beamed. Dallas thinks about how they don't talk about what happened to the baby, how he won't let her talk about it. It's selfish, he knows, but he wants to hold on to his memory exactly as it remains inside him, untouched by someone else's thoughts, reasons. There's no way of reasoning this thing. It's Dallas's way of honoring his son, a shrine of sorts that's quiet and private and his.

He remembers how for over a month Eli healed slowly, her "wound" she called it, all torn up again. And when she finally wanted him Dallas couldn't. Because he knew his son had been there. He knew the way she was inside was the reason his son died. He felt sickened by these thoughts, disgusted at himself for thinking them and he couldn't tell her. He felt anxious, restless and guilty. Hawaii was too small to fit the overwhelming damage his life had become.

Dallas took to driving around the island when he wasn't working, when he couldn't bring himself to go back to creating more structures, pressing down on the land, filling it up. Even the sounds

of carpentry were getting to him, monotonous pounding of ham-
mers, whining squeal of the tools, retching, rasping sounds of big
machinery brought to the sites, lifting things, aiming ever higher
toward the mountains, into the valleys, pressurized wood and glass
and concrete carving up the island like pizza.

One day, on one of his drives, Dallas noticed a young woman sitting on top of a car by the side of the road, legs dangling, her ankles
with their slippered feet pointing down, clutching a partially
enclosed cage with some animal in it. She wasn't that pretty, not
even as pretty as Eli, come to think of it, but when she climbed into
his Valiant, her bare-tanned knees almost touching the dash, Dallas
thought he understood what he needed. "Run out of gas?" he asked
her. He stared at the cage, scrabbling noise inside, flash of green the
color of a lime through the metal bars.

She shook her head, "Not hardly! Something's fucked-up.
Sounds like a lawn mower and I can't get the goddamn thing out of
reverse. Where you going?" she asked him, twisting her needle-
straight blond ponytail around her fingers. She plunked the cage
down by her feet; did the thing inside hiss or was that his own
breath whistling out? "Cool it!" she ordered.

"Is it scaly or slimy?" he asked.

The girl grinned. "It's a she, her name's Katie. You can pet her if
you want. I was taking Katie, she's an iguana, to the vet as a favor
for my friend. Katie is his and so is the goddamn car."

An iguana named Katie? Dallas looked doubtfully at the cage.
Two eyes like small bits of dark glass peered up. He could barely
make out through the metal mesh the ridges of green running down
its spine like dominoes. "I could go wherever you want," Dallas said,
inching the Valiant back into a line of cars moving up the Pali
highway, the Koolau mountains a steep green promise. "I could take
you to a service station," he offered as an after-thought. He looked
down at the cage again, the two eyes staring. Can iguanas glare?

"What the hell for? I'm ditching the damn thing. I've had it with
that car. I've had it with everything. Here I am, visiting this guy
who's supposed to be my friend. I'm from the Big Island for chrissake, and his iguana doesn't look so good. Don't you know, I tell

him, iguanas are rain forest animals? They need water, like, you should be squirting Katie every day with a water bottle, I told him, not filling her cage with half of Makapuu beach! He takes better care of his pot plants, I said. Also iguanas need attention, not just locked away in a room with the TV on. Like I'm any kind of an animal person or anything, I totally prefer anthropology. But it's just common sense." She dug out a slim paperback from her backpack, opened it to where a page was bent over almost at the beginning, stared at it disinterestedly. Katie made another frantic scrabbling noise then a plunk plunk, like a thwarted pirouette on newspaper.

"I see you're a reader." He smiled.

"Well, it passes the time, doesn't it? Mostly I'd rather watch the movie. I totally love movies."

Dallas laughed and the sound was strange. He tugged his free hand through his hair, smoothing it down, hoping she'd notice how it was still abundant and wavy though he'd turned thirty last month, how it fell the right way over his forehead and his face was good. It wasn't enough to want her. He wanted her to want him. Not the grief-filled way of Eli, expecting Dallas to pour his soul inside her so she could feel "connected," she called it. What, was he a goddamn extension cord? He hated the way his wife displayed their tragedy, making everyone around a part of it. Some things should be kept private. "What's your name?" Dallas asked, staring at the tops of her thighs, tan and hard in her shorts.

"Marnie." She yawned as if the question bored her. "Did I tell you that goddamn car belongs to my friend? Some friend! God, like did he want me to get stuck on the damn highway to get rid of me? He could've just driven me there and ditched me," she said, yawning again. "Or maybe it's his iguana he wants disappeared." Katie made a strange sound from some deep place inside what Dallas could make out through the metal door to be roughly a foot of green girth.

It knows, Dallas thought. The iguana knows. Dallas had a sense of something primeval, the dark eyes judging him in the way of animals, the silent omnipresence of a god. A sudden bump from the cage like a leap for freedom against the wire door.

Marnie made clucking sounds at it, then yawned with a wide-open mouth in his direction. "Poor thing's shriveled up as a dried out lemon. Maybe they'd IV it, who knows? Well, I won't get to the vet's now, that's for sure."

Dallas frowned. Braces. How old was she? Well, it didn't matter. What's age anyway, just a record of how many breaths a person breathes. A difference between Marnie and his own son came to this: how many more breaths in her functioning lungs. He stared ahead at pigeon-grey rain clouds hovering over the Koolaus like wings. Something about the flatness of her voice annoyed him, made him want to startle her.

"So Marnie, did you figure when you broke down in your friend's car you'd be picked up by somebody normal? Normal people don't usually stop for strangers, especially strangers bearing cages."

He watched her, the quick hard look she gave him, the way her mouth twisted then relaxed. She shrugged, "Whatever, but you don't look so dangerous to me. You look like somebody's father."

That stung. And not because he almost was a father, it was the idea she saw somebody that old. They drove in silence for a while, up the Pali heading over the pass to Kailua, the thick fist of clouds moving fast now over jagged broccoli-colored peaks then a downpour pelting the windshield like stones. Dallas flipped on the wipers. They were out of sync with the rhythm of the heavy rainfall and their erratic whining got to him. "This traffic is driving me crazy. Sometimes I think about Oahu filling up with people and buildings and cars to the point where we sink and disappear forever. How many sardines can you fit in a can? Would you want to go hiking?" he asked her suddenly. "I was thinking this morning how I haven't been on a hike for a long time."

"What, in the rain? You couldn't be that weird."

"Didn't you ever go mud sliding when you were a kid? You take a hike, and if the trails are wet you mud slide." Christ! he thought, realizing she was likely still a kid. "Well, I used to, anyway. Up the Nuuanu or Manoa trails. There's lots of things I used to do so sometimes I feel like doing them again."

"Yeah but in the rain? Why would you do it in the rain? You wait till the rain stops, so then you get the mud. I'm from the Big Island. That's the way we do it there."

He turned sideways a little and gazed at her. She was scratching her perfect knee, staring blandly out the Valiant's dripping windshield, wipers going scree, scree, screeeee. He tried to look where her breasts should be but her oversized shirt disguised whatever was there. Katie's small round eyes glowered up at Dallas through finger-like bars. Don't iguanas ever sleep?

Dallas rubbed his neck. "Damn," he whispered. He imagined crawling up a muddy Nuuanu trail with some girl named Marnie from the Big Island, sliding down into the cold stream, mud floating off their skin into the water like blood, heathery smell of the water. He'd push his body against hers, wrap those bare legs around him, all the while knowing what he'd go home to, the hollowness of a life alone with Eli, silence of their apartment so empty it echoes. The door to the baby's room was permanently shut now. Dallas saw to it when he came home one day and found Eli lying in the bassinet, curled up like a fetus using every possible space in the little bed, its wicker legs bowing crazily under the grown-up weight of her. The smothering sensation building inside him since his son's funeral became at that moment unbearable. "Eli, for god's sake, what do you think you're doing?" he shouted. He had opened his arms to her imagining for a second the impossible, that his wife like a child would come into them, that everything could go back to how it was before. "Get out of the bassinet," he pleaded. Then he yanked her out and she fell against him sobbing, "Benjamin! I want my Benjamin!"

"Don't ever speak that name again!" Dallas ordered. The barking of his voice—he knew how it sounded, saw the shock crumple down the ridges of her face. He couldn't stop himself. He felt such hatred for her, for himself, for the baby who died never letting Dallas even know him, the person who might have existed as part of him, his son. "It's over, Eli!" Dallas said. "We need to move on. First thing tomorrow we get that bassinet and all the other stuff out of here. We're not having more babies, are we? You can't so there's no reason to hang on to these things."

And then he started piling them up, baby things, a careening stack of them like colossal pancakes, beginning with the bassinet and everything else loaded on it: the stroller with the plaid seat, a portable changing table, swimming ducks on its plastic surface, piles of little clothes, diapers, ointments, thermometer, off the shelves and on the table, a musical swing Dallas's father sent from California, spindly metal legs lying in random pipe-like pieces never to be connected, a corduroy baby carrier, baby books, baby wipes, baby towels, baby this, baby that. Launched at the top of it all was the lemon-colored Pooh in the red vest, a monument of baby things filling up one corner of the room. When Dallas was done he turned to his wife who stood there pale and silent. "See? They're just things, Eli, things we'll never use."

Remembering this Dallas gazed out the windshield of his Valiant, wipers swishing back and forth, back and forth. If he shut off the engine they would stop; if he chased Marnie out of the car she'd run; if he let that creature out of its cage it would probably go for Dallas's throat! If he did so many things there'd be a reaction, a result, but he couldn't save his son. Dallas shook his head, trying to get this image out of it, Eli's face as she stared at his creation, the baby tower, what remained of their child, the ruin of his things. She said nothing. Just stood there, face grey and small as a pebble. And he saw his own face mirrored in hers.

The noise of the rain drove through Dallas like nails. He turned to Marnie sitting complacent as a cow. Katie was making a steady scratching noise against the plastic rim of the cage now, almost a plea, Dallas thought, the indignity of it, life at the will of someone else. He reached out, stroked the top of Marnie's head. Like rain he let his hand drift down the length of her ponytail coming to a stop at the back of the seat. "So where do we find a veterinarian?" he asked her, the Valiant already turning toward any direction she answered.

WHEN YOU'VE GOT NOTHING

HENRETTA HARLEY NAMED HER FIRST DAUGHTER CEDRA which isn't
a real name and it doesn't mean a thing. Henri simply liked the
sound of it. The girl, who recently turned fifteen, is sullen and stubborn and dazed by her own boredom. She's around Henri all the
time since they left San Francisco and she's driving Henri crazy. "I
don't know one single soul in Texas," Cedra declared, yawning.
Sometimes out of spite for the way the girl has altered Henri's life,
Henri tells her daughter that the name Cedra is dyslexic for cedar.
"You have the sense of humor of a piece of wood," Henri once told
the girl. Cedra gave her mother a glazed stare. Cedra's father is dead,
the same accident that killed Henri's little sister. Nobody, including
Henri, knew she was pregnant with his child at the time. Nobody
but Henri knows exactly who Cedra's father is. Sometimes when
she looks at her daughter Henri thinks of death.

And she thinks of her little sister Missy, and how uncanny it is
that the child they yanked out of Henri with forceps (even before
she was born Cedra refused to accommodate her mother), looks like
Missy—same cotton-blond wisps of hair, same startle of dark blue
eyes. Henri remembers the man who loved his Corvette more than
her, and she remembers thinking this was OK. When he made love
to her it was the kind that hurts, and at nineteen Henri thought

that somehow, somewhere along the line she must have deserved it. When he tied up her wrists and bit the points of her paper white breasts, she thought, forcing back tears, yes! Most likely she deserved it. After Henri's sister died and her whole family shut up tight as mollusks, Henri knew this was true. Her punishment was to be the one left. She was sure if Melissa had lived she would have been more of a woman than Henri is, taller, smarter, more beautiful; so Henri lives her own life as full of herself as she can be, and the uncertainty that was once a part of her has become a quietly seething rage.

October in Houston, still hot enough that everything sticks to everything else from a spell of air so humid it's like breathing into a fish tank. After Henri opens Dallas Hyde's letter, the third this week, she packs up the ancient Mercedes, sticks the two blond babies into their car seats in the back and orders Cedra to ride shotgun. The girl bellows out something about when will her mother stop bossing her around, and Henri says fine, Cedra can live in Houston and pay the goddamn rent. They were staying with a friend of Henri's who announced she'd had it with imperfect relationships and the Houston traffic, and was relocating to the New Mexico desert to join some sect that worshiped things far away and silent like planets. She abandoned her cat Hermit (named after the crab not the behavior), her apartment, and left a month's rent overdue. Henri gave Hermit to the landlord and when he said he needed the rent, Henri smiled her smile that is all in her teeth and not in her eyes, and she told him he could go to New Mexico.

Cedra blows a bubble the size of a bullfrog from a wad of green gum. They are on their way to Maine, where the leaves are the color of blood and the autumn air has the tang of an unripened orange.

• • •

Henri bangs on the Hyde front door and when finally it's tugged

open there's her sister Eli staring up at her, mouth hanging open and
slack as a fish net. Henri's wearing tight jeans and a tee shirt that
claims Texas Does It Bigger. Her yellow hair like a tangle of sunflow-
ers frizzes out from under a pointed cowboy hat. Eli rubs her eyes as
if she's been asleep for a very long time.

"Well, I've been in Houston," Henri says, "hoping to find me a
cowboy." She grins and hugs Eli who has stepped outside the door a
few inches. Her sister backs away from Henri, bumping up against
the wall of the house which needs a paint job, Henri notices. Why
for chrissake would Eli and Dallas want a blue house anyway? They
should pay somebody to demolish the wood siding and slap on some
brick. She steps inside her sister's doorway, peering into shadowy
corners of the tiny living room, the late afternoon light dead as dust.
"Christ, El. You live like this? This isn't a home, it's a cave."

"Where are your kids?" Eli asks, rubbing her eyes again, tugging
at her chin as she follows Henri into the house.

"The monsters are asleep in the car, count your blessings. This
place is going to be kind of tight for us all, huh?" Henri gazes around
the crowded room belligerently, blue eyes burning. "This what your
life's come to, El? Some defective little house in the middle of
nowhere? Rock Harbor isn't even on my map."

Eli's cheeks flush. "Maybe you have a defective map. Where's
Jumper?"

Henri flops down onto one end of the couch, a spring poking out
of the other end. She sticks her long feet up on the intricately
scratched coffee table and pushes her running shoes off, they fall on
the floor with two soft thuds. "I left the sonofabitch again. Too
many annoying habits. Do you know he snores in song? Snoring's
bad enough, but put a heavy metal melody under it and you can
drive an insomniac insane."

Eli shakes her head, still standing. The air in the house has
become frenetic, a sense of collision, as if ions and molecules were
making war. "I wonder if we should check on the baby. I don't think
babies should be left in cars, should they? Isn't there some law
against that?"

"Well, Jumper snores like the goddamn devil's got inside him,"

Henri continues, ignoring her sister, "or some Elvis impersonator."
Something happens inside Henri when Eli talks about Henri's kids,
she remembers this now—the word baby out of her sister's mouth
causes a clenching up of something taut and sour in Henri's stomach. "The man can't leave the rock and roll life, not even in his
dreams."

"That doesn't sound like such a huge crime, Henri. I mean music
is what he does, right?"

Henri shrugs. Jumper Harley was the one who came to her in
San Francisco when Cedra was a raging two-year-old and Henri's
most notable accomplishment in twenty-two years was the ability to
cry without running her mascara. He liked her better back then,
when she didn't know herself. That way he could tell her who she
was. Jumper Harley, used-to-be-famous rock and roll star, is the
father of Henri's two blond babies. They've had an on-off marriage;
most of the time it's Henri who decides to leave Jumper before
Jumper realizes he can do this to her. She can't stand the thought of
him leaving her.

Henri gazes over to where her sister's easel is set up in a partially
lit corner of the room. She tries to imagine what it would be like to
paint the life around her, to be captured by a canvas the way
Jumper's soul is stuck inside his guitar. Everybody, it seems, lives
some sort of a life outside of themselves but Henri. She stares at an
unblocked canvas propped up against the wall. Her sister appears to
be painting a montage of shoes—little shoes, strappy ballet shoes,
yellow galoshes, beat-up sneakers. "You're surrounded by mountains
and a killer coast line and you fill that thing with shoes?"

Eli chirps out a nervous laugh, then slides into a chair opposite
from where Henri's sprawled. "You sound like my husband. I'm into
the colors, that's all, Yearning Yellow galoshes, Roaring Red sneakers. Says something, don't you think?"

Henri leans forward, eyes fixed on Eli's pink face. "Are you losing
it, sister Elinor? I'm asking this because I got some damn strange letters from Dallas. That's why I'm here. To save you." Henri stretches,
ignoring the heat in Eli's eyes. "I can confess to you things aren't
hunky dory with me, either, so here's the deal. It's not really the

41

snoring that did in my marriage this time, it's Smoke."

"I didn't know Jumper smokes," Eli says flatly. "But so what. Questionable breath, a few extra dollars from the groceries budget but you folks can afford it."

Henri rolls her flawless eyes. "Don't be dull, Eli. Smoke is Smoky, VISION'S lead singer. Don't you remember? She's ancient. Looks it too. Says her hair's silver but it's grey as rain."

"Jumper's having an affair with his lead singer? I find that hard to believe. His gods were the shoes you walk in."

"Well, she's dug into our home, spread herself around and taken over. Like fungus. The shoes are harboring athlete's foot."

"She moved into your house?" Eli scratches her forehead, frowns.

Henri shrugs. "Yeah. Of course the kids and I had moved out a few months before but it didn't take that bitch long to roll herself in and become like the wallpaper, stuck to my husband. Turns out all these years she's just waiting for a chance to creep into our life in the permanent sense. Now me, I only wanted to try out a cowboy that's all. Just once with a cowboy before I was too old to ride."

There's a scratching at the door like an animal, the knob turns this way, that way. "Mama!" a shrill voice commands. Eli jumps up, race walks to the door and yanks it open. In tumbles three-year-old Morgan, baby Maple howling from the car. "You left us, Mama!" Morgan scolds as she marches inside, a mini-sized version of her mother, flipping stringy blond bangs out of her eyes, barely a glance up at Eli.

"Nonsense." Henri yanks the child down beside her on the couch, tickling her ribs, blowing on her balloon soft cheeks. "Cedra's in the car asleep. An earthquake or something and your half sister would unplug that goddamn Walkman from her ears and save your little asses, you can bet on it."

"I'll go get the baby," Eli announces, heading out the door. Henri looks after her for a moment, the determined thrust of her sister's small hips, then gets up and follows her to the door. "Could be my car's in need of a washing," Henri calls out, standing just inside. "In Texas we ride horses."

Henri watches Eli pull at the silver handle. The door opens with an expensive sounding sigh. Empty soda cans tumble down on Eli's feet, there's piles of used diapers on the densely carpeted floor, granola bar wrappers, squashed juice boxes, a headless doll and a half-eaten lipstick lying on the back seat, a trail of deep violet in its wake.

Henri shrugs when her sister turns around and glares at her. "Hey, so it's a third world Mercedes. My maid's on vacation." She grins.

The baby quiets instantly and gazes up at Eli, a frown squiggling across her pale brows. "Maple, are you Maple?" Eli coos. Henri watches as her sister holds out her arms, then she shouts, "That baby's fastened into her car seat, duh! Don't you know I'm a law-abiding citizen?"

Eli climbs in, pushing aside stacks of old newspapers and empty cracker boxes, unfastening buckles coated with something sticky. "Christ!" Eli calls out, "How can you drive something like this?" Henri shrugs.

Maple scowls and her brows crumple. "It's OK, sweetie, I'm your aunt. I'll bring you to Mom." Eli lifts the one-year old out of the car and she folds herself into her aunt's side, fat arms circling Eli's neck.

Eli walks back toward the house as Henri watches, Henri who knows her sister is breathing the milky scent of Maple's damp curls, the press of warm baby skin against Eli's arm. Henri wills her sister not to give her that look, prays it; she feels the sour knot that happens in her throat when she thinks about how her sister can't do this for real, that the doctors said Eli's too wrecked up inside and guess whose fault that is. For a moment Henri imagines giving her baby to her sister, giving all the kids to Eli, particularly Cedra, and running away to Europe, the South Seas, anywhere that's not here.

A half hour later Henri has taken over the tiny back bedroom, stuff from the backpack she was hoisting spread out across the floor and now Morgan's little bag too, its contents spilled. "Henri..." Eli hesitates, "it's just that there's only the one twin bed. I saw Cedra asleep in the front seat. She's so big. The last time I saw her was three years ago in California and she was a kid. She looks like you now."

"She looks like Missy. Baby sister Melissa, born again. I told Mom and Dad she'd come back to haunt me so naturally she comes back as the daughter I'd most readily put up for sale."

"How could you say that, Henri? Mom and Dad were devastated after the accident and Cedra's your daughter, your own flesh and blood."

Henri shrugs. "It's the truth, that's how. You got extra blankets? The babies can sleep on the floor. They're not verbal enough to argue. Cedra can sleep on the couch. She gives me any lip about it and I'll lock her out of your house. I'm tired of that girl's talk. Honestly, does she think we're a democracy?" Henri grabs a little wrist looming out in front of her, Morgan popping Maple on the head, Maple shrieking. "Morgan, you keep those fat hands to yourself or I'll eat your fingers, you got that?"

"Well, I have to say I'm wondering how long you plan to be here. It's not that I'm not glad to see you and the girls, just that this house is kind of small."

Henri drops the disposable diaper she was about to tape onto Maple, the baby hunkered down on the bed, chubby legs kicking wildly. "Christ, Eli, you think I'm doing this for me? Give me a break! Jumper's got his gold albums plastering our bathroom walls. You think I couldn't afford to stay someplace else? I'm here for you. Dallas wrote that he didn't think you were getting over 'your tragedy,' was the way he put it. Said you were into some weird shit with a criminal. Christ, you think I'd leave San Francisco or Houston for that matter, cowboy or not, and drive all the way out to this last frontier of the U.S.A. for me? And what's the deal with the criminal? Are you doing that pen pal bit? I read something about women who write to prisoners. Or maybe I saw it on 'Oprah.' It's a control thing. You always know where he is. I passed the prison up the road a ways. What's it like living in a town whose only hotel houses the state's major deviants?"

Eli sinks down onto the carpet, staring up at Henri. The carpet's old and clumpy, tufts of it sticking up here and there like scraggly brown rodent ears. "Dallas said that? I'm not getting over my tragedy?"

Henri finishes diapering Maple, swoops the baby up into her arms then settles her back down against her hip. She studies her sister. "Well, he said he thought I might be able to help you. But you know, El, he thinks I owe you. You know that, don't you? He's just like Dad that way. Maybe they're right, who knows? Maybe I've got some kind of major karmic debt to pay and I won't be forgiven for living until…who knows what the hell it takes? Maybe you give birth to the miracle baby and Melissa rises from the dead, makes Dad his Missy-baked chocolate-chip cookies again, then everyone can forget I even exist!" Henri grabs Morgan's hand who's humming to herself, rocking viciously in the wobbly wooden rocker beside the bed, the room so small every piece of furniture is an assault. She hoists Maple up tighter against her hip, the baby's pink thumb planted firmly into her rose bud mouth. "I'm going to find a store, buy some supplies. You do have stores around here, don't you? Maybe an outpost somewhere?"

She doesn't wait for Eli to answer or direct her. Henri never waits for directions. "You've got nothing to lose, El, having me here." Henri peers around the dark minuscule room, stares at her sister then shrugs. "What the hell? Looks like you've already got exactly nothing."

THE COLOR OF SALVATION

WHEN THEY BRING MORT BACK FROM THE "SUPERMAX" and he discovers Eli's gone he sobs, late at night in his cell, cold prison world silent as death but for an occasional cough, someone urinating, a Screw's steps and then his flashlight at a distance down the block. When he finally sleeps Mort dreams she is living in Texas where he was once, he dreams her there with him, her small body like a boy's tight on top of him, tight inside, like pushing through pounds of water, fighting it, coming up for a breath then diving in again. At one point he wakes up and remembers he's alone, has never been so alone. He hears the slap, slap, slap of the Screws playing cards down the end of the corridor, two of them, he knows them by their names and the names the inmates call them behind their backs. Life in prison is lived behind someone's back. Mort balls up his fist and punches the thick ridge of concrete beside his cot, runs his throbbing hand down the wall like it's her thigh—steel, eight inches of impenetrable steel inside. He shoves himself closer against the wall's cold, curls up like a snake and prays for sleep.

In the morning Mort sets about the business of uncovering Eli's whereabouts, a note to his source slipped inside his laundry bag, coded: new socks. You can get any information you want in prison.

You just have to pay for it.

He remembers the dream the way he remembers all his dreams, plays out their rich interior settings over and over as a way of passing the hours until he can sleep again. Houston. He'd been there, back when he was still a man. Business deal, air hot and wet as a boiled-over radiator, felt your whole life sticking to the insides of your suit. He made a lot of money in a week but no friends. The successful are looked at not as people but as something to topple. Crabs in a basket, the ones at the bottom pull down any that manage the climb to the top. Sometimes, though, when he allowed himself to think about it, the hollowness of it all ate at Mort. Sitting and drinking alone in the downtown Houston hotel room he had gazed out the window at a city that shuts down at dusk, no money to be made until the sun rises and it starts all over again, the heat, the mad buzzing of cicadas in the sidewalk trees, miles of steaming traffic on the chewed up highways. Money meant something to Mort in those days, the evils done in its wake easy enough to reconcile.

He imagines Eli there, Texas, her skin a cool white in the heat, the fire of her hair. He knows she's afraid of him and sometimes the feel of this fear ignites him. He sees her standing beside him, her tight little jeans, her bottom like two halves of a peach. He knows this: underneath any good love there's got to be some fear, because when the fear goes boredom sets in. Mort knows boredom. Nothing to look forward to, every day the same so that a better time is that one week in late May when the lilac bushes bloom outside the prison wall, and the scent, thick and sweet as a woman's neck intoxicates the senses, forces you to remember who you are. And the fact that you can't see it, only smell it, is like living in the dark with all your nerves tuned in to the one absolute thing that matters, the memory of it, the possibility of love. The truth is Mort can't completely visualize Eli's face anymore, just the sense of it, the curves of her cheeks, the way her eyes first met his then lowered. He had willed her to look up again and she did.

Mort knows she is meant to be with him. He wouldn't hurt her. How could he hurt her? It would be like hurting a part of himself.

He is her, and she him. She is the flesh that roams and he is the spirit. She is the red of his own blood. He recognized her, the first time he saw her in that art therapy class (another pathetic attempt to normalize the abnormal in prison, but that's a different story), the way she trembled when he showed her his painting, baring his ruin to her like emerging naked from the sea. She didn't look away. She is the part of him that is good, so how can he be good without her? How, indeed, can he live without her? If living is what he does.

Mort splashes cold water stinking of rust on his face from the basin at the foot of his cot, pees in the urinal to its side, flushes, hopes he isn't being watched. It's the lack of privacy that, finally, is the thing you just can't reconcile. He can take their hatred, the guards, other inmates, he's known hatred. But it's the way he can't sink down into himself anymore and just be with himself. The way everything here has a schedule, a time, and how he must be accounted for and counted six times each day. And a shower every other day isn't enough, not since Eli.

He has a secret he's kept from her, he doesn't want her to know too much at first because what then to tell each other for the rest of their lives? He sees their lives unfolding then refolding, together. He'll tell her at that time how he too was born in Hawaii and then found the truth, the cold hard seed of his life in Maine. It's fate of course, one more piece of it, and she doesn't know this yet.

After splashing more cold water on his chin Mort reaches for the shaving cream, does this job with quick, automatic stroking movements in the scratched up reflecting piece over the sink, no mirrors in The Rack, no access to glass. The humiliation of this, being treated like a child! He recalls working in the prison garden during past summers and digging out tiny pieces of glass from the soil, little shards of another time, other peoples lives too small now to be recognized for what they were. Mort runs his hand across his cheek. His flesh that knows just one hour of sunlight these days is spongy and white as a marshmallow.

But not to be bothered about this now. Now is Mort's thinking time, with the others at breakfast. He faked stomach pain; thinking is the nourishment he needs, without the slamming of doors, the cacophony of stereos, TVs, the sheer inhuman noise of it all. Could drive a man insane. In fact he must frequently remind himself he is himself, Morton Salvitore, not an insane man. Morton who had the best first ten years of a life, the best place to live, the best mother.

He remembers her slender white fingers like icicles in a place of color and heat, the cool touch of them on his neck, piano player fingers. Elaine Salvitore was tall, elongated neck and arms, and her eyes were the color of the slivered shells they gathered on Kailua beach, a bleached blue, almost lavender in some kinds of light, like in the evening. Mort liked it best when his mother walked with him in the evening. "These shells," she told him, "are all the broken people. Look how nice it is when you piece them together. You can almost make them fit." His mother smelled of the gin she drank. When she kissed Mort he liked the scent of it, sharp and pungent, a tickle in his own throat making him thirsty for something he didn't yet know. He liked the chink chink of the ice against the side of her glass, the sound that followed his mother whenever she approached, as urgent as the wind teasing the copper chimes she hung outside his bedroom window. "The Egyptians believed copper can protect you," she told him, "copper's as old as the world."

Mort remembers a particular lightness that must have been happiness, waking up without this fist in his gut, this knot of fear, of nausea, of nebulous grief that he feels now. There was a predictableness to his life then and he liked his place in it, the part he played in his mother's world. He liked how she got him up in the morning and fixed him a breakfast of soft boiled eggs and toast while he dressed, the toast dark and hot so the margarine sunk in. Once she burnt his toast and he told her that was OK, he liked it that way. After that for a whole year his mother burnt Mort's toast for him. She drank her gin and watched him eat, chink chink, the ice against the glass, against the tomato red of her lipstick, her smile sticking to her teeth the way the toast crumbs, the char stuck to his. "I do love you my little deer," she would tell him. "Are you my little fawn? You break my heart, Morton Salvitore."

In the summer they walked up the road together to the Pali Palms where his mother taught swimming lessons in a pool the color of the sky and shaped like a giant peanut. He sat at the side and watched her long arms pull through the water, tender and strong, the way she pulled the covers over him at night. Other seasons she put him on the bus for school and school was OK, he was able to sink quietly into things and not call too much attention to himself; he didn't get teased though he didn't have friends. He didn't need friends. He did what he was supposed to do, made the kinds of marks on his papers that his mother pasted little silvery stars on, told him she was proud. He lived for her pleasure, to get home off the bus and into his mother's cool arms enveloping him like water. His life could have ended that way, drowning in his mother's arms. He didn't question her further, the one time he remembers asking her about his father. "Dead," she answered. Mort didn't question it.

Until he was ten. And there was the cold war and the Cuban missiles. At school they were having bomb drills every week, the sirens yowled and they were forced to crawl under their desks and cover their heads with their hands. One day he got off the bus as usual and his mother handed him a glass of chocolate milk and a peanut butter sandwich, the smell of gin on her as hot and sour as the afternoon. She said, "It seems to me the world has finally gone and broken itself apart. As it turns out I am coming apart as well, Morton, on the inside. I'm sorry, my little deer, I didn't mean for things to turn out this way. It's just that I'm afraid I can't find the pieces I need to go on." Then she sent Mort to him, a father he didn't know about, who couldn't love him and whom he didn't know how to love. His father lived in Portland, Maine, a place Mort only knew existed from seeing it on a map at school. Later that same year his mother died without ever telling him why.

It was the headmaster who informed Mort, Headmaster Peterson at the school Mort's father sent him away to. "Son," the headmaster said after escorting Mort into his office, a tidy room with white walls, clean as a hospital and smelling of new leather and duplicating fluids, "It seems your mother was sick. Very sick."

Mort had looked up at him, not fully comprehending. "Do you understand?" the headmaster asked, pulling at his meticulously trimmed beard. Mort stared at the beard. He wondered how it would feel to have such a beard, silky? itchy? Like cementing yarn to your face, or scratching it with a hairbrush? Like wearing your scalp on your chin?

"Her presenting illness was cancer of some sort but that's not what she died from. Do you understand what I'm getting at, Morton Salvitore? Do I have to spell it out?" Headmaster Peterson peered down at Mort, sighed heavily, smoothed his beard a final time, lifted his face incrementally without ruffling the rest of his posture and gazed out the window. Then he said what he was known to say, Mort had heard the same words at least ten times since he began attending Maine Academy. "We are not handed happiness on a silver platter, son, we must earn it. It's the human condition. Love is always in danger."

When he's finished his morning routine Mort sits down on his cot carefully, hating the squeaking of it, the sound that reminds him it isn't a real bed, that he won't have a real bed or a real anything in his life anymore. Not this life anyway. He's going to write to Eli today; he'll pay plenty for her address, cartons of cigarettes and who knows what else. Won't be anything like what he had to pay to find out about her tragedy, however, the terrible weight he understood was a part of her. He found that out just a week before they dragged him off to the "Supermax" and he never got the chance to use it, to let her know he knows.

Well, you have to do it that way. To understand a person, to really know them you have to be able to crawl inside the wrenching pit of their guilt, the unbearable thing they've buried there in their waking life but must live again and again in their nightmares. The dead baby. He sees himself coming home from the hospital to Eli's life, sees her howling her despair in that empty room. He sees the empty baby bed and remembers his own emptiness, and how the baby was never a real person anyway, his source said, she lost it before it could become fully alive. He sees his own damaged life as it moves into Eli's, his arms holding her so tight he can feel her breath flutter against the wall of his chest, his arms that could hurt her, kill her, have killed before but are healing now, healing her. He needs to have this, this one last opportunity: that every time he sees her, his Elinor, the light from the chapel's window blazing red in her red hair like the light of his own salvation, every time he can be with her is one final chance to be human. No one else can do this for him, make him a man again with what her flesh understands.

"Dear Eli…," he calls her what the others call her but another thing she isn't aware of is that he knows her real name, the name he speaks in his heart, Elinor. "It's been too long since we last corresponded. You no longer have a job here. But I know you will be back to see me. Yours Forever, Mort."

He wants to tell her more. He wants her to know him, Morton, the real Morton not the image she has of him, not the beast she thinks he is. But not yet, time enough, the rest of their lives in fact. When she's ready she will ask him the question he knows she needs to ask, the one that doesn't have any certain answer, not in this life anyway: Why did you do it?

A man drinks, he will tell her, because there is nothing else. He drinks, and then there is perhaps a betrayal, a woman he thought he knew, or maybe it's just a hint of a betrayal but it sets his soul on fire somehow. Maybe it's the cruel memory of betrayal, after all, more than anything else. But this new possibility of grief, this drunken vision comes raging down inside him like a fierce wind, like a fire storm and it wipes things out. Wipes them out like the worst thing in the world that can ever happen and then is forgotten, or buried, or worse, never fully known. He doesn't remember. That's the god's truth. Did he black out? Did he pass out? Could he have loved her enough to save her? He doesn't remember. He woke up. Eyes still closed he smelled it, the rusty scent of waste.

Mort rises off the cot slowly, stretches. Every muscle aches from where they worked him over two nights ago, balled up wet towels wrapped around their fists so it wouldn't mark. It doesn't matter, he's glad to be back. At least at The Rack he can write to Eli, he can do his wood work in the shop and sometimes, when something of his sells and they pay him his cut, he can almost pretend he's functional again, that he's doing something that matters.

"Salvitore!" A Screw unlocks his cell. "Time to join the others, meal's over, get to work."

Mort nods, eyes down so the Screw doesn't see it, his loathing, his contempt. They don't like that about him, the way he knows he's better. Funny how life is, they hold the keys. He's found it's best to just move like a shadow, head down, blend in whenever possible. He's smarter than they are and they know this, best to pretend it isn't so.

He follows the Screw out the cell block, through Block B, down the metal stairs, three mechanically locked metal doors then up to the shop. For a moment he is in the hall outside the chapel and he remembers her there, the sight of her that first day when he knew she was the one, the late morning light a wintry pink in her hair, on her face, her skin as white as the white of an eye and, he imagined, as soft and slithery to the touch. He thought about that, the way she would feel, her skin against his, the exquisite fragrance of her and the sound of her voice, low and pleasing.

Mort shakes his head but her vision is still with him; even entering the shop that smells like wet wood dust, no sounds but the high steady scream of the plane, leveling a large piece of pine. She sits down at his bench beside him, her hand on his when he picks up the saw, back and forth, moving with his rhythm against the fine blond grain of the wood. The plane stops for a moment then starts up again, its high pitched wailing that cries out like an air raid siren: Take cover, a bomb's about to drop.

Inside Mort where they can't see it, behind his downcast eyes, his lowered head, there is another scream and the color of this scream is red. Red so deep you can't get to it, can't wash it away, a flow like a river that will not dry up, the color of his hands that will not wash clean. This scream inside him is his blood on fire and Mort understands that because of this he will never know God. And that the only way to cleanse himself, to become reborn is through her. His salvation. He waits like the dying wait. And he has all the time in the world.

WHAT THE DEER KNOW

Usually the dream begins like this: Clem in his wet suit fitted tight against his lean body like shiny rubber skin; his yellow oxygen tank the color of a Yield sign is strapped to his back; his skinny ankles are encased in webbed frog flippers and the knots of thigh muscles and elongated stretch of his calves are also a frog's, pushing up toward the surface from the murky depths of a hundred feet under. His scalloping tools are encased in the various pockets of his diving belt, and the net tote hauling his catch dangles from the belt so his hands are free. Clem parts the ocean like separating a gauze of heavy draperies, more and more of the swirling water moving down around him like falling cotton, soft yet profound. The undersea world is dark green, the world behind Stella's eyes when she sleeps is also this shade, not the verdant green of new life but the color of stagnation, of ancient life forms in a summer swamp, sucking, bubbling, murking, the sickly green of the primitive. Stella watches with the helplessness of the dreamer who understands but cannot affect, as Clem tries to part the water that is surging around him faster and faster like a waterfall, only it's the ocean, deep, dark and forever.

Used to be when Stella was a girl dreaming her troublesome dreams her mother would say, "Pinch yourself!" Stella's mother, the white of her hands, long metal object with a small hole at each end she called "The Instrument" clutched between her fingers, hovering over Stella's foggy still half-asleep face. Her mother pushed The Instrument against Stella's teen-age acne to "Free the germs," she called it and Stella howled. "Never mind, never mind," her mother repeated, the press of frigid steel under Stella's cheekbone, a sur-geon's knife, squeezing, popping, hauling the catch to the surface like a prize. Stella's mother guarded against the ravages of her daughter's young face as if it were a college education, Stella's place in her future. To this day she hasn't a scar on her satiny cheeks; to this day her mother can't put her arms around her daughter without examining Stella's face for its flaws.

This time when Stella awakens from the green-sea dream she pinches Clem, his sleeping breath raw and snarling beside her, "What the hell!" Stella turns away from him, closes her eyes again, the racing of her heart beat tap tap tapping like rain inside her veins. Lately she can't figure out if she still loves Clem but she needs to reassure herself he's at least there. "Go back to sleep," she tells her husband, "you're only a dream."

Later that afternoon Stella perches on a garden chair at her neighbor's house, her bottom burgeoning through the chair's plastic netting as if maybe she really is too fat, the way her mother tells her she is. "You'd better lop off a couple of those pounds or you'll lose that income!" her mother warns, meaning Clem. Stella sits up straight, wills the folds of her thighs back snug inside the inseam of her leggings, but crisscrosses of spandex smothered skin pooch out between the meshing like a black fleshy screen. Stella watches Henretta Harley light a cigarette, sucking the stuff in, blowing out a smooth cool trail of white. It is finally spring.

"I don't usually smoke, for your information," Henri says. "I'm using it as a stress buster, kind of along the lines if your stomach hurts pound your head with a hammer." She inhales another breath, blows, runs her tongue across her bottom lip. "Christ, can you believe it? My sister's moving back to Hawaii. I think she's actually going to do it this time. For months she's threatened him, warned him, told him if he didn't do god knows what to make himself a human person she'd be gone. She's got two suitcases packed, told Dallas the rest of everything else is his. Can you imagine? Just goes to show, husbands won't change."

"The lady minister I work for is from Hawaii," Stella offers. "Why would people from Hawaii come here? If I was from a place you could wear a bikini all year I'd stay there. Though maybe I wouldn't look so hot in a bikini. At least in Maine you can cover things up." Stella sighs and gazes out over the edge of the porch railings, out into the yard that's just like her own yard up the road a ways, deep and plain, the nearby woods pressing into it, like a yard here at all is an accident. Each blade of grass is pale and new, bare tree branches have softened with slender young leaves, and beyond the yard, beyond the forest, the lake is as silvery and shiny as aluminum foil, and then the opposite shore. Stella sighs again. "Life is so small."

"This state is too damn small. I don't mean area wise, just closed up. That's why *I* left Hawaii. That and being blamed for my other sister's death, but there's another story. Places that don't have enough highway connections make me nervous. What if you have to jam suddenly?" Henri stubs out her cigarette on the porch floor, stretches out long and taut as a pulled rubber band in her low slung beach chair. From inside the house the noises of her children and Stella's husband's daughter drift through the screens, droning, humming, whining sounds, and then Cedra, who's being paid to watch them, lets out a long high yip as if maybe one of them stepped on her, sprawled out in front of the TV.

"You have a sister that died?" Stella asks, her underarms suddenly wet, heart hammering. Why does the mention of death do this to her? It's as if every time Stella hears about a person who died, somehow she's known it all along; or maybe it's that she feels she knows them, that in dying they somehow became a part of her.

Henri doesn't answer about her sister and Stella decides not to pursue it. "Why don't you leave Maine, then?" she asks then reddens, hoping Henri won't think Stella wants her to go. On the contrary, Stella hasn't had a friend since she got married, six years ago.

Or at least she hopes Henri considers this a friendship. Actually, it's
Stella's dream to leave Maine. Just pack up and leave.

Henri rolls her eyes that are the intense blue of the wall behind
her. Stella remembers taking a walk a year or two ago and seeing Eli
Hyde, Henri's sister who *is* alive but is moving back to Hawaii,
painting this porch. She painted the railings, the floor and the steps
a redwood shade, and the wall of the house a deep blue, two unlikely colors that Stella would've never paired together but they looked
great. Stella had felt envious of Eli's smallness, the comfortable and
light way she moved about in her body, handling the paint brush
like it was an extension of something inside herself, that easy.

"Well," Henri says, "I can't say why. Isn't there some physics law
or astronomy or something about bodies having a tendency to stay
in one place? Supposedly energy's never lost though to look at my
sister's husband right now you'd damn well forget about that one.
He's near catatonic, spread out on his bed every day, sleeping hour
after hour. Maybe he thinks if he sleeps long enough he'll wake up
to a different life. It seems he figured she'd always be here for him,
no matter what. The last straw was one night when he got drunk he
asked her to let *me* have his baby, since she can't. Can you imagine?
He said I have three kids already so what's another birth? Does he
think I'm an incubator for chrissake?"

Stella closes her eyes against a sudden slant of sun burning out
from behind a fat cloud. She breathes deeply the heavy purple fragrance of blooming lilac. Run away, she thinks, just leave. For several years Stella has been collecting newspaper articles about women
who run away from their lives. She pastes most of them into her
scrapbook for Women Who Run Away, that she keeps hidden under
the bed. When that gets too full, before she has a chance to punch
in new pages, she plugs the extra articles into the dryer's venting
hole, confident that Clem would never use the dryer on his own
accord. Her latest entry is about a woman in South Dakota who
popped her husband off with a Saturday Night Special before she
ran away. The police found photos of her in his dresser showing her
bruised and naked and tied up. Not anymore. Not tied up anymore.

Stella likes to rehearse her own leaving: It's night time and Clem comes home late off the ocean. She hates it when he does that, racing the fading daylight from one hundred feet below the surface, all to pluck out a couple more scallops. And she hates the blubbery white taste of scallops. This time he's been bounce diving all day, down then back up, down then up, repeatedly, putting his catch in the boat then back down for more. She's told Clem about what can happen, bounce diving all day, then maybe he swims up too fast and he gets the bends, a deep burning pain that will only feel better if he goes back down again. At the very least there's this to worry about, she explained to Clem. It can be a permanently disabling condition, she has the article that proves it. It can feel like a heart attack, and then they have to depressurize you. Clem just laughed. He told her they need the money. He pointed out she's not exactly making enough for them to live on, is she? A lady minister's secretary? He uses that word, secretary, even though she's told him Reverend Ellen Barnes prefers that Stella be called her assistant. Ellen also doesn't like people to refer to her as a "lady minister," which Stella tries to remember not to say, at least not in front of Ellen.

Clem goes to bed finally, the way Stella imagines it, and she waits for the sound of his breathing to deepen, the raggedness of it growing into a snore, taking her time in the bathroom so that he won't wait for her to crawl in beside him. Stella's packed her almost-like-new Key West bag she found rummaging through discards at Good Will. She doesn't need much. Most of the trappings of a life are expendable when you get right down to it. And Stella walks out. Just walks out. Drives up Route One and then 1-A to Bangor, abandons their old Escort that's not reliable anyway when the snow flies and takes off on a plane to someplace else.

If it wasn't for Heather. Heather is Clem's nine and a half year old daughter from his previous marriage and Stella loves her beyond what Stella can understand. Reverend Ellen says love doesn't have to be genetic. It's all about different *kinds* of love, Ellen says. Sometimes when Heather stays with them Stella watches her sleep and imagines what it would be like to be her mother, to touch her, to hug her when she feels like it, braid her yellow hair; just to know Heather's child skin is Stella's own skin too. And she would never,

ever take The Instrument to Heather's face, even if she had that right as Heather's mother.

Stella won't have her own children. It's not a biological kind of problem, she explained to Ellen one day. It's just that nine years ago when Stella was a young woman with something fluttery and unsure inside her, she cut out her first news article about Things In The World That Can Break Your Heart, and pasted it into her now worn-out leather portfolio. The article, from The Portland Herald, told about the murder of Jenna Pierce. Stella was never sure what led her to this article, fixating on it, troubling about it, crying over it day after day—a story about something that happened in Portland, Maine, which could be a different state, for all the bearing it had on life in Rock Harbor, a hundred and twenty miles north.

The article, which was long enough to require you to flip to page eight at the back of the front section, showed a picture of Jenna Pierce from her high school graduation a year earlier, smiling out from the printed page the way pictures of the murdered do. Stella began to have dreams about Jenna, dreaming of her as a friend, a sister, even as a daughter, an integral part of Stella's own life, gone. She decided she would never bear children because she couldn't bear it if this happened to her own son or daughter. She couldn't stand the thought of walking her child to the bus stop one day, like a woman from New Haven, Connecticut, did, kissing her on the cool of her cheeks good-bye—and that's it, good-bye. The woman in this article never saw her daughter alive again. There was a photograph of a small coffin, with flowers on top.

Marrying Clem three years later gave Stella yet another thing to worry about; every time he dove into the cold green depths of the Atlantic Stella just knew there'd be the day he wouldn't come up again. She did love him, she must have, enough to go out in the boat in the beginning, the dark water surrounding her then appearing later in dreams all colored the same deep threatening green, and always about water or boats, the fluid sensations of instability and impermanence. Though not immortality. Stella won't believe in immortality despite being a minister's administrative assistant. She does the church books, makes the phone calls and bangs away on the ancient IBM office computer as if she knows what she's doing, but she won't believe in immortality. Stella just knows this is her one shot. If she can't get it right, that's it. No being reborn into a thin person's body without the migraine headaches she's been getting lately, no soul rising to a heaven without nerves.

Stella began cutting out articles about The Dangers Of Deep Sea Diving. And after a while Clem took particular delight in describing to her the depth of his dives, as far down as 100 feet where the underwater world grows black and uncertain, and so cold that when he rises up again his face is red and rumpled as a baby's behind. That was after she stopped riding in his boat, sitting at home instead in the upstairs of the duplex they live in, listening for his steps on the outside stairs. She began to wonder which she feared more: not loving Clem enough, or loving him too much so that losing him would be unbearable, or losing him before she could be sure if she really still loved him at all. Whether her love was in fact driven by the fear of her loss.

Henri gets up suddenly from the beach chair, her shadow with all that hair sliding over Stella. Stella opens her eyes again and tugs her hand through her own scant and greying hair. Barely over thirty yet already her hair is part grey and part gone, thinning for some reason that Clem says is her nerves, the doctor tells her is probably hereditary and her mother says, "Maybe you better get a wig."

"Well," Henri yawns, stretching up on her tiptoes, bare feet and ripples of sleek calve muscles under her cropped pants, "I can't decide what to do. Should I stay here and live my sister's life with her husband in this poor excuse for a house, or go back to *my* house in San Francisco where *my* husband is living with another woman? Smoky! Can you imagine being named after smoke? That's even more nauseating than being called Misty or Windy."

"I have an article about a woman who set fire to her house with her husband and his lover inside. She sent her kids to their grandparents for the night and her husband apparently thought his wife was with the kids. She circled the house with a can of his lawn mower gasoline while they slept. The article said she munched on an apple and watched her house burn. She had no regrets, it said."

Henri moves cool blue eyes down the bulk of Stella who is still sitting in the webbed chair. Stella wishes her eyes were like that, eyes that could stare at a person and pass judgment without saying a word. She wishes she could wear cropped pants and sport legs that look like they could do more than just get you around. She wishes she had a house in San Francisco or had even been there just once. "Well, thanks for sharing that, Stella. Honest to god you folks in the outback are weird. Maybe there's no place in this damn country I belong." Henri sighs.

Stella feels the beginnings of a headache, the flush in her face, a sourness in her stomach; although maybe the sourness is a parasite, she's begun to wonder about that. She gets this gnawing feeling right after she eats, like she can't possibly get enough food inside her. She's read about parasites. Half the things we eat have them in one form or another, and half the illnesses people get, even as common as the cold, are caused by some unspeakable little worm in their gut that's taken up residence.

"The problem is…" Henri is saying, "we should live in a world for just women. Men and women get down each other's backs in the worst way, yet look how demented they are up at that prison, living without us. Maybe men need women more than women need them. Maybe we should just shoot all the men. Maybe they'd treat us better if they thought every day they could be shot. That's why they behave up at the prison, you know. They got guards prancing around up there with something like M-16s attached to their shoulders."

Stella's heart makes one of those uncomfortable leaps and then a bump, like a roller coaster halted in mid-frenzy. The Reverend Ellen Barnes was recently invited to extend her ministry to Rock Harbor Adult Correctional and Stella lives with the fear that Ellen will ask her to help. Stella knows who's in that prison, murderers, rapists, the kinds of men who do the things that women run away from—until they can't. She knows the man who murdered Jenna Pierce is in that prison. Stella's been trying to think of a reason why she can't go that will be acceptable to Ellen, just in case. Ellen doesn't understand how scary life can be for real people.

Stella's head feels a rushing, hurtling sensation like a train moving into it and then the roar of the headache, full strength. She'll take Heather and leave now, go home to the empty duplex where Clem's presence is a dark green promise hovering unseen like a ghost, until later this evening when she hears his steps on the stairs. Then all will be well, for this night anyway.

• • •

One night just a few weeks later Clem doesn't come home, the way Stella always knew he wouldn't. The morning was windy and unsettled and a small craft advisory was in effect, they had heard it on the clock radio waking them before dawn. Clem pointed at the antique desk so covered with papers and envelopes you could barely see the gouges on its unpolished surface, at the unpaid electric bill, at another boat payment deadline they didn't make, over-extended credit card notices and the rent due at the end of the week. He walked out before the sun graced the sky.

Stella had considered grabbing Clem's legs below the knees, clamping onto his feet, forcing him to remain in their bedroom. Instead she yanked the covers over her head, pulled her pillow on top, hummed a nothing sort of tune into her ears and still she could not quiet the sounds of his leaving: a car door slams, the engine stalls, fires up, the whine of the tires as the Escort drives slowly away.

All night the wind off the ocean scratches around the back door like a wet and shivering animal trying to come inside, but no Clem. Stella keeps thinking surely these are his steps, his tired shuffle up the duplex stairs, each one another burden. No Clem. At some point she falls asleep, briefly, one of those sleeps that's merely assumed, never remembered. And she thinks she does hear his steps, she's sure of it, swishing and sliding and dragging up those stairs as if encumbered by, what? Kelp perhaps? Brown strands of it like her own hair used to be, around his ankles, hanging down like moss in the days when her hair was something and his body was a mystery and she covered every part every night with kisses; six years ago,

62

five, her hair sliding over him like the sheets she took off of him, back when there must have been love. How those slow nights lingered on, until the mornings when she would have to once again worry if he would come home off the sea.

Just before dawn Stella rises, lights the bayberry candle on her dresser and the cinnamon one down the hall, opens the shades so that the growing lightness, the milkiness of the sky can seep inside where it's still dark, where the shadows still hover in the corners. She tiptoes into Heather's room, gazes down at the sleeping child. Heather has the sheet worked around her small fist, pressed tightly against her cheek, as if her own hand is separate from her, something to hold onto. Stella feels a burning inside, an aching at the back of her throat and she fights the urge to crawl in bed beside the child, grab onto his Heather and sob.

She knows she will have to call Alyson, Heather's mother, but Stella can't yet imagine the words forming themselves against her own tongue, moving out of her own mouth, "He didn't come back." She used to feel jealous that Alyson had Heather, this permanent connection to Stella's own husband. What is forever? Clem didn't come home.

Later in the morning after Heather is packed off to school, after she fixed Heather a bowl of oatmeal with islands of brown sugar the way Stella herself used to eat it, Stella begins to clean. She sweeps the wood floors of the duplex, this time picking up the throw rugs instead of moving the dirt around them, shaking the rugs out of the window, the new morning air a sudden cloud of dust, and Stella thinks: he walked on these. And she lets the rugs fall down onto the new grass below.

In between her mopping then polishing the floors they appear at the door, two of them, Rock Harbor police in their dark blue uniforms. Stella doesn't invite them inside. She knows what they are about to say, has already imagined it a thousand times— Clem's Boston Whaler that they never even finished paying off tossing and drifting on the green swells like a person fighting to emerge out of a bad dream—empty. The police tell her that the Coast Guard has organized a search. Stella smiles, she nods, because she knew this is

what they would do, she's read it in at least fifteen articles about
People Who Drown, cut out and pasted into The Dangers Of Deep
Sea Diving. After a few days the search will be "regretfully" called
off. At some point, maybe as much as six months later, a fisherman
will find a part of Clem in his net's catch, Clem's wedding ring perhaps, an article of rotted clothing, even a jaw bone, and Clement
Dubois will be officially declared dead. But to Stella, Clem has been
dying for years. When she first understood that one day her husband
would not rise up from the green, Stella prepared herself for this
time.

After the floors glow like new skin Stella does the windows.
Then she wipes finger marks off the walls, scrubs the grout between
the tiles in the shower and throws out all those almost finished con-
tainers of lotions, sun creams, and half-used yeast infection prescrip-
tions from the bathroom closet. Stella attacks her medicines: pills
for her headaches, nausea, anxiety; sprays for when her ears plug up,
antihistamines for the pollen season, anti-depressants, anti-inflama-
tories, anti-tick spray to ward off Lyme disease harboring deer
ticks—throws them all into a plastic Hefty bag. Then she throws
the Hefty bag out the window beside the rugs, beside a broken
kitchen chair Clem never got around to repairing, all of Clem's
clothes, Stella's unflattering clothes, an umbrella stored in a box
kept near the door in case it looked like rain, and finally her scrap-
books—The Dangers Of Deep Sea Diving, Things Men Do To
Women, Women Who Run Away, Things In The World That Can
Break Your Heart—all scattered upon the tender spring grass.

Stella washes the bedding from the little alcove room they had
set aside for Heather's visits, pouring extra bleach into the water so
that even the sheets will sparkle, even though Heather won't be
coming back. For a moment Stella lies on top of Heather's bed,
careful not to wrinkle the freshly pressed Power Rangers quilt. She
inhales deeply, assuring herself that the room still holds that light
child scent.

In the late afternoon just before the sun starts its purpling slant
down into the evening, Stella pulls the secondhand bike Clem had
fixed up for Heather out of the garage, and she pedals into town to

the Corner Store where they sell bunches of flowers, tulips, lilies, and wildflowers. She buys a bouquet, climbs back onto the bike only a little conscious of the way her bottom hangs over the rose-pink seat, knowing what her mother would say; but what does it matter now?

When Stella arrives at the parsonage of Rock Harbor Congregational, Reverend Ellen Barnes greets her at the door. She is dressed in corduroy slacks and a button-down flannel shirt, more like a person than a minister, Stella thinks. Ellen puts her arms around Stella's shoulders, pulls her inside, shuts the door. "Have faith Stella, they're searching."

Stella shakes her head, slipping away from Ellen's grasp. "That's not why I'm here. It's getting too dark for the bike and the Escort is still at the docks where he parks. Can you give me a ride? I have these flowers. He liked tiger lilies." Stella inhales a deep, ragged breath that moves down inside her the way the water did him. She imagines the green water filling him the way blood flows inside a person's veins, sluggish at first maybe, then the full cold race of it to his head. She wonders if he thought of her when it happened, thought of how she was right, after all…his breath fully released and the green gush of the sea exploding up inside his lungs; and then the darkness, and then the forever.

Stella pictures the way it will be when Ellen takes her there, standing out on the rocky ledge, the tide moving below her, a slow cool slide of it, almost like she can walk right out on it, like she could deliver the flowers herself; almost the way Jesus was said to do it, walking out on the water like it's his path. "Have faith," Ellen repeats, patting Stella's arm. She walks over to the hall table, picks up her keys.

Stella feels the bouquet of flowers in her arms, imagines the ocean wind behind her and around her and through her, as if Clem could be on it, be a part of it; almost as if in the end he could have loved her enough, or she could have loved him enough, to be with her always. She remembers driving home late one night from her mother's house, Clem yawning behind the wheel, Stella wordless beside him, on a road in the middle of nowhere. It was almost dawn, the growing light a pale mist tucked over them, a supple wet quilt. And they came across two women bending over a dead deer beside a car with its hood crumpled, its windshield cracked and shivering in Clem's headlights like a cobweb. One woman was crying. The other held a gun. Through a shimmer of trees opening into a blue field Stella saw another deer, a buck, his horns silhouetted by an early sky the color of clay, standing without fear or the knowledge to be afraid, waiting for whatever it is we wait for.

YELLOW KITCHEN

WATCHING ELI PAINT, AN IMAGE COMES TO DALLAS of his mother painting her toenails. His mother was heavy and distant sometimes and their house was an angry place in the later years of his childhood, but not so much during this time he is thinking about now. He's a little boy, small for his age, scrawny, knees like two walnuts in his aloha print shorts called jams, bony shoulders hard as sugar bowl handles poking up under his favorite Surf Waimea tee shirt, stringy face. He's nine years old, coming home from school. He walks into the yellow kitchen and there's his mother, the back of her billowy and wide as the curtains that flutter in the window above the aluminum sink, overlooking Kaneohe Bay. She's sitting at the table, her chair thrust away from it and her right foot sticking straight up on its bare formica surface. She's bending over herself, her double-sized stomach, with great effort. Carefully his mother pulls the nail polish brush with the color Pearly Pink, her favorite, across each toenail. Her toenails are delicate, her foot short and white and puffy as foam.

Dallas can hear Kaneohe Bay from outside, the sucking noise it makes at low tide. The afternoon is warm and thirsty, Kona weather, the TV station his father listens to during dinner would describe it. Sargent Marty Kauahui is the Channel Seven weatherman and when he's done telling them about the weather he grins, salutes, says, "All pau!" Dallas's father salutes the TV back. "All done!" says his father, which means the same thing. Through the window Dallas can see palm fronds in their yard leaning and swaying in the humid breeze, above the long gnarly trunks they're attached to, the way his mother leans over the bulk of herself, concentrating, her brow dimpled, dragging the brush across those little nails. Why does this feel so sad to him, seeing his mother, who his friends joke about behind his back and to his face when they're being really mean, care this much about her toenails? He inches over toward her, folds down quietly in front of her on the yellow linoleum floor, has an idea that maybe she'll stop doing this to her toenails and touch him, maybe, stroke his neck with her hands, beautify him.

Though of course Eli isn't painting her toenails. Wouldn't waste her time, she'd call it, painting something as insignificant as toes. Her paintings have become smaller and smaller these days, Dallas has noticed. She doesn't even use her easel now, just a piece of pressed board on her lap and her canvas on top. She's painting small things, sets of them, a pair of little sneakers, laces askew, a pair of oranges, two spools of different colored thread, two crutches she borrowed from the neighbor's six-year-old son. Her still life period, she told Dallas.

It's late afternoon and they are out on the back porch where the light is good. Early autumn, before daylight savings is gone and the days get shorter and shorter, squeezed in between too many hours of darkness. Sunset happens by 4:00 in December. Dallas peers out over the field behind the house. He doesn't much care for this house, built in those architecturally constipated years of the 1950s. A house just old enough to have the beginnings of structural problems, but no grace. The field is what keeps him here. He's never lived anywhere where he can look out back and see only nature, nothing built by man. It helps him keep things in perspective. In the end buildings collapse. It's fields that are left. From the distance Dallas can see a flat silvery sheen like a new dime, Mirror Lake. A loon calls out, he's glad they haven't left yet. Something sad about the way most of the birds leave for the winter here. Makes him wonder if they understand something he doesn't.

Dallas knows his wife hates it when he watches her paint. Her eyebrows shot up at him when he came out on the porch, then she turned her folding chair away from his. Now they sit like two old people, gazing into their separate distances. Only they're not old, damnit! Dallas thinks, they're wasting away for no good reason. "I've been wondering about the adoption thing," he starts, staring at the back of her. He watches her shoulders stiffen, the twitch of her right arm, her hand holding the paint brush. "They told us we couldn't when we lived in Ohio but we haven't checked it out in Maine."

"Christ!" Eli says, still turned away from him. "We don't own a house, I don't have a job, you don't have a permanent job really, we have no savings and we've lived in three states in three years. Give it a rest, Dallas. We're not the picture of stability. We're not the parents they're looking for."

"That's if we want a baby," Dallas says, "especially a little white baby. I don't care what color he is, do you? And he can be older, a toddler, even if he's just starting school. That would be OK. No diapers." Dallas tries this last out with deliberate enthusiasm in his voice, what's the expression? Forced bravado? Tastes wrong on his tongue.

Eli stops painting. She stands up, walks over to the old picnic table the color of driftwood that's shoved up against the back wall of the porch. She found it at the dump. She found half their furnishings and a variety of other "We'll see in a year if it's useful" items at the Rock Harbor town dump. She is not one who covets ownership of furniture or appliances. Eli puts the board with her canvas on the table, comes back to the chair, sits down hard, leans over and screws on the tops to her oils that are spread out in an uneven line on the floor, plops her brush into some chemical in a glass jar then turns her folding chair around so she's facing him. "Damn you, Dallas," she says quietly. "You can't stop blaming me, can you?"

"All right now, Eli, I'm not blaming you for a thing here. I know you wanted your own baby but you can't do it, can you? The doctor said you can't do it. Does that mean we have to be childless? I want a kid, Eli. I've always wanted one. What's the point of even being married if we don't have a kid? We could've just kept living together, you could've kept your own last name, for chrissake. If we had a kid maybe things would go better for us together. Have you thought about that?"

Eli stands up again, moving closer to Dallas, towering over him in the lavender light as if she's a much bigger woman than she really is. "My own last name was my father's name," she says, "one man's name or another's, what's the difference? So why do we stay together?" she whispers over his head, the breath of her words stirring against his hair like wind.

"What do you mean?" His own words sound hollow. This is the edge they've skirted around, after all, like it's a cliff for almost four years now. Since the baby died. "All I'm saying," he says, "is that maybe things would at least be different between us if we had a kid."

"Are we glued invisibly? Some kind of emotional paste? Or maybe we're nailed together. Not a day goes by that I don't think about leaving you, Dallas Hyde. You've done so much that warrants it, you know. And I don't. I just don't."

"I want a child," he repeats. "I want to be a father. I want to feel some kind of reason for being here. What's so wrong about that, wanting a reason for living besides making a goddamn paycheck?"

Dallas has a sudden memory of his wife in labor. He winces at the way it comes back to him, all grey. As if Queens Hospital had lost its color that particular day, appearing only in black, white, but mostly in between. Dallas remembers Eli in the Birthing Room. Funny how when they first were shown this room, back when they were choosing a doctor, a hospital, back when the world was in color and they were going to be parents…this room was yellow, teddy bear wallpaper, pink oleander outside a large bay window. All this seemed to have disappeared when he brought her into Queens five months later, bleeding.

He remembers how small Eli looked, writhing about on the bed. He remembers her face, how her eyes pulled back into it, darkening with every contraction. "Oh, God, take me home!" she cried out and her words chilled him. Though everything seemed fine. The nurse assured them the baby's heart beat was strong and regular on the fetal monitor. Premature, yes, the baby was being born early but with a "strong and regular" heart beat. They were ready for the baby in the "Preemies" nursery, the doctor was ready to deliver. Everybody's standing by, Dallas was told. He had rubbed Eli's forehead with a cool washcloth. The nurse gave him ice chips to give to Eli, which she spat back out at him. Dallas didn't know how or who to be for Eli. They never even had the chance to go through Lamaze. He didn't have a clue how to help her. He wanted to take Eli's pain into his own body and be her. "Strong and regular," the nurse repeated, as they moved his wife out of the bed, onto a gurney. Dallas followed them into what looked like an operating room, not a teddy bear in sight. "Routine with a premature delivery," the doctor said.

But she did it for nothing. His wife went through that hell, for nothing.

Eli leans down over Dallas, into his face. He can smell the chemical she cleans her brushes in, pungent and sour. He remembers again his mother painting her toenails in the yellow kitchen, white afternoon light pouring in from the window, milky colored, a train of it roaring toward her as she hunkered down over those nails as if they were the only thing in the world worth such pure concentration. Dallas breathed in that chemical smell of the polish and the open bottle of polish remover sitting on the table. "Cutex," he sounded out the word on the label. "I'm a good reader, aren't I, Mommy?" he asked her.

He knelt on the floor, on his bare knees so he could be closer to her face, her scrunched up cheeks, flushed and round as tomatoes. He rubbed the back of his hand across one of her cheeks as she bent down over her toenails. If she would just look at him for a moment. She did, her little brush poised in the air, a glob of Pearly Pink at its tip like the head of a pimple. "Dallas!" his mother whistled out between her lips, her Pearly Pink lipstick that matched the polish, she bought them as a set at Woolworth's. "How many times do I have to tell you? Leave Mommy alone when she's doing her nails.

71

Leave me alone."

Eli's hand grasps Dallas's chin, raises it up toward her own face. He can't make out her features anymore, shadowed in the approaching night. "Dallas," she says and her voice sounds flat and subdued, "just because Benjamin isn't with us, just because you won't talk about him doesn't change the fact of him, you know. Adopting someone else's kid won't change a thing. Babies aren't light bulbs. You can't just screw in a new one when the other isn't shining."

SWEET BREATH

HE'S CRUISING ALONG ROUTE 315 GOING NOWHERE, and there she is. Her thigh is what he notices about her first. Long, really long, in tight jeans, she's stuck it out then curved it in and around a utility pole like a backwards question mark. She's blond, same as his wife, only his wife's hair is short. Everything about his wife is short. This hair swirls out and about like an animal's tail, like something with a mind of its own.

As he lets up on the accelerator, braking, coaxing the Plymouth Fury to an easy stop beside the girl, she whips her arm behind her head and yanks at the hair, stretching it down in front of her neck like a shield. She leans into the window he rolls down, passenger's side, takes her sweet time about it too despite the line of cars building up behind him. "What do you want?" she asks, peering in at him like he's the one with no right to be here.

"Shit," he mutters. An ache of something neglected tugs at his groin. She's barely more than a kid. Her eyes burn with newness. "Excuse me, but do you or don't you need a ride? I thought you were hitchhiking." His voice seems strange, a sound apart from the rest of him. It's been awhile since he's spoken to anybody.

"Depends. If you're a weirdo or a creep, forget it. Are you some kind of a pathetic loser?"

The driver of the car behind his leans on the horn. He flips him off in the rear-view, shaking his head, his own hair black as the road but for a slow creep of premature, just-over-thirty grey at his temples, and cut in an uneven line at his neck. He feels a surge of anger. The girl, the car behind him, it's like a conspiracy sometimes. "I didn't know hitchhikers were so bloody picky. Take a bus, why don't you?" A semi, emptied of its load, barrels by like a warning. The horn-blaster behind him, white car, probably a BMW or a Volvo, is writing down his license plate, he'd just bet on it. The girl shrugs, opens the door and climbs into the car.

"My stepmother has this same damn car, same color and everything. Goes to show you can't escape. Just take me anywhere," she says as he forces the Fury back into traffic, out of the right lane, shooting into the left where things flow a little freer. "Anywhere that's away from here." She tosses her hair over the seat so it's drifting into the back of the car where recently his whole life had been kept, a bag with his toothbrush and shaving stuff, his sleeping bag, a spare clean shirt and HOLLYWOOD—the book he's been reading about a guy who doesn't live his life the normal way but people love him, he makes a movie the way he wants to make it, it's a success naturally, and he lives forever with lots of money.

His eyes leave the road for a second traveling quickly over the girl. Her hair is the color of the moon and just as showy. A hank of it has blown across his arm that rests tenuously on the seat near her shoulder. She's left the window open even though the wind has teeth and it's about to rain. Not a yellowy blond, he rolls his eyes, stares straight ahead at the street again; she's hardly a real blond at all.

"Can't you get off this damn highway? I hate this highway. My last ride was an asshole and he left me here." Her eyes, a pale shade of an almost yellow, search his profile. Eyes like a cat's, he thinks. "I'm into your regular roads, country roads. I hate highways. On the mainland they go on forever."

"Where you from, Mars? You know," he starts, then tightens his lips. He remembers he didn't brush his teeth this morning. Does his breath stink? There was no fresh water in the park he stayed the night in, just a mud hole—Fishing Pond, the sign said. He shrugs. "Hell, how old are you anyway? I mean isn't this kind of thing pretty dangerous, you telling me to take back roads, away from civilization and all? Who am I? You don't know, I could be a mass murderer."

"Civilization, hah!" She throws back her head, her sleek neck long as a horse's. "Like isn't this Ohio? I got them mixed up on the maps we did in the fourth grade, Ohio and Iowa, four letter states in the middle of nowhere. Who cares anyway, what's the difference? I'm from Hawaii. The bars in Waikiki are open till four in the morning. That's civilization. Anyhow, I take rides from people all the time. Not everybody gets to drive their own Fury, you know."

"Right. So what. And you're too young for bars." He shakes his head. Why did he even stop? Not that he was going any place in particular, but this is supposed to give his afternoon meaning? He fiddles with the station tuner on the radio, sliding it up and down like scales, music, news, chatter, numbing and drab. He flips the power off.

"My father picked up someone in a bar. He brought her home and screwed her. I think he screwed her into something permanent, like maybe a socket because she's been with us ever since."

He smiles and sees she's smiling too, a little smirk. He feels that ache again, the stirring that starts deep in the pit of him, swells and announces itself proud as a flag. Something about the way she talks. Tough kid. He glances at her thighs, longer than his, longer than anyone's. "So what are you doing in Ohio if you hate it so much? You look like you should be in high school."

"School's bullshit. I'm going to stay with my mother. My real mother. She happens to live around here."

He maneuvers the Fury around a fallen tree branch. The roads away from the highway are rain-soaked, deeply pitted in places, the pavement may be as ancient as the trees. Not many trees though. Fields mostly, dull and beaten by winter, by constant rain. The sky is huge and grey as an old man's face, the grass bent and wheat colored. He takes his left hand off the steering wheel, laying it subtly upon his lap. He sees her, silver hair, legs wound around him tight as a vine. He'd be everything to her, lover, brother, though of course she can mean nothing to him. He means nothing. His loathing, his self-pity, this is what's alive in him. He'd put it in her, and then he'd be free.

• • •

She shuts her eyes, tilts her head back against the seat, its uphol-stery warm and familiar, a rich thick smell of plastic. The motion of the car under her is the motion of the world around her. It jerks, it moans, it whines, it moves forward too slowly, like a breath, like a sigh, like something broken. It stops.

The car door slams, "I'll be right back" he tells her. The sudden quiet is like the silent place inside her, empty, waiting. "Iron crow," her mother's letter had said. "I've got this iron crow in my yard, Marnie, it's so quaint."

"Don't you know?" her father said to Marnie. "Your mother loves her things more than us." But this was the way they had talked about each other, her mother, her father. And then her mother was gone.

"Such a tiny yard, hardly a yard at all, life in a trailer park," said the letter. "No room for you, baby." A trailer, somewhere in central Ohio she wrote, no return address.

Iron crow? Marnie pops open her eyes as if one might be perched on this dashboard, cold metal stare, leadened feathers. The dog in the trailer next to hers barks all night long, the letter had com-plained. Marnie could hear her mother's voice underneath the scribbled, jubilant script, breathy, a final, lingering sigh.

The man climbs back into the car, his face pink and mottled. "Sorry, I had to use a bathroom, a user-friendly bush as my wife used to say." Marnie stares at his hand as he shifts into first, reddish fin-gers, beefy and weathered like her father's. Her father's are sun-dam-aged from his years life guarding at Waimea Bay. That was when he was young, just a little older than Marnie is now. His last good years he told her once. Her own hands are smooth and long-fingered.

"You want to know something else? The woman my father keeps in our house doesn't let me keep pets. Not after the guinea pig incident, that's what she calls it. She marches into my room, doesn't even knock, says she wants to 'Throw open the windows to the ocean breeze.' Can you believe that? Like, we live on top of a volcano, not exactly prime beach-front you know? Then she says, she's got this shrieky, bitchy way of talking, 'Your guinea pig's gonna be dead by next morning the way you keep its cage. Look at it! That cage is pure filth. Do you even feed it? What if I took care of you that way?' What a major bitch. Like I need her to take care of me? I call her The Sleaze."

"What's your name, anyway? Mine's Harold." He stares at Marnie, she knew he would. While she's been talking to him she's unsnapped three of the snaps on her jean jacket. She's wearing not a thing under it.

"Harold? As in Hark the Harold Angels Sing? They named you after a Christmas song. OK, so your last name is probably Carol. Cute, really cute."

He shakes his head, pulls at his chin, gazes fiercely at the road in front of him. "That's Harold, my name is Harold not herald. Don't they teach you to spell in your school? So what you're probably all of fifteen, huh?" He pushes the gear shift into third, accelerates, slips into fourth. "Now let me tell you something. I have no life," he says. "My wife's gone and she's got our apartment. I quit my job. There's nothing so-called respectable about me but I've never done a thing I can't at least live with myself about."

Marnie sticks her foot up on the dash, short black boot, candy-cane striped sock, drums her fingers against her knee cap to the tune of the rain that falls suddenly hard. "I'm seventeen," she says, "almost. Also I'm a model. Did you guess that? The woman my father keeps sent me on this shoot in San Francisco. My father said I was too young to go alone. She said don't be stupid. It was a fashion spread and the photographer kept feeling me up in the different outfits. He's 'arranging me,' he said. When it was over they took me to the airport, left me there and I cashed in my Honolulu ticket for a ticket to Columbus." She unsnaps the last snap on her jacket, pulls it wide open. "You want me, right? Go ahead, why the fuck not?"

The Fury veers toward a ditch at the side of the road, dips, bounces back. Marnie feels its return like a curse. One whole week, nights alone in grungy motels, days spent riding busses, hitchhiking through all those flat little towns in the middle of Ohio, all those trailer parks. In seven, maybe eight of them, she sees iron crows on yellow lawns, between patches of dirt, of dust, of mud, standing staunch and vacant-eyed like real birds, only who wants crows in the first place? And iron chipmunks, iron squirrels, deer, every other trailer's yard, even on top of a couple tinny roofs there's imitation animal life. Nobody's heard of her mother. With the sleeve of her jacket Marnie swipes ferociously at the tears rolling down her cheeks onto her bare breasts.

"Maybe we should go find us a place to eat at," says Harold, his eyes fixed straight ahead on the road before them. "I'm starved."

• • •

"Well," says Harold, watching Marnie inhale a hamburger like it's her first or maybe her last meal of the month. He's taken her into Moynihan's, a little cafe in the middle of nowhere. Like a father he made her close up her jacket, comb her hair. A father, he thinks, that's what the others are thinking, staring from their tables at her, at him, then away again; old enough to be her father. He hates them, their smug, shut faces.

He imagines feeding Marnie until she's satiated and content. It would be dark when they go back outside, she'd lean against him as he leads her to the Plymouth, she'd be his willow and he her roots; he'd drive them to some park for the night that doesn't close its gates, that doesn't have gates. Some park that has water so he can brush his teeth.

Then, he'd say something completely outrageous to her like, See this belt? He'd whip it off his pants in one slick movement, the strike of a snake. Hit me with it, OK? Something really outrageous so he can remember he's alive. A terrible taste swells into Harold's mouth, like his own food coming up again, like venom. He covers his lips with the napkin, bites down on his tongue until it bleeds.

He says to Marnie after a slug of coffee strong as tar, his second cup—she's attacking an ice cream sundae—"So, you got a boyfriend in Hawaii?"

Marnie snorts, slaps at a drift of snow-colored hair near her mouth that threatens to mingle with her ice cream. "Oh, yeah, lots. Hundreds. They all like me just as far as they can see me."

"That business in my car with your jacket? What was that all about?" He signals the waitress for more coffee, its bleak taste a punishment he no doubt deserves.

Marnie lowers her eyes. She slurps the remaining ice cream, mostly liquid, up with a straw, picks up the long-handled silver spoon, turns it against her tongue, sucks. He thinks about her long legs under the table almost touching his, her bony knees, her hair hanging down around her heart-shaped face. A sadness sweeps through him. "OK," he sighs. "So, what?"

"You mean this jacket?" says Marnie. "This fucking denim jacket belongs to The Sleaze, the woman my father keeps, my so-called stepmother. Yeah, well, isn't that what everybody sees when they look at me? I just figured it's what you wanted, that's the reason you picked me up."

Harold's face is hot. He stares at his fingers, stretching them out and around his coffee cup. The room they are in has dingy, colorless walls, and he sees himself blending into it perfectly, a part of its walls, its ceiling, space, air, its nothingness. "Why should you do what I want, if it's what I want?"

"So you'd help me."

"Meaning what?"

"So you'd help me find my real mother. But, forget it, because I changed my mind anyway."

Harold cups his chin in his hands, it's scratchy, a two-day beard, nothing about him is fresh anymore. He closes his eyes. Last month it would have been his wife sitting across from him, her cold, vacant stare never seeing him, always looking around, down, out any available window. "It's dead," she had said finally one night, handing him his suitcase the minute he got home from work. "I can't feel myself when I'm with you. I feel more looking at your dog than I do when I look at you, and your dog drives me crazy. Always shoveling his nose around the carpet, always smelling bad. But at least I feel something when I look at him."

That's when he quit everything—his job (it was a nothing job, an accountant keeping track of other people's money, nothing solid, nothing built, nothing gained beyond his paycheck), his friends (they were their friends, couples, a way to get through the weekends), even his dog (he left his dog with his wife!), just gave it all up. To prove…what? It seemed so pointless now. As though when one part of your life falls apart you can just shrug off all the rest to emerge clean and free as something else. What was he but the same old Harold without a life? "Sometimes I wish I at least had a kid," he says to Marnie. "I think I could have loved it. I'd have done a good job loving it. A kid makes a person more permanent."

Marnie's eyes, pale as the evening light, study Harold's face. "You know what?" She leans toward him. The smell of vanilla ice cream surrounds her like perfume. "You know what my mom used to call me when I was a baby? She used to call me Sweet Breath. Of course I don't remember, but she told me. She said she would throw me up in the air, to startle me because I cried a lot. Then after she got my attention, she'd hold me close. She said I had the sweetest breath. 'Like a brand new morning,' she said, 'like something perfect.'"

Harold takes Marnie's hand lightly in his. Her fingers are cold, and he feels bad about this. "Oh God, oh God, oh God," she says, wailing it, sort of matter-of-fact. "I hate modeling, could you guess that? I'm going to be an anthropologist. I'll get to travel thousands of miles away and I'll dig up remnants."

"Remnants?"

"You know, things from the past, from people who lived hundreds and thousands of years ago."

Harold nods, solemnly.

"I'm not so dumb you know. People think because I look the way I do I'm lo lo. That means stupid in Hawaiian."

"Where do I take you now?" he asks. "I don't know where to take you."

Marnie shrugs. "To the airport, I guess. Can't wait to hear the bitching out I'll get from The Sleaze. I make a game of it. I count her words, take bets on how many she can spew before she has to inhale."

Harold hands the cashier his VISA, feeling a strange satisfaction at paying for Marnie's meal along with his. Like a father would. Outside in the parking lot he puts a tentative arm around her shoulders. She's taller than him and he laughs. Because he's the one who's leaning on her.

ONE TALE OF TANTALUS

ELI'S OLDER SISTER HENRI TOLD HER HOW IT WAS after the accident, Eli in a hospital room hooked up to a machine, squeezing its breath into her, out, into her, out. Eli likes to imagine she remembers this tender whooshing of the air and she sees herself, sixteen, forever damaged but she can't know this yet, crawling out of herself, out onto the cool trail of mechanical air. Eli's own last memory of the accident is of Melissa, her little sister. The Corvette is wrapped around a road-side monkeypod tree, as if it had tried to fly up into the tree's spiraling branches, a twisted metal bird the color of corn lifting its ruined wings. Eli's thrown against the door so hard the metal becomes her own skin. She's conscious for a minute maybe, long enough to see Missy's foot sticking up outside the door, the rest of her somewhere underneath, pale ankle, blue and white checked stretchy pants she got for her birthday, the same blue color of her eyes they would not see open again. Eli knew somebody would die. She prayed it wouldn't be herself.

Henri said when they got to Queens Hospital a nurse slung her arm around their mother's shoulders. The ragged noise of their mother's sobs hung in the corridor apart from everything else that was alive there, sounds that didn't make sense of the world, uncon-nected to what's already understood. Could this really happen, one moment it's Missy's birthday and the next she's dead? Henri told Eli their father leaned into a white wall and groaned. Mostly Henri remembers this: everything glaringly white that day, like it was already Heaven, like Heaven wasn't such a good place to be.

The thrill is what Eli remembers. Missy and Eli with one of Henri's boyfriends. Where's Henri? It didn't matter. They find out in the weeks after the accident she was with some other guy and because Henri's boyfriend grew tired of waiting for her, Missy died. That's how Father put it—Missy wouldn't have been in that Corvette if Henri were there.

Eli was a redhead with skin the color of old snow in a land where you're either Hawaiian-dark, Asian, blond with a tan, or you're not looked at by any boy, at least not any high school boy. Henri's boys were older. This one's roughness, the spicy male smell of him, the dark secret of him enchanted Eli. She lived in a house of women, Father lurking at the perimeters, the shadowy corners of their female world. "This one, that one," he called them, as if he were hesitant to identify them by their names. Or maybe it just didn't make much of a difference to him, except for Missy. When Melissa was born Father gave up on the idea of having a son and he loved her anyway.

Eli was intrigued by all things male. She studied the postman's legs, the tender curl of his black hairs when he handed her their mail, the fit of his blue shorts over his swoops of thigh muscles. She inhaled the man smell from her father's friend's cigar, sitting in front of her on the ride to school. She gazed at her father's friend's balding head, a lumpy clay bowl with his thick neck under it. She imagined reaching across the airy space that separated them, front seat, back seat, and touching his neck, the tight stretch of his skin like a lizard's, the way his hair, what remained of it, was cut slightly uneven at the back of his head like a ridge of teeth.

They had played junk and a po, the Hawaiian version of paper and stone, and Missy's fist was a rock slamming down on the scissors Eli's fingers shaped, so it was Missy who got to sit on the hand brake beside Henri's boyfriend, it was Missy's hand clutching him so she wouldn't fly out the open convertible as they roared down the

Tantalus mountain road. Baby sister Melissa, just turned fourteen, fresh-out-of-braces smile and tufted little breasts like deviled eggs. Maybe his hand crept up Missy's leg, rubbed against her thigh, pinched the soft new flesh of her hip. Maybe he leaned into her breast and she felt for that moment such sweet confusion, thinking she should pull away, wanting him to linger there and she would pretend she didn't feel it. Maybe he really did touch her while Eli stared unknowingly out into the rest of the world, sky, mountain, forest, Tantalus road, curved and deadly. Missy was touched. At least Melissa was touched.

• • •

Eli rests her head back against the sticky-warmth of the Escort's front seat, her eyes forced open like some kind of water torture, sweat from her forehead dripping down under her dark glasses, driving the glaring road that leads to Rock Harbor Adult Correctional. The afternoon is reduced to the mechanical noises from her car and the steady insectual whining in the fields she passes, grass shimmering like pale green smoke in the heat. Summer in Maine, a rare, grey-hot day, so humid the sky, the sea, the road, the air are all one, their natural boundaries diminished by the cloying immediacy of heat. Tantalus, King Tantalus she thinks, from the Greek myth. Punished for his greed he's forced down into the underworld to spend eternity hanging in a tree laden with luscious fruit; soon as the fruit is close enough to pick it slips out of his reach; when he bends down to ease his raging thirst in the swelling waters of the universe, they subside. Tantalus, forever hungry and thirsty in the middle of plenty.

Eli thinks about how when she dies she wants the last person she touches to be someone she wants to touch. Like Missy did. To die with the feel of someone else's skin against hers. Eli thinks about dying too much her husband tells her, she's obsessed with it he says. But Eli is surrounded by the cycles of death and she is the part that remembers. Like the grave in the pauper area of the old Rock Harbor town cemetery: Unknown, Unwanted Baby Boy. She brings him fistfuls of wildflowers, sometimes she even brings him little metal trucks, marbles, a stuffed animal, treats she buys at the Corner Store as if he were her own. As if she had a right to his memory. Unknown, maybe, but not unwanted.

Eli is on her way to the prison to visit Morton Salvitore. Sometimes she can't help it, she just can't stop herself from wondering if Mort touched the woman he murdered, really touched her, the press of his skin against her skin before he blew out her insides. She wonders if he loved her even as she lay dying, Roaring Red, the color forever painted behind his eyes. When he closes his eyes at night it's the red he must see, when he wakes up the color is there like a sunrise, a promise that nothing can change. Surely he must have loved her? And how outrageous, how sick, yet how willingly might a certain type of love become like this, consuming, the desperate need to hold on? Eli wonders if at the absolute second when it was too late to turn back, Mort was glad it wasn't he who would die; if in the blind panic of his act he considered dying with her but understood at that moment his urgency to live.

And she wonders why she's doing this, visiting somebody who killed. Mort never denied it. Would it be easier if he had, if there could be the smallest, lingering doubt? Eli remembers feeling at the edge of something unfamiliar and appalling, yet also compelling in some dark way, standing beside Mort in the art class, staring at his painting. She remembers how normal it seemed at times, talking to someone who did the worst thing a person could do. He was repulsive to her he most certainly was, that pallid, fleshy arrogance, yet so poignant sometimes in his fake leather jacket, so proud of a thing like that. Something about him drew Eli in. There she stood, breathing the same air he breathed, breathing his smell, the musky, unwashed smell of men who must live together, cigarette smoke fragrant as cologne. She was conscious of her own scent beside him, brittle, dry, more like onions than perfume, that many layers to peel away. There he was. There she was. She remembers the tingle of it, the slow cool thrill. She was alive.

Lately Eli has been compiling a mental list of the things she isn't. She isn't a mother or a good wife; she doesn't have a mother anymore and she isn't sure these days that she wants a husband, or at least not one who every moment in some way reminds her of these things she isn't. She isn't wanted. Eli remembers want: a dark cold stream, the touch of an arm against her own; a yellow beach, hot hand creeping slowly up between her thighs.

She remembers when Dallas stopped wanting her. It had been almost eight weeks since they lost the baby and still she dreamed him beside her, his perfectly formed baby body like a finely savored wine, aged in the way of someone who lives for a moment then dies: In your mind you examine the possibilities his life may have held, you make him love you without judgment, press him close into your arms that will always wait, arms hanging empty as the sheets on the clothesline, no small shirts, no diapers white as moths fluttering in the breeze. Maybe you make him into a high school athlete or somebody really smart, goes off to Yale, wins the Nobel, still finds time just to talk to you. It's the talking you miss the most. Your dreams shape him into the man but can provide no voice. Ghosts can't speak. Language is a gift of life.

Dallas had stopped talking. Not completely, he still mumbled words over dinner, the taste of something remarked on, the heat of a particular day. He had stopped speaking with any desire to communicate with her, it seemed. Though not all at once. After the burial his thoughts stuttered out in starts of sentences, and then he just became quieter, his words in shorter and shorter configurations like clipping string.

And he didn't touch her. That was the worst. Eli's arms clawed out in the night for something, for a baby to suck at her breasts that still leaked milk despite what they gave her to dry it up. Eli was afraid *she* was drying up. Sometimes Dallas wasn't even in their bed. She heard him in Benjamin's room during those first weeks before he locked the door permanently, just walking around. She heard the creak of his footsteps on the bare wood. They never did agree on a color for the carpet.

One night Eli begged him to make love to her. She wore the red silky thing he liked, unbuttoning it low between her breasts over the still discernible swell of her belly. He said he was worried she wasn't totally healed and she told him she would never heal, but not loving made it worse. They lay on their bed, on top of the covers and her whole body shook with something like desire, something like despair, and from that night on these two things felt like they were one to Eli, desire, despair.

Dallas ran his hand over her breast, lifting up the silky shirt. But he didn't remove the matching panties. He pulled them to one side, crawled down and opened his mouth between her legs.

"But I want you!" she had cried, "All of you."

"I can't," he told her. "I'm really sorry, Eli, I don't mind doing this for you, I want to do this for you. I just can't...do the rest. Maybe it's too soon. I feel like I need to be pure or something. Nothing makes sense anymore."

The next day Dallas was gone on one of his drives and Eli came to the beach alone. This is the memory that haunts her, even now: The hot, still afternoon, Waimea beach deserted of people, not even dogs roaming under a sky so huge it ached, water blue as night, waves beating the shore. It was like walking into some hole in the earth, some loud, sea slamming hole with the rhythm of the waves curling like huge lips, dropping onto the hot sand, chewing it up, spitting it out.

Eli lay down on the beach near a grove of browning, salt encrusted ironwood trees that marked the perimeter, not even a towel under her, breathing the salt spray, the scent of it tickling sharp inside her nose. She ran her hands through the warm sand wanting to bury her body inside it, tunnel down into its yellow, grainy darkness. She closed her eyes under her dark glasses, lying on her stomach, legs open slightly, the sun melting down her back like butter. She felt weighted, like she'd never be able to move again. That's when she realized the beach was no longer empty. She felt his approach more than heard it as he came out of the grove of iron woods, the heart-racing sensation of being alone somewhere, then suddenly you're not.

"Hey, lady. Hey, pretty lady. I bet you sleeping, huh?" She felt his shadow as he bent over her, the cool of it as if he were lying on top of her with no weight. "A nap in the hot sun, huh?" His voice was neither high nor deep; it sounded wrong somehow, not completely real, unctuous. She felt a ripple of fear, of nausea, and that profound sense of not being able to move, like half awakening into a dream, frozen, powerless, yet inconceivably curious.

The sand caved in as he knelt beside her, the smell of him, a tang of dime store aftershave and alcohol. He, whoever he was, was drunk, and probably stoned out of his mind, Eli thought. Her heart drummed. Maybe if she kept pretending she was asleep he'd lose interest and go away? Probably he was just one of the beach boys who inhabited Oahu's beaches at strange hours, the rest of the island at work and there they were with their ukuleles, their surfboards, their bleached and sun-damaged hair. He was curious about her most likely. A woman, lying alone on an empty beach when everyone else was somewhere else. Alone on an empty beach. Eli smelled him as he inched toward her, the woodsy heat of his closeness.

Then she felt it, or she thought she did, was she dreaming? Sun stroke? Or was there really the slow steady crawl of a hand between her legs, slithering over the backs of her sweaty knees, moving up. Her heart beat electrified. He believed she was asleep, must've believed it drunk or stoned, because how else would he allow himself to behave like this? Wasn't he afraid she would whip around, shriek, howl, produce a knife from somewhere under her and chop off his fingers? Wasn't he afraid she would do *something*? But if she moved at all, cried out, he might attack her. What would happen if she just lay there?

The hand pulled the crotch of Eli's bathing suit to one side the way Dallas slid aside her panties the night before. Blood roared through her veins into her heart like a missile, like her heart would blow up. Muscles at the backs of her thighs tensed and she willed her whole body down tight against the sand, breasts, stomach, the part of her his hand moved against. Eli imagined squeezing his hand between her legs, closing tight, squashing fat fingers until they popped like ticks. The hand froze for a moment then moved again. She whispered, "Get the fuck out of here!" into the sand where he couldn't hear her. Or she imagined she said this anyway. Her brain was swimming, swirling, pounding, wanting to explode—the thought of what would happen if he sensed she was awake, what was happening because he didn't.

She'd be dirty if she couldn't stop him. Like when she was sixteen, months after the accident and still "recuperating," Mother said, her word for keeping Eli at home, away from boys, their cars, anything that might take this daughter from her. Eli noticed him by the Manoa stream that ran through the back of their property, sitting on a slab of rock under a dense bush of gardenia, the pungency of its creamy blossoms rising over the dark smell of the water, up into her bedroom window where she stood, staring. It was like he was calling to her. Eli slipped out of her house and went down to the stream.

He was her age and she knew somebody who knew him it turned out, so he wasn't really a stranger. They smoked a joint together. Later they kissed. And they kissed again, and this time his hand squirmed down under the waist band of her shorts, touching her uncertainly where the doctor said she was broken. Eli had prayed she could be whole and normal. She would let him do this, and then she wouldn't see him again. If only she could be normal! She would hold onto the memory of him like a taste you can't get out of your mouth.

Then Father appeared, suddenly, on the grassy hill over the stream and he chased the boy away like a fly. "Shoo! Shoo!" Father howled. "Don't you dare!" he hissed to Eli, yanking her, sobbing and shaking back through the yard toward their house that was dark with shadows in the waning afternoon. He led Eli into the bathroom where a can of Comet had been left on the sink Mother cleaned. "Scrub!" he ordered her. "Scrub that dirtiness away."

On Waimea beach Eli's heart was beating inside her ears like the sound of the sea pounding the shore. How could she keep pretending this wasn't happening? She felt helpless, pulled into a darkness the way her father dragged her into that bathroom: "Scrub!" Then, so help her god—Eli remembers this part too clearly—a numbing sensation crept over her, a hot and shameful craving. Her legs relaxed, opened a little. She prayed he would keep believing she was asleep. She sighed so he would think so and the sound of her voice made her cheeks burn. Slowly his fingers massaged her. He couldn't see her face pressed into the beach, her eyes closed behind her dark glasses, but his hand had become part of her, insistent, possessing her. She shuddered, grit her teeth into the coarse sand forcing its way inside her mouth. She needed a full breath but was afraid to inhale, afraid he would stop, afraid if he heard the sound of her urgency his fingers would become the person and the person would want more. She was wet with desire, with despair, and shame. Please, she prayed, don't let him say a thing.

"OK, lady," he whispered. Eli felt the sun again on her back, heard the crunch of his footsteps as they receded through the sand away from her. She waited a long time, head down, afraid to move, afraid to look, afraid she might see him and both of them would have to admit what happened; afraid of its perverseness and what this must say about her because she let him.

But most of all Eli was afraid of the violence that had almost become something like love. And this is the fear that remains with her even now, thirty-two years old; that she really doesn't know what love is.

The prison rises up ahead through a startle of heat. Its red brick has aged almost to grey in places and the giant hump of the building looks like a mound, a home for ants perched on a bare hillside over-looking Turtle Cove, miles of sweating, glistening mud when the tide pulls out. There are no turtles. R.H.A.C. Bold black strokes on the white sign.

Eli turns into the driveway, gazing up at the thick bars over windows dense as a man's neck, metal grilles like cages. Her heart feels like it needs a jump start. She parks the Escort in a space under an elm tree that spreads its twist of rotting branches over the back corner of the lot. Dutch elm disease. Are even the trees on this property damaged? Eli parks back here so Mort can't see her car from a window, can't see her get out of her car, legs naked and pink with sunburn. She will tell him she's leaving, for good, going home. Then she will touch his hand.

Inside the prison is cool and sparse, the barrenness of concrete and stone. Entry room, nothing but a bench and a wide long desk. A tomb, Eli thinks, eying the first barred metal door with the walk-through metal detector in front. She hands her L.L. Bean bag to the guard at the desk. She remembers this routine, they check for contraband and later, she can almost hear it, they'll laugh about whatever it is she carries with her, the things of a life too important to leave behind even in prison, her wallet, hair brush, whatever book she is reading, a small sketch pad with a variety of pens, tops on, tops off. They'll take her keys and her license, assurance she'll come out. He peers inside, frowns, scratching one hand with the uncut fingernails of the other. "Eli Hyde? Thought you didn't work here no more." He shoves a clipboard with the temporary personnel sign up sheet toward her.

Eli shakes her head. "I don't. I've come to visit an inmate. Travis Hill said it's OK."

The guard snorts. "Well, you know, Hill ain't the be all end all around here. It's not like he's the warden." He yanks back the clipboard and pushes the black visitor's book at her. "The name's got to be on my list for allowing visitors. If he's not on my list you can't go in." Eli hesitates feeling suddenly uncomfortable, the thought of writing out his name, letters unfamiliar to her hand though the shape of them intrudes her thoughts. Morton Salvitore. She writes it, signs her name, the time, doesn't look at the guard's eyes when she passes the book back, just the hang of his cheeks, the way they roll down into his diminutive chin, waterfalls of flesh. This one never liked her much. No reason she supposes. Just a glitch in his routine.

The guard stares at Morton's name then at her. "Sit there," he orders, pointing at the bench. "They're near the end of a lock down so might be a while before someone shows up to escort you. You could come back another time?" he offers hopefully.

Eli crumples down onto the bench, feeling its hardness at the backs of her knees, the wood swollen from the humidity. Her legs are sweaty, everything on her is wet, clammy, and she feels her resolve slowly sinking, doubt rising up inside her like a flag. His letters have asked her to come see him and like a fool here she is. Eli never wondered how he got her home address. Mort no longer surprises her this way.

She tips her head back against the cool ridges of concrete behind the bench, closes her eyes. After awhile she hears the metallic slam of a door, the rubbery squeak of sneakers on the concrete floor. Travis Hill. He's wearing cargo pants and a thin aqua shirt that's too tight against the sleek elongated stretch of his shoulders. "Hi there," she says, face flushing.

"I'm really sorry about this, Eli, honest to god those guys are too much sometimes. Turns out Salvitore won't see you today. I don't know what his problem is. Says he's not feeling well, but who knows? Christ, Eli, I mean at any rate are you sure you want to visit that one? Any one of the others from your class would be pleased as punch to see you again and they're a whole lot nicer people, know what I mean? Made some mistakes. But Salvitore? Who knows what kind of a game that one's playing."

Eli nods, embarrassed under Travis's puzzled, concerned look. Her cheeks are really burning now. What for chrissake is she doing here, anyway? She tugs at the hem of her denim skirt, pulling it down to the tops of her knees, feeling exposed. Why the hell did she wear a skirt! "It's just that I got some letters from him. That's the reason I'm here. He asked me to come."

Travis frowns. "Well, heck, Eli, you know we're not responsible for the contents of letters they send. If I had my druthers we wouldn't let them send letters to folks on the outside. Just invites trouble, if you get what I'm saying. I mean come on, they're bored to death, no stimulation, you're a nice-looking woman, what are they gonna do?" Travis hands Eli her bag off the guards' station desk and walks her toward the door.

"I miss working with them on their paintings," she offers.

"Doubt I can hire you back. The Legislature in their infinite wisdom cut Corrections again this last round. Before long I may be out of a job since with no budget there's not likely to be much rehabilitation going on, not even the stuff that passes for it. But you can come on a volunteer basis, you know. I always welcome volunteers. Though damnit, Eli, you should consider staying away from Salvitore. There's something not quite right about that one. Also he's a manipulator. Gets people doing the damnedest things for him and the strange thing about that is none of us like him so much. Do you see what I'm saying? Because here you are. I'd hate for you to get sucked in."

Eli nods, smiles, says nothing but her heart is hammering. She hasn't decided how close to this whole business she wants to get again and right now she feels close enough where something inside her has broken open. They step outside the building and a wave of hot air slaps against Eli's face like it's trying to press her back in. "Actually, what I wanted to let you know is I've decided to go home to Hawaii. You can tell him that. Tell them all good-bye for me, OK? And good-bye to you too!" Eli is crying suddenly, great, gulping sounds, ragged sobs, her face pink and mottled. "Sorry, but I don't have a clue why I'm here!"

"Where's your car?" Travis puts his arm around her shoulders authoritatively and she leans into him, lets him walk her toward her car at the back of the lot. Eli knows this is where the segregation cells are, at the rear of the building, and she knows these have no windows. But for some reason as Travis pulls open her door for her, as Eli climbs into the Escort, she feels like she's being watched, like there are a pair of eyes inside the building grey as the afternoon boring down inside her, to that place of desire and despair.

"Don't fret over them, Eli." Travis pats the back of her head like she's his puppy or a little girl. "They're inmates. They do their time, then inside a year most of them are back again. How many of us change? And this from a guy who does rehabilitation for a living. They're attached to this place, Eli, you shouldn't mess with it. I've seen the ladies who try to change things. Frankly I don't get it. Why do they want a prisoner anyway?"

Eli leans out of the open car window, tugs at Travis's aqua shirt, drags his generous face down toward hers. "Kiss me good-bye, OK?" She forces her mouth against his, but it's Morton Salvitore's face that looms above her, fleshy and unreal, painful, pathetic. She has a sudden image of herself as a young teenager, body gangly and unformed as a noodle, following Henri who's parading down the beach at Waikiki, sister Henri stuffing then strutting her bikini, surfers, beach boys, soldiers, all gawking while Eli followed invisibly behind, her secret, savage thirst. Like Tantalus, forever unsatisfied. Again she feels this burning at the back of her throat, this sour, hopeless taste.

Eli pushes Travis away, fires up the Escort. She sees him in the rearview mirror, Travis Hill, red faced, vague and big as a tree just standing there, watching as she peels out of the prison driveway. On the seat beside her is a small plastic car with rubber wheels, for the Unknown Baby Boy's grave. Eli reaches over and snaps off one of the wheels. She clutches the damaged toy while humming a ridiculous tune from her childhood, "She wore an itsy bitsy teeny weeny yellow polka dot bikini, that she wore for the first time before...." Eli was too small then to recognize a truth, words that echoed with emptiness, like hollering down into a canyon and having your own voice bounce back at you, same as before.

LOSS

WHEN SHE RETURNS HOME FINALLY IN THE LATE AFTERNOON Dallas
watches his wife undress. The muted light flowing in through the
window is a dusty dirty gold. The color reminds him of horse droppings, and how he used to find time in his life to do things like ride
horses, motorcycles, hike, surf the turquoise waves off Oahu; how he
used to live his life that way. Dallas feels a tightness in his chest like
a hand is squeezing him from the inside out, the way he feels when
he remembers the years of his life that have been swallowed up by
his marriage and it seems he hasn't a thing to show for it. The light
casts shadows on his wife's bare back, a pattern of leaves from the
oak tree outside when she bends down to unbuckle her sandals. He
stares at her back, moving his gaze up toward the beads of sweat glistening like tears on her neck. "It's so hot," Eli remarks without looking at him, "I could just die." Her spine is supple and lean for a
woman so small. When he first met Eli, Dallas thought she was a
ballet dancer, her springy light way of walking, as if she's part air and
not so committed to the ground her feet touch upon. Dallas wonders if the man who wrote the letter to him put his hand on Eli's
back, under her shirt, the trigger finger of a killer maybe, tracing the
hard ridges of her flesh flowing like dominoes down her spine,
touching her, the impersonal yet possessive way one might finger a

piece of paper.

Dallas clears his throat violently, makes a sound like spitting, swallows it back down again. "So, damnit, I want to know! Who the hell is this prisoner? I warned you about that bloody job, Eli, I knew something like this would happen." He shakes the letter at her from where he sits, waving it about in the darkening room like a flag of surrender. Her surrender though, not his; he'll see to it that she never sets foot inside a prison again. He stares over at her two packed suitcases. "You're not going anywhere," he tells her.

His wife doesn't answer, but he senses the freezing of her movements for just a moment, the bristling of those sweat-beaded hairs on her neck. The bulk of her red hair is pushed up at the top of her head in a clip; she releases it now and waves tumble down over her thin shoulders. She stands in only her bikini underpants, facing him. He feels nothing like desire. The light outside the window flattens. Thunder heads are rolling in.

"Well? I got this letter, you see? From the prison. Delivered to me at the construction site. For chrissake Eli, special delivery, in front of everybody. From the fucking prison!" He pitches the blue envelope at her. "Prison blue," one of the welders had announced, snickering. "Friends in high places?" he asked Dallas in front of God and the rest of them. Well, Dallas hates this particular job anyway, a goddamn office building for a bunch of techno-nerds. He'd rather be working on somebody's house. That's the problem with carpentry. You've got to go with the seasonal stuff that pays the most because there's not enough work in the winter. His talent's wasted on something built for utility only. His work is intricate, like art, a client once told him. He's a wood turner and can turn a bowl on a lathe into something too beautiful to eat out of. As a kid he could carve a hunk of old beach wood into anything. He'd much rather build kitchen cabinets than the kitchen.

Eli stares at the envelope on the floor, in front of her bare feet. Finally she bends down, picks it up, opens it slowly like she really doesn't want to, at least not in front of him. He watches her cheeks fire up. She's guilty as a hooked fish.

"So what I want to know is, how the hell can this stuff go on in front of all the guards? You said guards stayed in the room while you were there, or was that a lie?" Dallas has a sudden vision of prison as anarchy. Throw the criminals into a giant building, lock them in there, let them fend for themselves. Kind of a LORD OF THE FLIES goes concrete and metal.

"Dallas…" she hesitates, her voice muffled, starts again. "This man, Morton Salvitore, was one of my students. He got a sort of crush on me is all."

"A sort of a crush? He says you 'leaned down over him while he painted, and you were wearing a loose blouse.' Blouse, Eli? Since when do you wear a blouse, not a shirt! Is he a ladies' wardrobe expert or something? Does he march on both sides of the street, a little light in the loafers sometimes? I'll bet he can't hit a nail straight to save his life. For chrissake Eli, this is all pretty damn sick! A goddamn criminal?" Dallas gets up out of the overstuffed chair he was sitting on while interrogating her and moves toward her. She backs up against the bed, sits down hard as he leans over her. He can smell the flowery Hawaiian perfume she wears that her father sends sometimes, and he imagines the man in the letter inhaling her, he sees her bend over him, a cloud of her cheap scent settling down upon him like dust.

Eli becomes defiant, cocks her head up at Dallas, the dark intensity of her eyes like a crow's. "Who the hell are you to question me, anyway! While I was teaching that art therapy class you were taking your therapy in the entry level ranks of female bank personnel."

"That's over," he snarls. "We agreed not to mention it. What I want to know is what you are doing. You've had those goddamn suitcases packed. Is he making a break? Are you running away with a criminal blouse designer?"

Eli crushes up the letter, tosses it against the bedroom wall, yanks the covers back on their double futon bed and climbs in. Then she tugs the covers over her head even though it's hotter than a heart beat, howling, "Don't be such an incredible idiot, Dallas! Come to think of it, don't you even dare speak to me right now. My life is nothing. I have nothing that matters and you ask me what I'm doing. Go away! Just go."

Dallas's face itches like a razor burn. He thinks about that letter and his embarrassment getting it at the site. He stares at the small cloistered shape of his wife, blankets wrapped around her like a shroud. He has a desire to move away, leave her before she leaves him, go somewhere, anywhere. "I could divorce you, you know," he says. "Fraternizing with a prisoner! For god's sake, Eli, couldn't you have picked a car salesman or an insurance agent, somebody normal?" The taste of a move is in his mouth, new air, new faces, forget this old life. He thinks about the letter again, the whiny yet determined voice of the writer: "I've been spending some time with your wife," the letter said in its loopy, anal, makes-no-mistakes handwriting, "It seems we're destined to be together."

Dallas yanks the covers off Eli, grabs her by her bare shoulders and hauls her up against him, pushing her head under his armpit where the blue-black circle of wet on his tee shirt is like a bruise. "Please, Eli?" he whispers fiercely, "Don't leave me! I promise you, if you leave me things can never be the same."

PREY

THE REVEREND ELLEN BARNES IS DRIVING STELLA DUBOIS in the church van, a dark blue minivan with the words Rock Harbor Congregational painted in white on either side, with cloud grey seats inside, a generic neatness and the hum of the heater's fan blowing its steady breath across their gloveless hands. She shifts smoothly from second into third. Years ago when her father taught her to drive he said, "There's two things a woman's got to know, pop a goddamn clutch and kick some sonofabitch where he doesn't forget." So far she's done only the first.

The van takes to the winding Maine roads with the grace and familiarity of a thing born to do exactly what it's doing. They stop at the only town light, a flashing red warning beside the sign that says Leaving Rock Harbor Please Visit Us Again. It's here the Plymouth pulls out in front, turning from the crossroad where the orange light blinks caution, a dead deer strapped to its roof.

"Oh good heavens," Ellen says, "So why do they do that? Is this transportation or a trophy or what?" An older Plymouth, Ellen remembers this vision from her youth, tail fins like sharks prowling the hot Honolulu streets she grew up in, tanned elbow hanging out an open window, white tee shirt, bulge of male muscle. Only a child and yet the sleek sight of these cars, rock and roll beating out secrets from inside, odors of oil and exhaust and plumes of cigarette smoke spiraling upwards toward a sky that seemed bluer then, caused a restlessness to stir inside Ellen, a yearning for something that never did quite materialize. Her mother called Ellen a dreamer. She'd shake her head, her hair sprouting pin curlers in neat metal rows like a Slinky. "What can you get from dreaming?"

Stella says, "Why do they do what? If you mean hunting, a deer's a winter's worth of dinners around here. There's kids go hungry without it. But I hate to see a wild animal strapped to a car, there's no dignity." She doesn't look at Ellen when she speaks, stares out at the deer, its eyes opened into oblivion. Six months ago Stella's husband Clem didn't come back from diving for scallops. She sits beside Ellen like something frozen.

Ellen reaches over and touches Stella's wrist, the place where her coat sleeve doesn't cover. The coat is vintage something and it's too small. Her skin feels cold. "I know it seems unlikely, Stella, but they never found any trace. He could be, I don't know, somewhere. Stranger things have happened. People get amnesia and disappear. Maybe he hit his head on the bottom of the boat coming up, just enough to make him forget. Don't give up hope. God's ways are unfathomable."

Stella shrugs, says nothing. It's late November and the land is tinged with a glazing of frost. They follow the Plymouth up Route One, narrowing road unfurling beside the bony outlines of mountains, frigid Atlantic on the other side, its salty breath inching inside the slightly cracked window of the van. Ellen has a fleeting sense of something lost. "How's Clem's daughter doing?" she asks.

"Heather lives at her grandparents because Alyson, that's her mother, goes off with some Neanderthal who hates kids. I hardly ever get to see her and I was practically another mother. When I do she doesn't talk. She's got that look a person gets when their life's in the hands of somebody else." Stella rubs her eyes, tugs at a strand of neck-length hair. "Sometimes I think about the way it used to be. I think about being at home, my home, and she's sitting beside me and I'm combing her hair. To me, Reverend Barnes, that's God. Sitting with Heather, combing her hair."

Stella closes her eyes, tips her head back. "Let me know when we get there, OK?"

All this time Ellen's trying to ignore the dead deer, neck lolling and bumping against the back window of the Plymouth, body strapped tightly to the metallic green roof, stiff legs anchored on one side so that only the head moves, the long and graceful neck. "How can anyone slaughter such a life?" she whispers, peering over at Stella who doesn't answer. Probably there isn't an answer, Ellen guesses, not in Maine, anyway. She imagines its last breath, final bit of white air frozen on the black nose, the way condensation from a warm house freezes against a winter window. It's definitely dead, tan fur matted and darker where she supposes the rifle's bullet exploded at the back of the neck. Killed on the run.

She imagines this deer last summer when it couldn't know this fate, neck pulsing with life, grazing the field behind the parsonage, Ellen's home for two years. Perhaps it lifted this very neck in a moment of instinctual warning, curious smell, sense of impending danger without the language to understand such things. Ellen watched from inside the cottage, behind gauzy curtains the former minister left. She felt a yearning, a desire to be ruled by a power unlearned, purple evening, sweet crunch of the uncut grass, breathing the musky breath of another deer beside her. A craving for how it might be to feel right in her own skin, alive without the knowledge of what life is, just that it's worth the fight to hold onto.

Certainly no persistent voice inside Ellen calling her to the ministry, a field that's not a cool stretch of lavender evenings but instead late nights of uncertainty, the loneliness of a life belonging to everyone but her. Seminary! the voice insisted. She never imagined the calling would come from a voice that was hers in its sound but not its reasoning. Had she thought God Himself would speak?

The Plymouth hits a rut in the road and the deer bumps hard against the back window, its head twisting around for a moment so that Ellen sees the tongue is out, just the swollen black tip as if it had been about to kiss. Ellen knows they do this thing, kissing. She observed the deer in early spring, unsettled time, large buck bumping up against a doe, mouths nuzzling. It reminded Ellen of eighth grade, thirteen and the child parts of her peeled away to a white-hot core of something else, quivering, profound. Lani Jenson's "make-out" party, Kailua Beach, tang of the salt air erupting inside Ellen like the new movement of her blood between her thighs. That night the moon coated every shining thing like a vision, a postcard of somebody else's life. She wondered if this was her life, lying on the beach with pimply Donny Lott, his tongue inside her mouth, electric sensation somewhere between wonder and disgust and then his fingers, shy little crabs skittering under her shirt. She wondered if God would punish her for what she felt.

Reverend Ellen Barnes considers stopping at the next intersection, wherever that might be on this mostly deserted road moving north, letting the Plymouth get well ahead of her. "Stella!" she says and Stella jumps. "You're not bothered at all by that deer? I find it, I don't know, disturbing. What chance does the poor thing have against a gun? That man determined the end of that deer's life. It's against the laws of nature. Survival of the fittest doesn't account for firearms, if you ask me."

Stella shrugs, eyes still shut. She keeps Ellen at a distance as if Ellen is God's own apprentice. They do that in Ellen's church, treat her kindly, respectfully, and never let her forget she's not one of them. "Well, I don't think it's right," Ellen says, "hunting with a gun. A bow and arrow, maybe. Better yet they just slug it out."

She concentrates on the backs of the mens' heads inside the car, two of them in the front seat, driver's head tall and narrow, close cropped hair she guesses is red. She imagines his raw face, squinting eyes set hard against the slant of the late morning sun. His companion wears a baseball cap and, Ellen would bet on it, a flannel shirt under his blaze orange hunter's jacket. Scrunched up shoulders, beefier, eyes small and tight as bullets. She's seen these men, the severity of lives lived in a remote place worn onto their faces, necks, etched into their skin, voices, every breath. She feels her inadequacies to serve them. Rock Harbor Congregational was considered a beginning ministry yet Ellen senses a quiet need here, more so than in the generous stone churches of New England's cities. She's head-

102

ed to one of their houses now. The call that came in the black of early morning, the death of somebody's father, a man whose wife was a sometimes member of Ellen's congregation before it became her congregation, who retired his family to a camp in the woods and is now dead.

When she was a child Ellen used to play "funeral" with her sister. After their father killed the giant cockroaches lurking in the unlit corners of their kitchen she and Jane gathered the brittle carcasses. They rounded up decaying coconut rats, stiff mynah birds, even an occasional fish washed up on a sandy beach, eyes round holes of emptiness, providing all with proper burials under the mango tree in their back yard. Now, as Reverend Barnes, Ellen feels that in memorializing somebody who's died, offering comfort to those they've left, she can be true. More true than the words she speaks each Sunday, genuine when she writes them, pouring over The Bible, books and papers from Seminary; yet somehow when greeting her parishioners, morning sun through cathedral windows lighting their faces as she looks out over them, Ellen feels a wrenching inside. Who was she to give them her words? The awkward, red-faced girl who let Donny Lott roam inside her clothes, sweaty hand slipping beneath the waistband of her shorts while she pretended to sleep on the beach? What sort of sanctity was this? She didn't even like Donny and spent the rest of eighth grade hot with the shame of his secret.

Just when Ellen thinks she can no longer bear the sight of the dead doe in front of her, shackled to this car, these men, the Plymouth lunges off onto a dirt road on the right, no blinker, no warning, disappears. Almost as suddenly Ellen sees her turn on the left, "Between two white pines," the voice on the phone said, "near a pond about frozen enough for a ice fishing shack."

When the young man at the door lets Ellen and Stella inside after a studied look up and down them both, he leads them to a faded sofa, stepping over piles of yellow newspapers and a fat cat spread like a sponge on top of a greying pillow. The cat doesn't grace them by opening its eyes in their direction. The young man points at the sofa and Ellen and Stella sit down. "His name's Barclay," he says, indicating the cat. "Barclay only pretends to like me so he can stay inside. I'm Scott."

Ellen expected to say her usual right off, but instead is silent and stares around the tiny cabin, dark, cluttered, no sign of female anywhere; hunting things—two rifles pegged up on the raw wood wall, fishing poles, a bow and arrow, tinny dishes in a sink that has no cabinet under it, just a frayed peach-colored curtain partially hiding the pipes below. Scott Barker, the dead man's son, follows the direction of her eyes. "You wanted a mansion or something?"

Ellen smiles, she hopes a warm one. She unbuttons but doesn't remove her wool coat. The cabin is cold. The only visible heat source, a fire in a wood stove, is mostly an anemic glow. "Is your mother around? This is Stella, my assistant in the church office. Stella told me there's a Mrs. Barker."

"She doesn't live here anymore," Scott says, eyes shifting over toward Stella sitting stiffly at the other end of the couch, looking like she'd rather be anywhere else. "I don't feel right about it," Stella told Ellen. "Sometimes I dream about somebody who's going to die and there's not a damn thing I can do about it."

"I don't have to live here, either," Scott says. "I'm nineteen but I didn't have a better place to go so I thought, what the hell, it's free." He perches at the edge of the sink, long legs, torn jeans, unlaced combat boots.

Ellen rearranges herself on the couch that's losing its stuffing on one side. It's the only real piece of furniture in the room. She pats at the stuffing, a nervous habit she has as if trying to put things back in their place. Scott points at the stuffing, "My dog did that, so guess what? Dad shot him. No second chances around here. I'd offer you my bed to sit on, but it's up in the loft. Dad slept where you're sitting."

Ellen feels a chill of something distasteful and averts her eyes from his face. It's not usually this way, she thinks. Scott has a good face, strong lines, the child in it long since hardened into the man. She stares at his legs, the way faded denim wraps itself around the elongated stretch of his calves. She imagines the softer, sweeter touches of the parts of his body under his clothes and a wave of regret sweeps through her, then the despair for thinking these thoughts.

"My mother's the one told me to call you. She lives near enough, but I won't see her before the funeral. She's got a boyfriend and he can't stand me. Steven's Funeral Home took Dad. Figured that's cheaper than having the ambulance ride Dad up to Steven's since he was already dead. Dumb name for a mortuary, the guy probably couldn't spell his last name. Though maybe Steven is his last name, you can't tell." Scott jiggles his right leg, drums a couple of fingers on the metal rim of the basin and shakes his head. "I bet you don't know why they call them stiffs. Dad had a heart attack in the outhouse last night and by the time I got out there and found him this morning he was already like a plank of wood. Do you believe in God?"

Ellen glares up into Scott's face, her heart pumping a strange violence inside her veins, ramblings of his words like dry leaves skipping on a wind, harmless, meaningless, yet causing an unfamiliar quickening inside her. Though pale, his shock of black hair, unshaven chin, and thick eyebrows give the appearance of a darker person, ancient yet ageless.

Stella says, "For chrissake, can't you see she's a minister? Asking her if she believes in God is like asking a doctor if he believes in aspirin."

Scott shrugs, "My dad was a plumber but he didn't believe in his own shit. Anyway, she looks normal enough." He glances at Ellen's breasts and Ellen reddens, tugging at a wave of brown hair that slipped out of the clip she forces it into. "I'm just wondering because I've seen animals frozen and Dad looked no different. It took two of those mortuary muscle-men to even lift him out of there, so I don't guess anything's going to be rising from him like a soul or something."

Scott doesn't seem to expect a response and Ellen says nothing. He jumps down off his perch, twists the faucet on and a splash of silvery water comes out, slides a bent kettle under it. "Coffee?" he asks them, "I only do instant though."

Stella shakes her head. Ellen nods, relieved to be back to something known. She wonders if Scott's always this frenetic, or if their presence makes him nervous. Ellen is waiting for something like despair. "Your mother's making the arrangements and she wants me to do the service? That's why Stella's here. She's going to take down the particulars and she'll help your mother. OK if she takes some notes?"

The kettle lets out a screech and Scott yanks it off the small burner. "Yeah, but I can't guess what you'll say about him. See Dad lived a life that was more of a undoing of things than doing them. He shot my dog. When we lived in Rock Harbor he gutted my computer because he thought I was getting too far away from him on the Net. He moved us out here to his hunting camp when my mother got too friendly with the neighbors, but she taught him a lesson, she left him. My dad would've wanted you, you know. He wasn't bad looking. He looked like me, just older and fatter. So much fatter, in fact, a heart attack wasn't unexpected. My mother used to say, Herb, if you don't drop some of that baggage you're going to have a heart attack! Dad had high blood pressure and he got fat just to spite her, she said. Could you be with a man like that?"

Scott hands Ellen a cup of black coffee in a cream-colored mug with a deep gouge on one side. "I hope you don't put anything in it. Dad said milk's a peripheral food. I've been drinking coffee straight since I was ten." He plunks down in the middle of the couch causing Ellen's lighter frame to move in a little toward him. Stella gets up, strides across the small kitchen area. "I think I left my notebook in the car," she says, "I'll go look for it, OK?"

"Sure thing, but I still can't guess what you'll write," Scott says.

Ellen sits up straighter, forcing her face into a bland, expressionless expression. This young man is breaking all the rules of death. He doesn't seem to want comfort, and she's suddenly too aware of how close he is, the musky young-man smell of him, slope of his rounded shoulder under a thin white tee shirt. "Aren't you cold?" she asks, then blushes.

He shrugs, tapping his foot against the wood floor, "I'd have to go out and chop wood. Dad wouldn't let me yesterday, said we needed cooling off. Dad didn't get his deer this season so he's been like a mad man. Shot his own damn dog the other day. Can't tell you what old Sarah did to deserve that."

"Good heavens! What's the matter with you people? There's such a disregard for life around here. I mean, don't you even feel a little grief?" God, Ellen thinks, patting her hand against her chest, forcing down the small angry beatings of her own heart, Now he'll see what a fraud I am. Ellen's own father used to tell her she liked animals better than humans. Should have been a vet, Ellen thinks.

Scott doesn't answer. He gazes at the unpainted wall. Ellen can hear Stella outside opening the van's sliding door. There are only two windows in the room and Ellen stares out of one. She notices the sky has flattened to a dull grey, the color of an old nickel. "Do you know what?" Scott asks, still not looking at her, "Last summer a buck came up on our porch. What do you know about deer, Reverend Barnes? Luckily, Dad was somewhere else or he would've shot him like the buck was an intruder, even though it was out of season. I was coming back from fishing. The sight of him standing near the door made me drop my bucket. Had a couple trout in it too. He wore a full rack and stood taller than me. He was just hanging out by our door like it was his camp. We both stared at each other for about a minute before he bolted. It was strange, because for that minute it was like our roles reversed, like this was his place and I was the animal, the one who didn't belong. I never told Dad. You're the only one that knows."

"Why do you think he went onto your porch? That's not in the nature of a wild animal."

Scott grins and Ellen sees his teeth are clean and straight. Her father used to tell her you can almost trust a man who takes care of his teeth. Ellen thinks about how Scott's barely a man, and how neither one of them has a father anymore to tell them anything. Scott folds up his long legs and his knee bumps against her thigh. Ellen feels that aching inside. Surely there's something she's supposed to say.

"Well, you're a minister. Are people so different from animals? I just figure it's in all of our natures to do the unexpected. I mean, who makes the rules? Who decides that a buck can't walk onto a person's porch? Who decides he can't just walk right through the door and make himself at home? If there were rules would Sam, that's my dog, get shot by my father? Sam was my friend. Would my father, a plumber, end up dead in an outhouse for chrissake, clutching his favorite tool?"

Scott is laughing, scratchy, high, hysterical. Ellen wonders if this is the laugh before the tears. She hopes it is, because tears she can understand. Tears are why she answered her calling. Grief is familiar, true, and she can be useful to him if he would only express it. She wants so much to be useful. Scott shoves his head between his hands, face down, so that only his black curls are visible, leaking through his fingers like things wild and apart. Tentatively Ellen puts her hand out over his head, not touching him, lingering over hair she imagines coarse as a sheep's, gnarly and knotted and warm. She hopes Stella won't pick this moment to walk back in. Ellen can do this thing alone. "How do you feel, Scott?"

"He wasn't that bad a man, you should know this if you're going to tell things about him at his funeral. He was the best he knew how. When I quit school he said, That's OK, there's other ways to be smart. I've been thinking about going back. I wish I told him, that I might give it another shot. I'm supposed to feel terrible because he's dead, right? Isn't that the way? But I don't know how to do that. You tell me, Reverend Barnes, how do I feel!" Scott whips around suddenly, pushes his head against Ellen's shoulder and without even considering it she pulls him into her chest, stroking his neck, letting his face slip down against her breast as though he's her son, her lover, the missing pieces.

"Think about something sad, the saddest thing you can think about," she whispers. Ellen's hand glides lightly through his hair, thick curls, not so coarse, slippery almost, as if they're glazed by a sheen of frost or the white of an egg. She moves her arms around Scott's shoulders, pressing him tighter against her, sensing the fluttering of his heart near hers, knowing he's finally crying but she won't say the usual to him.

Ellen thinks about the dead doe strapped onto the Plymouth, her beautiful neck now hanging drained of its blood on somebody's porch. She thinks about the doe's lover, big buck, afternoon sky the color of metal, air cold as death, standing on the porch beside her. She thinks about Stella whose husband is part of the sea now, who sleeps in their bed alone. Ellen remembers when she first came to Maine, Stella and Clem took her on a hike. They went off somewhere and Ellen lay down on a flat warm rock near a stream. She must have fallen asleep because when she opened her eyes a giant hawk swooped suddenly down over her, his wing span broad as the afternoon. She could feel the air shift and move as he cut through it, she could see the intricate patterns on the undersides of his wings, he was that close.

Ellen wraps her arms tighter around Scott who's sobbing, a ragged, wounded sound. She breathes in his musky smell, sensing his skin, his bones, his blood. "I think I understand why they hunt," she whispers. "They want to know what it feels like to be God."

WHAT IS HAPPENING TO STELLA DUBOIS?

WHAT IS HAPPENING TO STELLA DUBOIS? Anxious, plump, pink-faced Stella, never been anywhere in her life; now it looks like she's done the world, skinny in her too-tight jeans. Her mother says, "For Pete's sake Stella, aren't you a little old to be acting like you're this young?" And Stella's hair, there's even less of it these days, like the hedge clippers got to it, a crew cut dyed the color of a lemon. She's pierced one of her ears in a multitude of places, and one hole at the side of her nose, radiant glass nose-ring the color of Henretta Harley's eyes.

"Wow," Henri says, shaking her head at Stella's outfit, the jeans and the low cut chenille sweater, breasts scooped up like ice cream cones. "You're a regular slut these days, Stella."

A regular slut, Stella thinks. She likes the sound of it, an identity at last.

They are sitting at the polished wooden bar in the Breakwater Lounge, slurping down frothy glasses of rum something, paper umbrellas poking out of pineapple chunks wedged onto the rim. Not much night life in Rock Harbor, Maine, Stella's scouted out what little there is. Canned music whirls out from speakers above them and the air is blue with smoke. Stella removes her umbrella,

110

folds of spotted purple tissue paper stuck onto a toothpick, and drops it into her purse. This is how treasures happen: Stella finds them, bits and pieces of the life she's living like collecting fragments of sea glass, then she carries them home and plunks them into a ceramic jar labeled COOKIES. For Heather. Stella doesn't bake. And the child's visits are not nearly enough. The infrequency of them hurts Stella's stomach and her throat, that aching sensation of wanting to cram too much into the little time she's allowed. It's almost like Stella's the non-custodial parent in a divorce, except that she doesn't even have these rights. Just a visit now and then when Alyson wants time to herself and the grandparents, whom Heather lives with now, are someplace else.

"Damnit," Alyson whined the last time she brought Heather to Stella's duplex, "I just need some space once in a while and Clem left me next to nothing to support his kid on. What, was this an immaculate conception? I met somebody else and he doesn't like kids. Is that a crime? Do I get a life?"

That night Stella sat up with Heather, who was sobbing from a nightmare in the alcove room. The child wove her thin arms around Stella's neck and Stella felt that stabbing, burning, slashing in her gut, knowing those arms weren't for her. Heather had a dream her mother died. Then there was nobody but her grandparents.

That was last month, eight months since Clem dove into the Atlantic never to surface again. Reverend Ellen who's been ministering to inmates told Stella what happens when they lethally inject a prisoner. "The first one anesthetizes his facial muscles," Ellen said, "so he looks at peace. Inside his organs are writhing in agony. The second implodes his lungs. But if they electrocute him? Sometimes his hair goes blue with flames. What this should teach us is there's no easy way to make dead what God intended to live. I'm thankful Maine doesn't have the death penalty. I couldn't bear to be called to a place that takes the Lord's work into its own hands."

Stella said nothing, but she had wondered what it takes to kill a person, what lines are drawn, what limits are pushed, what paths are irreparably crossed. And what it is about being human the killer gives up, whether he's the murderer on death row, the doctor who administers the injection, or the one who switches on the chair. Stella had prepared herself for the event of Clem's death, but not for her own grief. So this is how she came to think of Clem's drowning, like a lethal injection, the way the green sea imploded his lungs. In the weeks that followed, for a while, Stella had tried to pretend Clem wasn't dead. She let herself act like she believed it when people said They never found his body, just an empty boat…maybe, maybe?

At night she would imagine Clem beside her, Stella clutching Clem's pillow, Stella stroking her arm and pretending it was his. She'd carry on whole conversations with her husband, hearing his own voice in her mind as easily as hers: Clem, she'd say, I told you so! Didn't I? Didn't I always warn you if you dove that deep, one day you'd be careless and do it without enough air in your tank? But Stella, didn't they tell you? I dropped my bag of scallops, 140 pounds worth! I went back down to get them. They found the bag, remember? Now, Clem, there's no excuse, is there? Well? Yes, honey (she pictured him hanging his head like a little boy, though really he never called her those sugary names), you were right. Stella would smile, hug the pillow closer, pressing her body against the pillow as if his pillow were Clem, remembering how that felt, making love to him back when she believed in love. So don't be dead anymore! she'd plead, a whisper, almost asleep, imagining him on top of her then floating over her the way his ghost might.

Sometimes Stella pretended she rescued Clem, down at the docks with her flowers, standing on the rocky ledge, and there he was floating in the ocean below her. She saw herself without even thinking about it dive into the freezing black water, a wrestler's hold around his neck, dragging him like a dog to the rocky beach then breathing his life back into him through his open mouth, from hers, forcing his heart, his lungs, to come alive again. He would sputter, a trickle of green sea flowing out of his mouth like blood.

But as the weeks became months and the search was long since called off and everybody else's life returned to normal, Stella began to hear an unfamiliar voice inside her, like a brand new person was trying to talk her way out. When Stella tried to pretend Clem was beside her it was this new voice hissing: "Give me a break! You'd of had more tender moments with a pickle." This person was definitely a blond, no more grey hair, when Stella's not even thirty-two. And she stopped eating so much. Food couldn't fill that empty place, so why even try? This person—secretly Stella calls her Jenny, the woman Jenna Pierce might have become if she'd had the chance— Jenny understands that except for Heather, there's no such thing as love. Something else happens between a man and a woman. Stella sees the way they look at her now, her skinny, blond, new-person self.

"I'm a risk-taker," Stella says to Henri. She winks and grins at the man with the ponytail on the opposite side of the bar who's been eying Stella and Henri, and now just Stella.

"Taking risks like mountain climbing maybe. Sky diving? Go for it! But multiple bed partners in this day and age is crazy." Henri slurps down the last of her rum froth, motioning to the bartender for more. "It's like Russian Roulette. And in some places they treat AIDS victims like Lepers, you know. You should be more like me, one at a time. See them through, you never know when some sleeper might be the one."

Stella snorts. "We're talking fantasy land here, right, cocktail Disney World? Anyway I'd rather live a full life and die early than an empty life that lasts forever."

Henri flips a fringe of bangs off her forehead, glowering for a second at the ponytailed man panting at Stella. "You sound like a goddamn bumper sticker, Stella. Christ, it seems everyone who gets in my life gets under my skin. I'm no shrink but this is not a good way to handle grief. What kind of example are you setting for our kids, for Heather? Why don't you talk to that minister, what's her name?"

Stella lets out a sharp laugh that sounds more like a bark. "I don't see Heather enough to be any influence whatsoever. And as for Reverend Ellen Barnes, she has no idea what's going on in this world outside those prison bars. She's being eaten up by her ministry there, especially this one inmate. He murdered a woman named Jenna Pierce. Ellen thinks she's been 'called' there to help him in some way. Well, who's been called to help me? If people like that deserve help, what about people like me?" Stella's eyes tear up and she blinks these back immediately, willing them sucked dry. If she cries her mascara runs and the white parts of her eyes turn the color of a tomato. She's had too much rum, Stella decides. She peers hard over the bar at the ponytail. He gets up and strolls slowly toward her, like he's on an invisible line and she's reeling him in. "You know," she whispers, "there's people I've been so mad at I could murder, people who treated me that bad. Like I was nothing. Like I was as good as dead. But I didn't. I wouldn't. That's the difference."

"For chrissake, Stella, the thing at stake here is your own life, right this minute!"

"You can only lose what's valued in the first place," Stella says. "Isn't 'losing your life' a strange expression? As if it's something you can keep track of, put in your pocket for safe keeping?" She thinks about Clem, how if she truly valued him surely she could have found a way to keep him from going out to sea, surely! She pictures a miniaturized Clem in the pocket of her too tight jeans, squashed into place. Now don't you go getting lost again, she'd tell him, I warned you about the dangers of deep sea diving. Now look what you've done, you've gotten yourself drowned, you've gone and imploded your lungs!

Stella pats the side pocket of her jeans, slides her hand over her hip, down her thigh. The ponytail who's sitting on a stool beside her now breathes in her every move. She knows what's next. Animated conversation, significant eye contact, a ride in his car or hers and later the rolling, rolling, rolling, she's on top of him, he's on top of her; the cold crush of the green sea filling her for this one night.

HEATHER'S HAIR

IN THEIR GRANDFATHER'S HOUSE THE THING they are forbidden to do is throw away anything that still has a life to it, that still has a use. This includes paper napkins after a meal which Grandfather inspects for spots, grease is OK but maybe not spaghetti sauce; old shoes, their leather stripped then born again as patches for Heather's and her half-sister Miranda's jeans; even their grandmother's first car, a VW Beetle the color of a tangerine, its inner workings tinkered with, gutted, other parts from other VW's sutured in until finally it "Relinquished the ghost," said Grandfather. Now it sits in the driveway, a hive for the wasps he's certain in some secret way help his garden. No use telling him honeybees are the pollinators. Grandfather says that if somebody took the trouble to make it or God creates it, it has a use.

This also applies to their hair. They are forbidden to cut it because God grew it. Heather's half-sister Miranda sees nothing strange about this. She has a thick ponytail and is obedient as a horse. Miranda is two years younger than Heather and is skinny and weepy and weak. Their grandfather's hair is silvery as January air, and their grandmother's careens down her back and is the color of a shadow. Heather loves her grandmother's hair. She loves watching her grandmother wash it on Saturdays, flipping it into the sink in

115

front of her, pulling her long hands through it, her shampoo that smells of mint beading up like frog's eggs.

But Heather wants her hair short, like the boys' hair where she used to live with her mother before her mother made Heather and Miranda live here. Heather wants her hair short and sometimes she wants to be a boy, and she wants to be a teenager instead of forever ten. If she were a boy and a teenager then maybe her grandfather wouldn't boss her around so much. "Do this, Do that," and Miranda does nothing because she's the little one, he says. This morning Heather had to set the table for breakfast and she stepped on Miranda's foot, the ear of Miranda's pink bunny slipper. It couldn't have hurt, she hardly got to the skin at all. Yet Miranda shrieked when she saw Grandfather was watching and Grandfather told Heather to get the spanking board, Grandmother's vegetable cutting board when Heather isn't being spanked. Miranda hissed, "Your daddy is drowned!" And Heather said "Well, you don't even know who your daddy is!" That always put everyone on edge.

Heather wants to be a teenaged boy and she wants to be somewhere else. She wants to be back in Rock Harbor where she lived with her mother, not on this bumpy road in the middle of Maine, tangles of dead machines in beat up yards, cars without engines, bikes without wheels, rusted snowmobiles, old refrigerators. Is there anything so useless as a refrigerator trussed up like a turkey? Heather thinks, sitting on the newly painted steps to the back of her grandparents' house. "Hetter," her grandfather calls out to her from an opened window, "if those stairs are not dry yet, you and me, we are going to have a problem!" Heather's grandparents are from Poland. When they speak her name it rhymes with wetter because this is the way they talk. They were poor in Poland, her grandmother told Heather, so everything they have now is a gift.

Heather stares out into the yard. Behind it where the grass stops there are giant black woods that stretch all the way up into Canada, her grandfather said, to the frozen place where the continent stops. "The woods make you disappear if you aren't good," he told Heather and Miranda. Like their mother did. "Just drove away and she never looked back," says Grandfather, about every other day. "Dropped off her daughters like she's delivering the goddamn mail." Sometimes their mother comes for a visit, for an hour or part of an afternoon, and once for a whole weekend when their grandmother had the flu. But she never takes Heather and Miranda back with her, wherever she goes when she leaves. And she doesn't say that she'll return, even though Miranda always begs her to. "Promise you'll come back!" Miranda demands, spoiled brat that she is.

Heather wants to be a boy, maybe even an adult boy so Grandmother won't wash Heather's hair anymore, Heather screeching and wailing when Grandmother combs the tangles out afterwards, screeching and wailing when she pulls the mass into two wet braids the color of mud. "Hush, Hetter," her grandmother says, "you're too big a girl to carry on this way."

But once Heather starts screeching she can't seem to stop, screeching, wailing, crying and then screaming, for her mother who drove away, her father who didn't come back from diving for scallops, almost a year ago but still Heather waits. Without a body there's no proof is there? Stella, Heather's father's wife, says Heather shouldn't think this way. "He's not coming back," Stella says. "We have to believe this. At least it's peaceful where he is," she adds. Stella has dreams that tell her things, "Knowing dreams," she calls them. In her dream Stella saw Heather's father swallowed up by the green sea. Sometimes Heather even screeches for Stella whom she hardly sees anymore and when she does finally see her Heather doesn't know what to say. It's as if Heather has no language for the things that have happened, because if she tries to talk about these things her grandfather says, "Hush! It's bad luck to speak of the ones who passed." Heather's whole world has been blown apart like a milkweed pod, drifting little bits of what she used to know floating away.

Before she goes to sleep each night Grandmother tucks Heather in, perches on the bed and says, "Let me listen to your prayers." But Heather doesn't know who she is praying to, she sees a great big smoky face in the sky with lips of wind that blew it all apart. Her mother found somebody else to love, does God make that happen? Grandmother says, "It just happens, Hetter, these things just hap-

pen." Who made her father drown, if her father really did drown?
Her father could swim. Her father taught Heather to swim! In
Mirror Lake, her father's legs like two tree stumps pulling Heather
down between them, her breath blown up like a balloon in her
chest, then rising to the surface breathing the green bubbles of air,
great gulps of it, shining airy bubbles and her father saying, "Good
girl, good girl!"

In the night, in the small upstairs bedroom she shares with
Miranda, Heather thinks she hears her father sometimes, coming
back from the sea. What will he look like now? In her own dream
Heather sees the Swamp Thing, her father a mass of kelp, dragging
up her grandparents' stairs, swish, swish, opening the door to the
bedroom with a hand bony as the carcass of a fish. Heather shrieks
and Grandfather calls out from their downstairs room, "Hush,
Hetter, or I get the spanking board!"

Later when the house is silent again and Heather is still, her
blanket pulled up over her face even though it's spring and the night
air is finally warm, her grandmother slips up the stairs, the quiet way
her grandmother has of walking in this world, like her grandmother
is a shadow of her own self. She sits on Heather's bed, strokes the top
of Heather's blond head, the part that isn't covered by the blanket.
"Sleep, Hetter," she whispers, "I will be here for you."

Two months later it's summer and Heather learns about fireflies.
It's not that she didn't know fireflies existed, she used to catch them
in jelly jars during summers past, just to make her half-sister Miranda
scream. "Let it go!" Miranda wailed, her breath bursting out in short
little gasps. "You're hurting it! It has to be free!" Miranda was too
slow to catch fireflies. When she ran into the house to tattle,
Heather opened the jar and released it.

"Let me tell you about fireflies," Grandfather says one soft July
night with no moon, stars smattered across the sky like cottage
cheese. They're sitting on the back steps, Grandmother and
Miranda inside watching TV. Heather can see the blue light from
the TV against the closed curtain and her heart beat jumps a little as

it always does, sitting this close to her grandfather. She can never be sure of his mood, of what he might say. "Never mind, bite your tongue," her grandmother says to Heather when Heather's mouth crinkles up like she might talk back to him. But what would she tell him? That he makes her so mad? That sometimes she's scared of him? That she wishes he loved her, just a little? Tonight her grandfather's mood is like the dark, tender and lonely.

They stare out at the back yard, alive with pokes of light. The lights are orange as match heads, hovering over the longer grasses near the woods, chasing in and out of the black spaces between the trees. "Do you know why they do that, Hetter? Because they're looking for love," her grandfather says. "That's what they do. Male fireflies flash to attract the female. She perches on the grass and she chooses the male she wants. She flashes back and he comes to her." Her grandfather sighs. "Here it's a feminine world. Could be what's wrong up at that prison," he says, pointing through the darkness in a vague direction. "They flash but there's nobody to answer." Heather's grandfather was a guard at Rock Harbor Adult Correctional. It was all he could find when he came to this country, her grandmother said. "You know it's the last thing he would do, even if they deserve it, keeping other men from being free."

"But," says Grandfather, "the surprise is that sometimes the female doesn't want the male for mating. Instead, maybe she is hungry. She mimics the flash of a smaller species and when he zooms down to her she eats him! The male is not so aggressive, you see. He just flies and flashes all night until a female calls to him. That much isn't so human, huh, Hetter?"

Heather doesn't know what she's supposed to say. She never thought about fireflies behaving the way people do. They flit about on a dark night and their lights are proof that it's finally summer. "What makes them light up?" she asks.

"They have some organ near their tail with lots of light cells, kind of like our own nerves, and this thing in their brain sets the shine to a pattern." Grandfather lets out a long breath. "If people could do that, can you imagine the light our world would have?" Heather's grandfather stands up slowly. She can hear the skritching sounds his knees make, close to her ears where she sits. Heather is very still in case her grandfather's mood has suddenly changed, in case he remembers he's mad at Heather for knocking over her milk at dinner. Her grandfather doesn't say a thing. He walks out into the yard, into the fireflies' lights. Soon he is swallowed up by the blackness, his shape disappearing like ink erasing.

PART II
FIVE YEARS LATER

There are no trees in prison
because their branches would be shaped
into weapons,
because their leaves might hide
a fugitive,
because their tops might overshadow
gun towers,
because trees, like men,
need deep roots to grow.

—Joseph Bruchac

HEATHER'S HAIR (II)

SO WHEN SHE'S FINALLY FIFTEEN HEATHER CUTS her hair off, handing the rope of it to her grandfather, a fierce new glint in her eyes, new breasts, a swagger when she walks. "Now we won't waste it," she tells him, excited by the bloom of her defiance.

"Go to your room!" her grandfather howls. But Heather's already halfway up the stairs, to the room where she spends most of her time, now, when she has to be inside their house, door slammed shut, her new life pinned to the walls, posters of current rage rock bands, pictures of anorexic models, poems her grandparents wouldn't understand. Her half-sister Miranda has moved back with their mother. "I don't have room for them both," her mother said. Who made the choice?

A month later Heather dyes her hair Radical Red and then she shaves it off completely. "When chickens get teeth!" Grandfather growls, scowling at her luminous head, waving Heather away from the dinner table.

"OK," Heather says, "I won't eat!" She marches out of the kitchen, tossing her perfectly clean napkin into the trash.

"Oh, dear," her grandmother moans.

"Bring that goddamn napkin back to this table!" her grandfather barks.

But Heather's bolting up the stairs, the burn of tears in her eyes. If her father were here! she thinks. Heather's father who disappeared into the Atlantic has become like a prince these days, a fantasy who might somehow materialize into flesh again, making her life OK. These days when Heather throws herself face down on her bed she tries to picture her father the way he used to look, the color of his eyes, his hair, the shape of his mouth. These days she can't often remember, it seems there's always a part missing, a puzzle without all of its pieces. Mostly Heather tries to recall his touch, the slide of his fingers down her arm, the blanket feeling of his hand wrapped around hers.

Later that night Heather's grandmother slips into Heather's bedroom, furtive and light as a bird, her silvery-dark hair coiled and mounded on top of her head like a monument to some reptile. She hands Heather a plate of pot roast in brown gravy, carrots and mashed potatoes. "We had bread pudding for dessert," her grandmother announces. "I made it from white bread. You know how Grandfather likes his white bread. In Poland we only had dark."

"He can't make you keep your hair long," Heather tells her grandmother. "It's your hair not God's."

Her grandmother strokes Heather's naked scalp with her cool long fingers, says, "It feels like a peeled egg, Hetter, like a peeled egg."

Then it's summer and Heather goes to California with her friend Cedra. They are staying with Cedra's stepfather and his new wife on the northern coast where the cliffs are as big as mountains and the waves at high tide crack against them then slide out, hissing. She doesn't come back to Maine until it's too late.

"They didn't discover the cancer for so long and when they did she was gone in just a few weeks," Heather's mother tells her. "She didn't even complain," Miranda says. They're talking long-distance to Heather, each on a different telephone extension as if this is some chatty event. "She bit down on the covers when her pain was too much," Miranda says. Miranda's thirteen and thinks that having breasts makes her an adult. "We would've called before only Grandmother didn't want to spoil your vacation. Are you having fun?" Heather's mother adds politely.

Heather remembers how when she told her grandmother about going to California her grandmother sighed and said she'd never been to California, not even once; maybe next year she would go to California with Heather. Heather wishes more than anything in the world she had found some way to bring her grandmother to California. Maybe she would have won the essay contest at school, bagged groceries all year at Shaws, and then her grandmother could have gone to California, just once.

Flying back to Maine the space outside the plane's window is high, light and empty, the air (Heather knows this from her physical science textbook) precious and unable to sustain life. She tips her head back against the seat, closes her eyes; the humming of the jet's engine fills her ears like the humming of insects outside her grandparents' house. This summer Heather missed the fireflies.

She pretends her grandmother made it to California and was there with Heather, walking the hot yellow beach, a long cold drink of iced tea afterwards. Heather pretends these things because she just can't think about what really happened, can't think about going home to her grandparents' house and her grandmother not there. Heather imagines herself as a faraway rain cloud about to burst. She feels an incredible knot in her stomach, a fist of something sour and unreal. She wonders if this is what it is to feel somebody's dying. Heather never truly believed her father drowned, what is grief supposed to feel like?

A strange fragrance hangs in her grandparents' house, it is unfamiliar to Heather but she's certain it's death. Her grandfather is in his recliner when Heather's mother and Miranda drop Heather off, his head bowed. "We'd come in," Heather's mother sings through the open door, "but it's getting late."

125

Heather's grandfather raises his head, waves or perhaps dismisses them. "I was having a nap," he snaps. Her grandfather looks smaller than Heather remembers, smaller than the way he looked at the beginning of summer. His house looks smaller too, the rooms dark and hollow even though they're cluttered with objects from a lifetime of never throwing anything away. It's Grandmother who is missing.

Heather doesn't know what to say to him. Grandfather motions her to sit down on a chair beside his chair, her grandmother's chair, smaller, the color of a plum. Heather's grandfather points at a cream-colored album on the coffee table her grandmother once polished every day. The scarred brown wood still shines like washed hair. Heather passes the album to him and he opens it, fingers trembling. Her grandfather has gotten old. She's been gone just one summer and everything has changed. "I made this collection of her, you see, Hetter? Pictures of our life together. You're in it, too." He hands the album to her.

Heather gazes at her grandmother in the photographs, her grandmother's hair hugging her shoulders that Heather never got to hug again. Did she even remember to kiss her grandmother before she left for California back in June, so anxious was she to leave Maine behind? Heather turns a page and there she is with her half-sister Miranda, little, lots of hair on them both. And there's Heather with her cut hair, red hair, shaved head, her twisted, know-it-all smirk.

She stands up suddenly and wraps her arms around her grandfather's neck, tells him good night. Heather rarely hugs her grandfather, he doesn't resist. She feels the bird-thin bones around his shoulders and neck, and she imagines her grandfather light as a breath now, or a cloud, the last hold on what Heather has known, drifting away.

She doesn't go upstairs to her room. Instead, Heather heads down the hall into her grandmother's room, yanks open the closet door, stares hard at her grandmother's clothes still hanging there as if her grandmother might slip in and put them on. She presses her face against the clothes and breathes the light mint scent of her grandmother. "Why cancer?" she whispers to the clothes. The few times

Heather had forced herself to think about her grandmother dying someday, she imagined it peacefully, her grandmother asleep and Heather old enough to bear it.

Heather pulls out a skirt her grandmother wore over the years, patched, repatched, seams torn, sewn up again. The skirt is pale grey corduroy, an elastic waist with over-washed cotton hanging down. Heather puts her grandmother's skirt around her head, slips into her grandmother's bed that is her grandfather's bed, too, lets the material with the light sweet fragrance of her grandmother drift down upon her neck, her shoulders, her chest. She wraps her grandmother's skirt around herself like it's her grandmother's hair, like it's one more Saturday and they've washed it, they've combed it. Heather is wearing her grandmother's hair.

THIRTEEN YEARS

MOLLY PIERCE HAS BREAST CANCER and they've done just about everything to stop its spread to her other parts, radiation, chemotherapy, lumpectomy, even a new age nutritionist's diet of apricots and raw carrots and lots of mineral water, no fat. Now she waits. Jenna Pierce, Molly's sister, was murdered thirteen years ago and recently Molly moved up from Portland to Rock Harbor where the prison is, to live whatever time she has left in the shadow of the man who did it. As if maybe being nearer to him she can be closer to her dead sister. Maybe she will come closer to answering those questions that rock Molly's nights even now, her dreams where for a moment she sees him leaning over Jenna the way he looked in the newspaper photo, a man whose mother must have held him sometimes, must have felt something for the person he might have become. In the dream Jenna's green eyes the color of Molly's own eyes fly open and for a minute she's real again. Molly relives that last moment when everything was fine, over and over. Maybe when the answer finally comes she will know there was a reason.

Peter and Mona Pierce, the parents, can't believe how just thirteen years ago they lived a regular life, two healthy almost grown-up daughters, a house and two cars. If only they had known that was the gift, that the things they kept working for they already had, two healthy daughters, a house and two cars. "Just a few more years," Peter used to say, "and we'll be set. We'll skip a vacation this summer, just a few more years we'll have enough." These days Peter has piles so bad he can't sit sometimes, has to lie on his side. He has colitis and gets so bloated he fantasizes taking a long, thin and silvery sharp skewer, pop! Whatever's inside him that's in so much pain explodes.

Mona is fat. She hasn't stopped eating since it happened and now with Molly's bad breast she's started drinking, too, sometimes before she's even finished her morning pancakes, scrambled eggs and sausage, she's got a vodka tonic in her hand. "Well, it's summer," Mona whines, "so it's too hot for coffee." Nothing much matters, anymore. They sold their house and one of the cars to pay for some controversial cancer treatment Molly's insurance wouldn't cover and it didn't work, anyway. Though they try not to think about it and they certainly never talk about it, Peter and Mona just can't believe this is happening, that their lives could go this far down. They can't believe they had two daughters, sacrificed whatever it was they had known together to do whatever seemed right in raising their girls; soon they'll have nobody at all.

Sometimes Peter blames Mona, sometimes Mona blames Peter, though they never say this to each other. Inside Peter breathes a fiery hatred for the man who did this to Jenna. What's left inside Mona, as far as Peter can tell has been buried under an avalanche of flesh.

Molly Pierce is driving a leased Corvette with the top down, wind ragging through a whole new inch of hair growth. No more chemo for her; no more getting so sick you want to die anyway. She's running up her credit, doing all those things she wanted to do but couldn't convince herself she could ever afford to do, like this car. So when she sees him at the side of the road, thumb out, wearing a prison guard uniform blue as the night and standing beside a broken-down VW, Molly thinks, What the hell?

"I'll bet you're going to R.H.A.C., you're late for work and you ran out of gas," she says after she's screeched off Route One and popped open the passenger door.

"Used to be you could trust a VW but this new generation just isn't the same." He shakes his head, grins, then climbs into the Corvette after staring at her for a moment, up and down. His eyes are the grey-light color of the afternoon.

Molly hasn't had a man look at her at all for a while, except with that face of tragedy her father wears. Now she's got enough hair to appear real again and her thinness could almost be a fashion thing. The object here, Molly thinks, is to feel real. She slides her hand down over the poke of her hip bone for just a second, against the fit of her jeans, then back onto the shift, slipping into first. He's younger than what she figured a guard would be, no belly bubbling out over his wide black belt. Molly inhales, releases her breath in a slow soft whistle of sound. There's that uncertain quickening in her gut, that feeling of being all wrong on the inside, something else on the outside.

"Do you know someone named Morton Salvitore?" she asks after shooting back onto the highway, the roar and the power of the Corvette's turbo. "I thought maybe you would since you work at the prison." She accelerates and the evergreens on either side of the road become a sudden fleeting childhood memory, of riding with Jenna in their parents' cars, naming the things they passed, big tree, yellow house, fake ducks in grass, old lady rocking on a white porch.

"Salvitore's on my cell block. Why, you know him? I can't believe you'd know someone like that. You're way too nice to know someone like that."

She shrugs, takes in the scent of the wind. Houses, yards, fences, the containments of human life, flying by.

"The thing is he's a con artist. That's typical but this guy's really a piece of work. Now he's trying to pretend he's got religion and is redeemed. Maybe that lady preacher buys it but not us, no siree. They get inside, these cons, and they finally realize it's all over, that there's no way out. We know what they've done and they can't pull anything over on us or hide anymore, so then they want to be for-given. No such thing if you ask me." He straightens his belt, thrusts out his long legs against the floor board's rich carpet and Molly can't help but notice the knots of thigh muscles under his prison guard pants. She rolls the ball of her hand over the gear shift, angles, then thrusts it into fifth gear, cruising speed.

"If you ask me, a man kills a person there's got to be a punish-ment for it. Don't you think? What kind of a society would we be if at any moment we could all get shot and nobody's held account-able?" He grins at her. "So what's your name?"

"Molly," she answers, "and the name on your badge says Scott Barker. Now can we skip the next twenty minutes of polite ques-tions? Because I don't have much time." Molly comes up too fast on the bumper of a U-Haul, blares the horn then pulls back a little, swearing quietly.

Scott stares at her long and steady. "Well, sure. I can live with that. The truth is, I have a lot of time. I was coming off duty in fact, but I was afraid if you knew that you wouldn't feel it was so urgent to give me a ride. My VW's not going anywhere, it's the damn clutch again. I've got all the time in the world."

Mona is there, inside all of her flesh. There was a time when she thought she could hide under it, that maybe the weight of her own skin would squeeze down upon her, smother her inside until all that's so terrible disappeared, all the shaken up, nervy parts of her that can never forget, no matter how many donuts she stuffs into her mouth, no matter how much vodka she pours down her throat.

Sometimes when she's having an especially bad day, when Peter is gone wherever Peter goes when he's not slunked into his recliner, staring at the TV (once he had even forgotten to turn it on and there he sat, staring), Mona gets out the photo albums, plops them down on the glass coffee table beside the Ding Dongs and the Ho Ho's and a pitcher of vodka sunrise, and she slices them open like a surgeon. Thirteen years gone by and still she's trying to find the clue, the reason, the sickness underneath the patina of their lives that allowed this to happen.

They all looked so normal, that always strikes her first, the average American family living out their typical lives. The girls in their braids, Peter at his barbecue, life in their own little yard. "It's nothing," Mona whispers, chewing on a generous bite of Ding Dong, "Tell yourself it's nothing." She talks to herself this way when she looks at the photo albums, like talking to another person. "Mona," she says to herself, "you and he were good parents. You loved them best you could. Nobody can blame either of you." And yet she can't help looking closer into Peter's face, wondering if there's a distance there, the twist of his mouth, the way his eyes seem to gaze out of the picture. Is that it? A father who appeared to be part of them but really wasn't? Is that why Jenna went for those older men? Was she looking for a father in her killer?

The police said it appeared Jenna didn't know him that well, that maybe she just met him that night. Nobody seemed to know much about him. But then again nobody seemed to understand about Jenna, either. After Mona has enough vodka sunrise in her she does the worst she can do. She imagines the way it was before her daughter died, those last few hours of the life Mona brought into this world, nursed, and loved more than anything, more than her husband, and secretly—oh so guiltily!—more than Molly. Molly is Peter's daughter, her distance, her ability to make shared experience, even pain, just hers; just like her father. When it happened, Molly was almost twenty and living at home, a student at the University of Maine. She abruptly got a night time job at McDonald's and moved into her own apartment. Though their house wasn't a home anymore, Mona understood that. When something like this happens it's like the very stuff your life is made out of is shredded. Nothing can be put back the same. Still, Mona can't forgive Molly for leaving her alone with the silence of Peter. Molly didn't even come home for her birthday that year and Mona had made a point of remembering it, marking it on the calendar the way she always did.

This is one way Mona pictures it: Jenna, beautiful Jenna who had graduated from high school but was still unsure of her future,

132

still new and open to so much, meets him at the Radley Hotel restaurant and they go home to his apartment for coffee. (The police said they had been drinking but Mona only accepts this possibility in a second scenario.) In this version he's nice to her and she likes him. He's older, a downtown Portland businessman, and maybe Jenna sees some future in it, maybe she sees him taking care of her the way Peter didn't, the way Mona would have if only Jenna had stayed home that night, Thanksgiving night, after Mona had prepared turkey with all the fixings. What was inside Jenna that made her need to go out, what restlessness, what want? What could Mona have said, offered or done to keep her daughter at home? If only Mona had thought to tell Jenna she loved her, at least that! before her daughter walked out the door.

Then, maybe, things got a little out of control, lying on his bed where the police found her. What could he have demanded that Jenna couldn't give? Maybe she said no and he got angry. But still he must have felt it, must have known the goodness in her? In this scenario Mona refuses to see him as all bad because if she does then she must also see the fear inside Jenna, the horror when her daughter realizes her mistake. And that is too, too painful. Mona sees that he is agitated, angry at Jenna's reluctance. So he shoots her. But it doesn't make sense! Oh, god, the hours Mona has spent trying to make sense out of the most terrible thing that can happen. Mona sees him covering Jenna's pretty green eyes with his other hand so she won't know, so he won't see her staring up at him, still trusting him; so that maybe in those last few moments she was allowed to hope.

On an impulse Molly pulls off the main road onto an older, winding road leading up into hills that are pink under a slant of late afternoon sun. "We'll take the scenic route since you have the time," she says to Scott. Somewhere in these hills, she thinks, a rock-strewn valley or a flattened area between two deep green ridges, there are blueberries growing. Somewhere there's children picking them and a woman wearing a wide, low hat, and a black dog runs wildly through a yellow field. Molly can count the trees as they drive past, their branches and each tender leaf, if she looks closely enough, if she wants to do this. These days she allows herself her impulses. These days she figures if Scott doesn't like her, or if she decides she doesn't like Scott after all, she'll just turn around and go back. "It's all urgent with me," she says.

And then Molly remembers something really crazy—the time her old college poetry professor put his tongue in her mouth and she thought she saw God. It was the year Jenna died, a month or two before that happened, and Molly was invited to the poet's waterfront condominium to have dinner with him and his wife. He met Molly, who was driving her parents' Pontiac, in the parking lot and gallantly flagged her into a space waving his linen handkerchief like a toreador. Her poetry professor used to make her laugh out loud, those silly, charming things he did. He was at least seventy, bent over and white as a cotton ball, and she had felt honored to be his dinner guest.

It was in the elevator up to the seventh floor that the old poet suddenly cornered Molly. On tiptoes and leaning his quivering little self up against her he slid his tongue into her mouth. When the elevator doors sighed apart Molly was too surprised to speak, her mouth hanging open, her heartbeat hammering, and there was the poet's wife grinning like a chipmunk, pudgy cheeks, all sweetness and full of small graces.

Throughout dinner Molly forced bites of Beef Wellington down her throat, each piece of meat a reminder of the red curl of the poet's tongue that was in her mouth first, the churning secret of this while he chattered on about everything else. His wife asked Molly polite questions about nothing in particular. "Are you a fan of my husband's poetry?" his wife asked. Molly felt as if she were living somebody else's life.

The poet was talking about how God worked through him in his poetry, how the voice of his poems really wasn't his own but God's instead, and Molly drank more and more wine though she wasn't really old enough to do this. She was trying to drown away the taste of his tongue that was more than just texture, that had become inside her mouth something as ancient and irrevocable as the poet himself. And as her own tongue grew saturated her thoughts clouded up then burst forth like rain, a brief shower of illumination, and a sort of wet, peaceful blankness came over Molly. She thought of how the poet said God worked through him; she thought about God working through the old poet, the words of his poems coming from God's own mouth, perhaps. And there it was! It was God who kissed her! Not the quivering crinkly little whiteness of the poet whose class she would drop before ever finding out whether her lips were worth an A or a C. It was the unfathomable appearance of a deity himself, the greatness of His words, the power of His breath, the slick, wet slide of an immortal tongue darting across the desert of her mouth; God would make everything right.

Then there's the other vision, the one Mona has when the vodka sunrise is gone and she's not kidding herself anymore with the orange juice, with the red squirt of grenadine syrup drifting at the top of her glass like a cloud of blood. No, it's vodka straight from the bottle now and Mona is furious with the jiggle of her own flesh lifting the bottle to her lips, like a pocket full of pool balls her underarms hang down, and she remembers how the last time Peter mounted her, whenever the hell that was, he groaned like he was climbing up a mountain of her, groaned and sighed and all of whatever it was Mona might have been feeling turned cold and bitter with the taste of her need—vodka, the lip of the bottle thrusting against her own mouth.

It goes like this: He spies Jenna in the Radley Lounge, through a crowd he picks her out the way a crow zeros in on an insect, something smaller, more helpless, weaker than the profound failure he is. She has been drinking and he offers more to her, and then he takes her to his nest, pliable as a worm. Mona has to see it this way, her daughter so drunk that her own spirit can't imagine what will happen to her. He lays her down on his bed and he does it to her. Oddly enough Mona must see this part too, her beautiful daughter known in the flesh by the man who kills her, because Mona can't fathom

that he would just shoot her. She can't imagine there would be
nothing else but this cold and violent act, the .357 down her baby's
throat. Despite what the police said, there had to have been something else! Maybe he put his hand on her breast and felt her heart
beating under it, felt the life that was there and understood in the
end how terribly wrong he was.

Mona hurls the empty vodka bottle at her husband's empty
recliner, listens to the visceral shattering of it as it hits bare floor
instead. Thirteen years and nobody can give her a reason why. How
come this monster whom she can't name, because if she gives him
his name then he becomes a man who is this minute living, breathing—why was he allowed to be the last person in the world to see
her daughter alive? Why couldn't Mona have held onto Jenna that
night, Thanksgiving when they had so many things to be thankful
for but must have forgotten them; held onto her like when Jenna
was a little girl, crawling up into Mona's lap because there was no
safer place to be? For thirteen years every time Mona drives past the
Radley Hotel she feels her breath strangle up inside her, her failure
to save her daughter like a noose around her own neck.

Mona takes a bite of the Ding Dong, chews, chews, and it turns
into a chocolate mess on her tongue. She is crumbling inside, flesh,
bones, organs, all turning to dust. Mona inhales another bite, forces
it down the hole of her throat.

Molly pulls over to the side of the road, a quiet, grassy area near a
field with short summer-burnt grass. She turns off the engine and
the ringing of insects lifts out of the waning afternoon, the fading
sunlight high and gentle. She doesn't look at Scott who is looking
at her, she can feel his eyes on her, questioning and dry as the grass.
"Shhh," she whispers, though he's said nothing. Molly turns away
from him, gazing out of her window that faces the field. She can't
see the ocean beyond but she knows it is out there, a long, low permanence of grey and blue. She knows the prison is there too, near
the sea, and the man who took her sister's life, inside. What was he
thinking during the moment that he did it, when it was too late for

anything else? What does he think about now, every minute of every day he has left?

Scott says, "I'm going over behind that tree. Wait for me, OK?" He opens the Corvette's door, climbs out then shuts it, a taut, extravagant sound. Molly watches him, the fit of his uniform against the backs of his legs, then she slides her hand up under her shirt, running the tips of her fingers over her left breast, the scarred area where she first discovered the lump. Even then she had wanted to run, not telling her doctor for several weeks, living each day with its own private message of her mortality.

One afternoon after the radiation treatment and a chemotherapy cocktail Molly's hair fell out in the space of two hours, whole long strands of it, bunches like old leaves littering the burnished wood floors, Indian throw rugs, imported cane chairs, the things of her apartment. She had thought about this, seasons, fall, the drying out and the dying of things. And she cried for what seemed to be a symbol of lost womanhood, a pair of blunt scissors taking care of the rest, pale tufts like little ears sticking up all over her head. Recently Molly's doctor told her a last bit of hope was a mastectomy. Not a guarantee, the doctor said, but what else is there? The strange thing was that Molly had thought about dancing then, about the way this feels, her chest pushed up against a man's, and what would it be like if she had one breast? Would he know she had only one breast? Can a man feel a woman's two breasts, the rhythm of her movement against him?

Scott is walking back toward the car, not looking at Molly whose hand is still under her shirt, holding what used to be. Molly wonders if he dances, but she won't ask him. Because now she can see herself, through this field past the old trees lifting their branches like skirts, and the bones of the land, the hips, the ribs, the ridges, and sun-baked flowers with their dizzying scents. Molly sees herself dancing, naming all that is alive this minute around her.

COCKS

THERE WAS THIS OCTOBER DAY TEN YEARS AGO when a storm swept in from Penobscot Bay, tearing off the remaining leaves that clung haphazardly to the trees in their yard, pale gold leaves, old tan, dead brown. Bucky remembers coming home from Rock Harbor Middle School and noticing these trees, stripped, lifeless. He stared at them for a long time before going inside; he had felt a cold, unnamed fear. Bucky called for his dog Sherman, forgetting for a moment that Sherman had recently died. His heart just quit. Nothing could be done.

He feels this fear again, this old loss, standing on the buckling, termite-chewed steps of Marnie's Hawaii house where she lives with her new boyfriend, father of her baby. Marnie leans toward Bucky just inside the screen door, staring out at him, not opening the door. "I heard about your Grandma Shirley," she says. "I heard in the end she couldn't even remember who she was. What a bitch that would be, losing your marbles and dying from Alzheimer's. I bet she didn't even know she was dying."

Behind him the late afternoon light pales. He peers inside her cramped house, into the darkness and shadows. Marnie's boyfriend's fighting roosters are trapped in tiny chicken-wire cages at the side of the yard. They shriek, and she shrieks back at them, "Shut the fuck up! I hate those cocks," she says.

"I've been back on the Big Island since the funeral, for over a month now. You never called."

Marnie shrugs. "Hooch didn't pay the goddamn phone bill. They unplugged us."

"Dammit Marnie, it's just that I thought maybe we could be together. We used to talk about it."

Marnie presses her face against the screen, flattening her nose. "Are you kidding? No offense, but I like my men a little edgier you know? You study bugs, for chrissake."

"Entomology."

"Whatever. Hey, like I've got total freedom here. We eat when we damn well want to, watch TV. A real life."

He frowns and looks away from her face, so close to his own through the screen. "So where's the baby?"

Marnie gazes into a distance of sky. Then she yanks open the door, steps out beside him. The door makes a sighing sound as it shuts. "I named her Mark."

"Mark? You had a girl and you named her Mark?" He stares at her. She looks sunken, her flesh from being pregnant seems to have deflated too suddenly. It hangs on her bones like rice bags. "Well. Can I see her?"

Marnie shrugs. "Sure you can, but you'll have to ask The Sleaze. My stepmother took her to some folks to hanai. That's a Hawaiian thing. To you haoles, you white people, it's an illegal adoption. To us it's just somebody who takes a kid we don't want." She leaps down from the rotting steps, pacing about the over-grown yard. "I'm still a model, anyway. I'm still skinny."

"Marnie in case you haven't looked in the mirror lately, guess what, you're also still white!" Bucky follows her, prickly crab grass grabbing at his ankles, the sticky smell of red plumerias from two heavily-laden trees pulsing into the muggy air. "I don't get it. You said we couldn't be together because you were going to have some-body's baby. Now you don't have the baby but you're with him any-way. What's the deal?"

She whips around, hard yellow eyes. "So what's in your future,

Buck-o? Bug books? Graduate school? Boring!"

Bucky feels a sudden stab of pain over his eye. Sweat rolls down his forehead. "Do you actually love this guy?"

Marnie pounces at him. She pushes him onto the grass, on his back, climbs on top. "It's not always about love Bucky. God what you don't know! Are you being loved, Buck-o?" She exhales down into his face. He can smell her last meal, something tangy and sharp with onions. He can barely breathe, the way she's camped out on his chest. "Well?" She crosses her legs, bounces a little and his esophagus makes a scrinching noise.

Bucky feels helpless lying under her. Like an over-turned beetle, he thinks. The Burying Beetle is a type of Carrion Beetle. They dig under the carcass of a small animal until it falls into their hole. They bury it, food for the larvae, their eggs are deposited on the corpse. Bucky seizes her leg. "I wanted to be with you, is all. I thought we had something." His forehead's beginning to throb. He tries to shift her weight off his chest. "God has an inordinate love of beetles," said the biologist J.B.S. Haldane.

Marnie slides back a little and rolls around on Bucky's stomach, like she's floating on an inner tube, like he's the water. Her long fingers play with the waist band on her shorts. "Here comes the crab!" she says. "That's what Hooch says when he wants me, when he's sober. Otherwise he just takes me."

"For chrissake Marnie! That's no kind of love." His head is spinning. God may love beetles, but what Bucky has learned is there's always someone meaner. And they're the ones who win.

"Give me a break, Buck-o, you don't know, you just don't know. I've got my things here. I live here. I've got a bedroom, a full-length mirror, all my clothes are here, I've even got furniture that's mine. This is who I am."

Bucky's migraine comes on in little stars, fragmenting, dissolving into a pulsating darkness. He shoves her off him, clutches his neck, then rolls on the grass away from her so that he's facing the cages with the fighting roosters, their grand and colorful displays. They strut about in their cramped quarters, black eyes shining like glass. Which one will become a bloody mess, broken, sliced up from a razor blade tied to the skinny leg of another, neck hanging to one side like something wrung out, squeezed dry, like a used-up rag? He thinks about how like these cocks, there are people walking around with invisible blades, cutting up other people, winning from the sheer surprise of their violence.

He turns and stares at Marnie who sits cross-legged in the grass, gazing at him, her own eyes empty as plates. She smiles, a slow, languorous movement of her lips which Bucky notices are chapped, a thread of skin hangs down like a crumb. "Anyhow," she says, "I named her Mark to give her a chance. Mark's a white boy's name. You guys have all the luck."

GHOSTS

THERE WAS A TIME WAY BACK WHEN ELI would do anything to make him notice her. "Look at me, Daddy!" she'd shrill, hanging by her knees upside down on the wobbly back yard jungle gym. It's her little sister he stared at, Missy, who held on with her hands. Henri's the one got yelled at the most, the oldest, supposed to have been his son. Even that would have been OK since at least he noticed her. When Missy was born she became Daddy's little girl. Elinor was the middle daughter. "This one, that one," but what about the other one? What about Eli?

These days Eli's father sits by the plate glass living room window staring out, his bald head white as an egg in the light shining in from the afternoon sun. He's barely recognized Eli since she left her husband and came back to Oahu to be with her father, and he depends on her completely. "No good sonofabitch," her father used to say about Dallas, cheerfully, as if he expected this daughter would have married nothing else. These days when Eli mentions her husband's name her father cries out, "Capital country of the city of Texas!"

"Alzheimer's disease," her father's doctor said, "they become like children again. Could be a blessing of sorts," the doctor said, "he never did get over the loss of your sister, and now your mother's

142

gone too. I suspect the life in his mind was just too sad to hold onto."

Eli's father calls Eli by her sisters' names, her mother's name, and names that shouldn't be used at all. He is as dependent on her as a puppy, and she cares for him in this painstaking way, wiping his nose and mouth when things from inside leak out, bathing him, her hand slipping across the pointy ridges of his ribs; afterwards she powders his skin where it has become raw. She changes her father's socks when they don't match, chooses what shirt to wear with which slacks, yanks the tea kettle from his hand when he's about to heat it up with the iron, "No, Daddy, don't you dare!" Words he once hollered to a teenaged Eli when she let a boy explore her under her clothes, sitting on the rocks of Manoa stream below her father's bedroom window. Had Eli hoped her father would see the woman in her, since he didn't acknowledge the little girl? Now, when her father wanders their neighborhood, searching for whatever it is he thinks he has lost, Eli leads him home, holding his hand, pulling him neatly beside her. Missy is dead. Henri doesn't want him. Eli has her father now.

And what would her father think if he knew this same boy came back to the house when nobody was home but Eli? What would he think of his daughter opening the door in her slip, her panties, no bra, pulling this boy inside? What would he think, "this daughter," leading this boy to her bedroom, kissing him urgently inside the door, her room clean and pink as the insides of a shell? With a sweat-warmed hand this boy pushed Eli down on the bed her father bought for Henri, handed down to Eli when Henri got a new one—pushed her down and her slip came up and she was laughing and gasping at the sight of this boy, his pants below his knees, the tops of his thighs thick and tight as two palm trees swaying down upon Eli's opened legs. He thrust into her once, shuddered and was done. Then he was gone, leaving Eli with a burning between her thighs and a strange new sense of who she was in this world. She straightened the things in her bedroom, knickknacks on the knotty pine shelves, pictures on the pale pink walls, clothes folded into neat little piles on the vinyl chair, as if the boy had been there long enough to touch anything at all.

There was an evening last week when Eli couldn't find her father. She called the police who sent a helicopter beaming through the night skies, over the Koolau mountains, behind their Manoa home. They discovered her father cowering between the ginger bushes in somebody else's yard, naked, calling out Eli's mother's name. Eli brought him home, tucked him in bed and stroked his damp forehead that smelled of the prickly sweet fragrance of white ginger. "She's gone, Daddy. I'm who you got now."

There is this structure to things: Eli works on her paintings during the nights that her father sleeps and when he's awake the hours are defined by his needs. She has established routines around her father's care—up at dawn to lay out his clothes, helping him dress, feeding him his oatmeal then cleaning up the spills, washing his dishes, mopping the floor where he pees sometimes, leading him to his chair by the window, sitting him down like bending the legs of a large sagging doll, caving him in at his knees. Sometimes she ties him loosely to the chair with the sash off her robe, those days when his eyes are somewhere else and he's prone to wander. Then it's soup for lunch, soft foods so Eli won't have to bother with his dental plates, a nap in his room so she can clean up his mess, an hour to gaze at a yellowing newspaper, her feet on her mother's couch and he's up again—the cycle of chair, meal, clean up, and finally sleep, all over again.

Sometimes her father bellows at Eli, curses her; sometimes he lays his head down into her arms and weeps. Once when she caught him running out the door into the night, the green smell of the mountain air and the dark scent of the Manoa stream rising around them, she tackled him down onto grass already wet with dew, his body bone-light and ragged as an ostrich, shouting "No, Daddy! You can't do this to me! I won't let you!"

Was it then Eli first sensed they were being watched? Breathing sounds from behind the plumeria tree, in, out, in, out, as she lay on her sobbing father like a lover might or the child she might have been so long ago? "Let go of me!" her father howled, "I don't want to be buried here!" Eight, almost nine years ago, it was Eli's father

who had said, "God's sake Elinor, that baby took one breath. It barely qualifies as living at all. This is no kind of grief. You can't bury
yourself this way!"

For weeks after their baby died, until Dallas padlocked what
would have been Benjamin's bedroom, locking away what should
have been Benjamin's life inside it, Eli kept seeing phantom babies.
She'd be sitting in her chair, rocking, her arms clutched around that
hollow place inside her where the baby had been, her dreams of
who the baby would be, memories of the feeling of his life inside
her, little beatings like butterfly wings against her own flesh; she'd
look over at the other chair and a baby would be lying in it, funny
shaped head, arms flailing for just a second until it became an empty
chair again. Or she'd go into the baby's room, sure she heard the
sounds of him in the cradle he never used, crying for her. "I'm coming!" she'd call out to the silent apartment.

She'd be slumped over the kitchen table drinking tea, the steam
of it rising up into her half-asleep face, her numb body, and her eyes
would catch for just a moment the darting in and out of tiny baby
legs, too small and frail to have ever propelled Benjamin's breath-
starved body, yet for this one moment whole.

IN THE MIRROR DIMLY

SOMETIMES WHEN DALLAS THINKS ABOUT HIS FATHER it's the orange rope he sees, a coil of it tied to and wrapped around a jutting rock, the ocean cliff off Hanaumu Bay. He sees his Aunt Barbara, his half aunt, her heavy hair the color of the rocks, the hard man-like muscles of her calves under her short muumuu that blows up in the night wind. She bends over and he imagines her black hair swooping down against her hands like a shadow as she knots the loose end of the orange rope around her ankle. Dallas remembers his father's own hand around that ankle; he saw them outside the window of his parents' bedroom, his father and his aunt playing football in the back yard. Dallas was ten years old, his father wouldn't let him play. "Tackle! They're playing tackle of all things," his mother whispered, shaking her big head, its puff of dried corn-colored hair. "Well, she's not exactly your real aunt, you know, not completely." Then his mother went back to her afternoon television programs, her "stories," which in later years were never turned off. Dallas watched his father's hand wrap around his aunt's ankle, sliding up that muscled calf toward the hard brown top of her thigh.

His mother explained the truth of Barbara's death to Dallas five years after it happened. He was thirteen when a fisherman found her muumuu and the rope, and that year, the height of his parents' war he was told it was "an accident." Dallas missed his aunt, the one person in his family who went to the mainland, graduated from college and came back a rebel, her untamed hair, her M.G. sports car, her laugh that sounded like there were actually things that amused her.

Throughout the years after his mother told him and sometimes even in his dreams, Dallas imagined Barbara as she tied the long rope, saw her jump into the incoming tide that sucked up under the cliff where a cave was, then pulled out again. The rope held her so she wasn't swept into the ink-colored sea, and she remained tethered to the rock in the darkness, drifting about in the deepening water like a thing trapped. With every thrust the tide rose higher, each new wave of it pulsing around her face so that she couldn't take a breath until it slipped back out again. Each breath had to last longer and longer, as the ocean bloomed around her.

Dallas likes to think she got away. Likes to imagine in the end her life meant something, and she reached down between the cold rhythm of the waves, yanked the orange rope from around her ankle, slipped off the cumbersome muumuu and swam to a distant freedom. He sees the surge of the sea around Barbara, her long hair floating out and away like a manta ray, something that belongs there; like she's already gone.

Dallas thinks about the damage his father did, but these days Dallas can't condemn this thing enough the way he knows he should. His father must have felt something so powerful he was willing to sacrifice everything else. Dallas once asked his mother why… his father who divorced his mother and moved to Los Angeles, his mother who in later years never left her couch, poised like some massive statue, a monument to consumption and television and her array of cosmetics spread out upon the glass end tables, guaranteed to make her beautiful.

"How should I know?" his mother said. "There's a sickness sometimes between a man and a woman. Makes them want what they're not supposed to have. Barbara was pretty. She graduated college, but turns out she was dumb as the rest of us."

● ● ●

These days if somebody were to suggest to Dallas he's stalking his wife, would he laugh? Dallas Hyde? Who could have any woman he wants? He sees it more as a sort of game. Eli walks out on him and goes back to Honolulu. A couple years later Dallas also moves back but she has no idea he's there. Turns out he just couldn't bear it without her.

So he follows Eli at a distance when she goes into town. From outside her father's house he watches her inside, moving about in her life without him. He takes pride that he can do this and she doesn't have a clue. Dallas gets as close as he dares, just to see Eli's face again and know that in some way she is his.

Well, wasn't their vow "Until death do us part?" Has Eli died into this new life, taking care of her old father who Dallas never thought she gave much of a damn about, anyway? If she did it's news to him. Why is she here? He's discovering there's lots of things he didn't know about his own wife. Like her toe stretches over the bathroom sink to peer at herself up close in the mirror, he didn't know his wife was so vain. When she was living with Dallas, immersing herself in her paintings, sometimes Eli would barely wash her face. She'd tug her red hair back into a ponytail and fly out to do some errand in between letting the oils dry, dressed in baggy sweats and a paint-stained shirt. Once he told her he preferred a little makeup on a woman, just enough to give her that polished look he appreciated. Made him feel valued, thinking she cared enough to look good around him. After hearing this Eli used up the rest of what little makeup she owned on a painting, azure eye-shadow sky, mascara tree branches like a Japanese-inspired landscape.

So Dallas had an affair or two; well, who could blame him? It wasn't about sex. He just wanted to feel valued. He was lonely, and tired of sleeping single in a double bed.

Now, Dallas watches Eli smear lipstick the color of blood across her pale lips. He's crawled into the over-grown lantana bushes underneath the living room window, pokey leaves, branches thick and grizzly as an old man's beard. He sees Eli stick her face down in front of her father's. "Look at me Daddy!" Dallas hears her plead. If Eli peered closely out of this window, the one her father eyeballs constantly, she would see Dallas folded up like an animal in these ridiculous bushes, laughing at her. Though he's not a callous person, he wishes she could know this. He's changed in some pretty significant ways. He even goes out of his way now not to massacre those creepy things that come into his territory, spiders, cockroaches, even the long strings of ants the color of charcoal that flow in and out of his rented kitchen, windows, cupboards, under the table, no place sacred; he lets them live. He was never one for bugs and this used to enrage Eli, his "random killings," as she put it. Sometimes it seemed like she loved all life forms except him.

Spying on Eli makes up at least a little for the long months in Maine without her, when Dallas used to drag himself awake every morning. He no longer had eyes for Eli's sister Henri, sleeping in the next room. He wanted his wife. Henri's kids were getting on his nerves, taking over the place as though he had by mistake stepped into someone else's house, theirs not his. Henri said she was waiting for her husband to "beg" her to come home. "I'll just be here a while," she said, "a rest stop that's all." Two years later Henri was divorced, and Dallas was feeling that he wasn't a part of his own life anymore. It was because of Eli.

So even though Dallas felt a little guilty at first, Eli so absorbed in her meticulous care for her father that she had no idea he was watching her, he felt some satisfaction knowing things he shouldn't know—like the oatmeal she eats every morning when she used to skip breakfast; and intimate things like the way she pawed through her mother's dresser one day, pulled on her mother's slip then dropped down onto her mother's bed, crying. Dallas remembered how after Eli's mother died their father refused to let Eli and Henri remove their mother's belongings. "It's my house!" their father bellowed, when he had a voice for these things. "Do we need to be reminded every moment she's not coming back?" Eli had pleaded.

Dallas feels close to Eli the way a voyeur feels close to the person he watches, almost a god of sorts, knowing her in her most intimate ways, behind the mask she puts on for the rest of the world. It's like being on the inside of her skin, understanding her life when she can't be aware of his or even know he's become a part of hers again.

Sometimes at night Eli stands close enough to the window where he could touch her against the glass. He imagines doing that, his fingers lightly stroking where her breasts are, the curve of her stomach. Maybe their marriage was always this way, a skin of something brittle yet transparent between them, that close to shattering.

In her father's house Eli is surrounded by all that has changed. Still Dallas refuses to let himself feel sorry for her, the bottom line is she left him. She wrote to him and said she wanted no more contact; she was the one who hung up when he tried calling her, tried to make things right again. "They can't possibly be right again," she had shouted in his ear, 6,000 miles away, "because they were never right in the first place." For god's sake they had a baby together and he died! She used to beg Dallas to say this to her, to talk about it with her when he could barely taste the words on his own tongue.

And there's the letters. Rock Harbor Adult Correctional, the standard prison blue envelope with the disclaimer on the outside, that the contents hadn't been evaluated by prison officials. Not many of them anymore, but Dallas makes sure he gets to the mailbox most days before Eli just in case. The way he sees it he's saving her, though from what he's never been exactly sure.

Dallas remembers a particular night back in Rock Harbor, being unable to sleep and watching his wife sleep. He had thought about his father, his mother, his relationship with his wife, and how everything and everyone in his life seemed so unconnected to the real Dallas, the person he was afraid he was. The person who was afraid. Eli was sleeping fitfully. She kept calling out her sister Henri's name. "Henri! Henri!" Dallas climbed out of their bed quietly and wandered into the hall. He paused in front of the back bedroom, its door partly open. The moon was high and full sending a bolt of white through the window. He saw a sprawl of baby arms and legs, little fingers, feet, covers kicked off, Morgan and Maple asleep on the floor. For a moment Dallas's stomach did something strange and there was a hardness in his throat like swallowing stones. Inching further into the room he could see the light in Henri's blond hair, a hank of it drifting down off the pillow, the sleek curves of her shoulder and hip.

The next morning Dallas drove to Rock Harbor Adult Correctional to meet Morton Salvitore. He wasn't sure why he was visiting this man whom he was certain he should hate. But he had been feeling increasingly drawn to the prison, a place where hope is a fragile thing and that easily broken, he figured. He was curious to know about the life inside, a life that must be less than his own, yet he felt an unexplainable tie to it, a sense of what it might be like to wake up each day with the same slice of grey sky through the same grey bars, same everything that couldn't change. He understood the despair of this, of not being able to change a thing.

When Dallas entered the building its bricked-in darkness also seemed familiar, like a home you don't want to go home to, but there's nowhere else. He felt a small regret, knowing he would come just this once. Because what could he say to this man, Morton Salvitore, besides insisting he stop sending them letters? Threaten him, perhaps, if he refuses? Dallas felt a coldness inside him when he thought about threatening Morton Salvitore. He couldn't see an end to this thing and he couldn't name the thing that he was afraid of, but coming to the prison filled something inside him, for that moment anyway, a space like a spare hour of a day where there is nothing else.

In the visitors' room he sat at a narrow table facing Morton Salvitore. Dallas had glanced around the room nervously, avoiding the man's hard stare. He gazed for a few moments at a slant of dusty light that flowed in through a barred window. This was a man who killed someone, after all, a man who might be in love with Dallas's own wife for chrissake. How do you look at someone like that? At the next table he noticed the silvery scars on another inmate's arm, the inside part, beginning near his wrist, creeping up. "They're called courage cuts," Mort whispered, leaning into Dallas's face, following the direction of Dallas's eyes. "They take apart a Bic shaver, cut across and up their arm, just enough to make a bloody mess. The name's a lie. The real courage is to cut down."

Now Dallas is again at Eli's father's mailbox and Eli is somewhere else. He notices the prison blue immediately but the scrawled handwritten return address looks different. Dallas slips off across the street where there is a dark stretch of tropical forest leading down to the Manoa stream, banana trees, ginger bushes, croton and ti leaves. He perches against a lava rock wall and carefully slits open the envelope with his pocket knife. A scent of rotting guava hangs in the thick air and the nearby stream whispers like a slight and steady wind.

"Dear Eli, Please consider writing a note to Morton Salvitore. I understand your hesitancy, but I must tell you he is very ill. My job is not to judge the worth of this man; I know he's done a huge wrong. It is also not my place to forgive him—we have a higher power for that! Working with Morton has been my greatest personal challenge, and though I doubt that he has come to accept the Lord, or even his own truth, I do see there is goodness in him. You would not be sorry writing him. You are one he worships. Reverend Ellen Barnes, Prison Chaplain."

Dallas presses hard against the wall, the coarse and jagged lava cutting into the backs of his knees. He needs the feel of something solid. He thinks about the letter, about the truth of it, and whether he has a role in it. Should he return the letter to the mailbox so Eli will find it? Will Eli write to Morton? What if he gets better? (Dallas wouldn't put that past Morton Salvitore, coming up from the gates of hell, a love sick Pluto to fish out Dallas's own wife.) But if Dallas doesn't put back the letter, then he is the only one here who knows. He imagines laying it on top of the mailbox, letting fate decide, sees the warm afternoon breeze as it rises and swirls about, catching an end of the envelope, twirling it up into the blue air. Dallas sticks the letter in his pocket and goes home

Back in his apartment, night time, the Waikiki "jungle" a smattering of two story buildings, palm trees, jumbles of voices and odors, salt air mingling into the burning of marijuana from open doorways, the greasy hot stink of the streets, Dallas remembers how it was a woman's scent that first drove him away from Eli. A year after the baby died, when things were supposed to return to normal, it was as if Eli had become this sanitary object, this brittle, odorless person and he longed for the way a woman's fragrance can drive you mad, make you forget, breathing in the flesh and spirit of someone else for however long it takes to step out of your life. Dallas knew that Eli knew. He saw her, nose pressed against the collars of his shirts, the scent of others brought into their bedroom, cologne, flowery deodorant, hair spray, some other woman's armor to face the day. Eli's tragedy had become her armor. He had tried to touch her, hadn't he? He felt Eli shiver and shrink, some integral part of her that didn't even seem connected to her own flesh. And then he couldn't touch her.

These days they are separated by glass. Dallas watches his wife care for her father, wiping drool from his chin. He wonders if it's their baby she thinks about, the touch of the wash rag on her father's skin that is, after all, as much a part of Eli's own flesh as Benjamin was. Does she ever think about Dallas? He watches her watch herself in the mirror. Is she seeing his face, imagining it, not realizing that if she looked close enough into the mirror she might catch his reflection in the window behind? It occurs to him that they might go on like this forever, Eli caring for her father like her father is her son. Dallas watching over them both like God.

PRETTY JIMMY

THE WAY PEOPLE TALK NOW IT'S LIKE THEY ALWAYS believed he'd
come to no good. Pretty and dumb is what most of them call him.
Pretty Jimmy, he's got these wicked green eyes like beer bottle glass,
he's tall as a tree and shaped so sweet, like something you want to
bite into. Jimmy comes from a family of dumb and pretty people,
something about a stepfather who had a slew of fine looking step-
daughters, who married one that was better looking than the rest
but without a brain in her head and she gave birth to a pretty
daughter who gave birth to the golden-haired uncles, the green-
eyed brothers and sisters and so on. One of those probably had
Jimmy. Who belonged to whom wasn't always exactly clear. They
were all dumb and most of them pretty. Jimmy was the dumbest and
the prettiest.

If it wasn't for Led Nash Jimmy might be with us still, hanging
out in the park during the summers, all two months of our summers
here when the shadows breeze down long and leafy and green as
Jimmy's eyes, and you open your mouth and suck in a breath full of
air so tangy it's like drinking the sea. Led's a bad one, we all agree on
that, and he took to Pretty Jimmy like something stuck onto the
soles of Jimmy's shoes. Maybe he figured with Jimmy's looks and
Led's own conniving they'd get someplace other than Rock Harbor

Adult Correctional, which is where Jimmy is now of course. Led's own people pimple the place like it's the Nash homestead.

My neighbor Scott Barker is a guard there. He told me about Jimmy being on his cell block, about how Jimmy's so good looking and stupid and sincere that the other inmates don't quite know whether to make him out a victim or a hero. So Scott's taken to protecting Jimmy, kind of, "Keeping the buzzards at bay," he calls it. Scott isn't too bad looking himself, though he's a little old for me, my mother said, as if what my mother says makes any difference. Since her divorce she's become the world authority on boyfriends.

Some of us think Jimmy got kind of a raw deal out of this; even my friend Heather is beginning to think this way and she's the reason he's in prison. Here's how it happened: Led and Pretty Jimmy took to hanging out in the park with us last summer when the weather was damn hot for Maine, "sultry," my mother called it. Made my mother want to be with her latest boyfriend more than us, it seemed, and since Heather was mostly staying with me at my house, her grandpa not being well and her mother—who knows where her mother was—Heather and I ended up spending most of our evenings just hanging in the park, my little sisters home watching TV, nobody watching Heather but me. I'm older than Heather but I'm not exactly the guardian type. Life was sweet enough. There's not a whole hell of a lot else to do in Rock Harbor.

So let's say it's last summer again and Led and Pretty Jimmy start coming around. Most evenings you'd see them lounging near the lightning-split oak where the druggies hang, before the light goes completely dead and the night breezes are tripping through Jimmy's long brown hair that's the color of dark taffy or caramel, something rich, tasty, and smelling like a woodsy shampoo, I'll bet; and Led just leaning against that tree with his vicious smile, eying the girls who saunter by like he owns them, like he screwed each one of them. Lord, that Jimmy was a good-looking one though, standing there with his dazed smile and his shoulders jutting up hard as rocks under his tee shirt. I can't blame Heather for starting the game with him, even though we warned her about him being so dumb, and we warned her even more about Led, who like I said stuck so close to

155

Jimmy it's as if Jimmy sprouted an extra ugly arm.

Probably it was Led who noticed Heather before Jimmy did, making her eyes at Jimmy, her moves, the way she'd swing by a little too close, scratch up against his arm like a branch might, something caught on him, shake herself loose, toothy smile just for him. Heather's one of these bony types the guys go for, wears her jeans tight below her flat belly and her shirt cropped up, and this particular night Led puts his hand there against her skin and he says to her, "Have you met my man Jimmy?"

Well, now, normally Led putting his dirty paw on her stomach would cause Heather to have a small fit, she's a jumpy type if a little reckless. It's because her father drowned and her grandmother died, and with her mother and half-sister who knows where I guess Heather feels kind of left out. Though she won't talk about it. She's grown inward like a toenail or something, tough on the outside but you know she's hurting. This time Heather didn't jump. She just drew back a little away from Led, inched up closer to Jimmy, "Hi" she said. And he said hi back. I remember he looked kind of embarrassed and pleased, and really sweet. I guess that's what comes from having no brains, nothing up there to worry about the way you appear to the rest of us. You can be just plain and simple and nice.

Maybe that's what Heather wanted that night, I don't know. It wasn't like her to leave with those guys, all alone, Led driving them away in his bad-ass car, slapped on decals of stars and skulls and heavy metal emblems, cartoon ladies' torsos swimming on the paint job like mermaids. He gets noticed in that car, I'll give him that, no looks and a whole lot of meanness.

The rest of the story I pieced together from what Heather told me and what my friend Scott got from Jimmy himself. Jimmy's just too dumb, Scott says, to understand they don't do that at The Rack, inmates blabbing to the guards. But Scott's a good guy, and like I said before he's trying to protect Jimmy from the prison pecking order which has the babybangers—that's their word for the child molesters—getting it first, then the rapists. Since Heather just turned sixteen, depending on if somebody really wanted to nail him, Jimmy could be both, Scott told me.

So they took Heather to the trailer Jimmy and Led rented just outside town, this shacky double-wide, a string of wire mesh chicken coops out back from when there used to be a egg business on the property. So many used-to-be businesses around here you wonder what anybody has to get up to in the morning? Anyhow, they took Heather inside and she said it was pretty nasty, piles of dirty dishes, yellow newspapers all over, cats lying everywhere like pillows, and antlers mounted on the wall—eight pointers that Led said he jacked one night, proud of it too, shining his car's headlights into a field to blind the poor thing, then firing.

They had a few beers and then a few more, and Heather told me she was starting to feel kind of good, that the room sort of swirled and softened around her and even became magically cleaner. Jimmy, who couldn't finish a sentence to save his life, stopped trying to talk to her and just looked at her with those dazzling green eyes. Heather said she felt a rush of something really nice, sitting together on the couch that stunk of must and mud and the cats they shoved off, and Jimmy who smelled of some kind of male perfume he slathered all over just for her, she said.

If it wasn't for Led maybe the evening might of ended right there. Heather told me about this, holding hands with Jimmy, not talking because there isn't much you can say to Jimmy and have him reply in any usual way; it's like his brain is missing the art of conversation or something, one person talks, the other responds, only Jimmy might answer to something said five minutes ago or even yesterday, if he got it in the first place, that is.

Well, Led disappeared for a while, Heather said, probably thinking that way Jimmy could make the moves on her. When he came back reeking of some hard liquor and found them still just sitting there, maybe Led decided to help things along. So this is the part I'm not as clear on, because this is where Heather got fuzzy when they drugged her, or Led did, snapping a popper up under her nose. She said there was this intense sharp smell like flesh burning in ammonia, and then her head was sinking and she couldn't see and she was calling out for somebody to help her because she thought she was dying or at least going blind.

One of them, she believes it was Led, tugged her jeans off and her bikini pants, and lay her spread-eagled on the ratty couch. She's sure it must have been Led because all the while she's breathing the stink of that liquor, a hot cloud of it looming over her. And she's hearing them conversing, Led's voice insistent, Jimmy's a small whine and then a wail and a whoop. It scares Heather, this new sound of Jimmy, and her vision is still all fuzzy and pokey and weird, so when Jimmy lies down on top of her she fights him off like she's drowning.

That's what Heather told me, that for a second she thought of her father swimming frantically up under the thick green mess of sea water that kept expanding—the more he tried to fight through it, the more it howled down on top of him. Heather pummeled Jimmy's pretty face and she shrieked and cried and sobbed into his face, and maybe he would've climbed back off her at that point, he really never had a mean bone in that big body of his, too dumb to be mean. But Led's holding him down, she can hear Led roaring on top of Jimmy, "Do her! Do the bitch, can't you see she wants it? Do her or you're not a man and you're no friend of mine."

Jimmy's moaning and wailing in her ear, "Heather? Oh Heather, Heather, Heather?" like her name's a chant, like he's pleading with her, or maybe it's the only thing he knows to say; maybe he just wants a friend, this poor dumb slob, whether it's Heather or Led, and now Led's saying he won't be his friend. Heather punches Jimmy again and this time she's really mad, the popper's wearing off and she hollers into his face, "Get the fuck off me, you stupid pig!"

Well, there's something about being stupid that can make stupid people really wild when others point it out. Something about that word maybe, coming out of Heather's own mouth. Maybe he trusted her; maybe he really did like her and he thought there actually was a chance she could like him back. Maybe he didn't understand she was only sixteen, younger than most of us; didn't know her life the way I know her life, living the hurt of not enough love.

Anyhow he did it to her. He raped Heather and one of them beat her up too, hit her in her jaw so the next day her chin was the color of red cabbage, a fist full and it hung a little crazy like her teeth were too big on one side. I'm not sure Heather would have reported it. She was embarrassed, I know that, and sick and quaky inside, and it was me who brought her to Stella Dubois, a kind of stepmother of sorts who Heather never got to live with but seemed connected to the way families are these days, scatters of them here and there. But it's like they're shackled to each other in chains when something like this happens.

What I'm saying is, I didn't know what else to do. I didn't know where to take her, who to tell when Heather came creeping back to my house later that night, all busted up inside. She couldn't stop shaking. I took her into my bed and I held her near me like she was my puppy, shivering and whimpering, like I could protect her, my skin against hers even though it was already too late. I cried along with her because, dammit, I didn't know what to do. My mother was at her boyfriend's. Who tells you what to do when this kind of thing happens?

So the next morning I took Heather to Stella and there's no convincing Stella that if it weren't for Led the whole thing probably wouldn't have happened. Stella was out for flesh. She wanted the guy that did it. She wanted him put away and she would do whatever it took to get him. She said she wasn't about to let any man go around preying on a girl anymore, she wouldn't stand for it she said.

I'm not saying Jimmy didn't deserve some kind of punishment. He's a dumb guy who did something really bad to Heather. It's just that I'm not sure he understood exactly what he did. I think Stella would have shot Pretty Jimmy herself if the police didn't get to him first. She hired this fine looking lady lawyer from Portland who eyed Jimmy up and down on that stand like he was filth, like he was a slug, slimy and useless. Maybe that lawyer thought this of all of us, who knows? We're just people who live in this micro town in the middle of the Maine coast. Most likely Heather would never have gone through with that trial but for Stella prodding her along.

Truthfully though, I think nothing much was left inside Heather one way or the other. I think when these things happen to people who've had a lot of bad luck, who haven't had enough love, they just kind of give up. They go through the motions, whatever these are, they get worn down and faded and maybe they start to won-der how much of it really matters, anyway? Sometimes they feel like they're nothing, like there's nothing inside of their own skin but their skeleton.

I should know. My mother named me Cedra. Which means exactly nothing.

THE TRUTH ABOUT ANGELS

WHAT IF MORT WAS WRONG? What if it didn't happen the way he allowed himself to remember it? What if it really wasn't Thanksgiving, Mort didn't spend it with his father because his father never really liked him and there was no Jenna Pierce staying with him, nobody to come home to at all? What if it happened on no special day? What if he had nobody, nothing to fill up that void as even now he is filling up inside the spaces he must breathe into, this thick murderous advance? What if it wasn't anger, passion or despair that made him do it but instead just a sort of bland emptiness, a boredom of spirit, and there was never any reason at all?

There are things Mort knows to be certain and death is one. He feels the rot inside, the wrongness, and he knows he won't rise. If only Elinor would appear, Mort's angel, fold him up in the red wings of her hair. He holds onto her vision as the proof he has lived.

There is this desire in Mort to be touched just a little, the soft sure pressure of another's flesh. Perhaps the cruelest element of his life in The Rack is this lack of innocent contact, the skin on skin that the outside world takes for granted, a firm handshake, a pat on the shoulder, the accidental brushing up against a woman whose scent lingers through an open door. These things remind a person he is not alone.

And he feels alone, more alone than he has allowed himself to feel in a long time, lying in the infirmary, sleeping bodies in the beds on either side though it is almost afternoon; when there is no hope sleep comes as a temporary solution.

How is this happening? He remembers the beating in the shower, was it three weeks ago, two months, does it matter? The inmate named Toad that Mort refused to pay off, and a herd of his cohorts, of course. What is skin, anyway, a physical manifestation imprisoning who he is on the inside, dragged about through these years, becoming less useful, more prone to ruin and distress? His face ground like a hunk of meat into the slippery cold tiles and the sound of the drain in his ear, sucking. Afterwards that snarling Screw they called Blow behind his back, who's always hated Mort, took his turn too before bringing him down here, a kick in the chest like a horse might, swift and black and emotionless. Mort had a different feeling inside him when it was over, lying in the bruised and throbbing heap of his own flesh, his crushed chest bone; a sense of something moving out of him, slowing him down, life pulling closer to its end.

The infirmary is murky, plain grey walls, same impenetrable concrete as Mort's cell. From his bed he can't see outside the one window, only can he imagine the wide flat field past the prison wall, stretch of the uncut grass and then the open ocean beyond. When Mort first came to R.H.A.C. he used to pretend there was this possibility of escape, creating some distraction then climbing up and catapulting over the towering wall, the razor-wire fence, with the strength, the sureness, the youth he once had; slithering low through that field like a snake, biting with his own good teeth through a rope securing a boat that in his dreams was always there, his furious but quiet paddling, slipping lightly over small waves like something that takes to the water naturally, a salamander, a seal, skimming his way out to sea and beyond.

What if he did it for no reason? What if he's been locked away in prison these thirteen years for no good reason at all?

He hears Reverend Ellen's brisk voice outside the infirmary, the mechanical door buzzes open and she is escorted in by one of the Screws. "For heaven's sake!" she barks to the Screw, "It's 85 degrees outside, 95 in here and you've got a blanket over him! No wonder he's so ill. Suffocating on the inside from pneumonia and barbecued on the outside from incompetence."

"Hey, Reverend, don't blame me. Do I look like a nurse? They told me he's got fever so keep him covered."

Ellen yanks the blanket off Mort and for a moment her hand grazes his neck, he feels the coolness of her fingers on his hot skin. He remembers his mother's hands, her cool long fingers sliding through his hair, unkempt, uncut, the way she liked it. Didn't she know he would have done anything for her, been anything she wanted, grown into the man who wouldn't disappoint her?

And then Mort can't help it, at least he doesn't think it's deliberate, but water from his eyes makes its way down his cheeks, he feels the slide of it leaving wet trails like what a snail makes, or a slug.

"Oh," Ellen whispers, sitting beside Mort on the bed. If he had it in him he would hold her; if only he could hold onto her, just for now. Mort hasn't touched a woman since the night he shoved the .357 against Jenna Pierce's screaming mouth. Perhaps it really was only to quiet her? He was never that way with women, at least he has this pride. Mort's no rapist. But he's always hated noise. "Oh my lord, Morton, what are you doing to yourself? You're burning up!" Ellen takes a handkerchief from the pocket of her slacks, pats it gently against Mort's eyes, wipes the sweat off his forehead. The handkerchief smells like laundry detergent and for a moment he has an image of it, clean and white as a moth, fluttering on a clothesline in the sun. It's these little things he's missed the most, after all. Laundry drying in the sun, the small life of a thing like a moth. Once while he was working in the prison garden a humming bird flew near him. It dove down to suck nectar from some tubular-shaped flower and Mort heard the whirring of its wings, so intense it was like Mort's own blood was rushing, electric, beating with this tiny, vibrant, temporary life. That was the last time before today Mort had felt tears on his face.

Ellen bends down low beside his ear so that only he can hear her. "Try hard to know the truth now, Morton Salvitore. It's between you and God."

163

• • •

Mort inhales another tight, choking breath as if his air is being replaced by water, like sticking his head into a filthy fish bowl and trying to breathe life from the green viscous liquid, the primordial soup, the rest of him still hanging desperately on to the aerobic world. The exhale pulls back away from him with a ragged, squeezed out sound. There is coldness within him, the kind that doesn't get warm. He felt it that night, he remembers this much—the coldness, the blackness that was inside him, more so than usual on this particular night, as if everything had been slowly building up to it. And there it was.

Thanksgiving was the one day of the year when Mort's father came to see him. On this particular Thanksgiving, thirteen years ago, his father talked about "My family," his new wife and daughter. And didn't Mort think about somebody named Jenna? Wasn't she supposed to be beside him in the Radley Hotel dining room, listening to his father drone on and on, telling Mort about everything that was wrong with his life?

"Drink, drink, and more drink," his father said. "What's to become of a life lived this way?" Mort's father, his calculating way of firing out his words like a sharpshooter, the perfect fit of his hair piece, expensive cut of his pin-stripe suit, rattled on, and the fiery thirst inside Mort became a volcano. He gazed around the dining room, his eyes like small grey stones, white tablecloths, silver utensils in neat rows, seasonal centerpieces stuck together by some florist using silk and dried up flowers, and didn't it all seem so contrived and unconnected to the things Mort understood? They were the only people eating, it seemed everyone else had a home to go to for Thanksgiving. Mort sat in that empty dining room silent as a rock, staring at his father who could not look his own son in the eyes, and he saw his father was just a reflection of someone else, some person Mort would never want to know. He thought about how if he had met his father at a business event and his father gave Mort his card, Mort would have thrown it away.

"Where will you be on Christmas?" his father whined. "In a

month, drinking like you do you'll as likely be dead. Ever seen the sight of a person drinking himself to death? I can tell you it's not pretty. Your entire body will shake and shake like a goddamn spastic, and you'll be completely incoherent. So even if you change your mind and want somebody to save you? No one will understand. No one would want to understand."

Mort thought about where his father would be, spending Christmas with his family, and he thought about this person named Jenna who was supposed to be there, sitting beside Mort, taking up his side of things. Where would she be on Christmas? He became more and more agitated thinking about her, how it would be later at home in his Portland apartment, waiting for her. The apartment was in an aging brick building, in a tidy and quiet neighborhood of mostly older people. Mort had found this desirable, the appearance of this, a business man living this settled life. Outside he would hear wind rattling through the sidewalk trees as he listened for Jenna's steps, the click, click, clicking of her high heels she would not be wearing for him. She'd breeze in, late as usual and they would play their little game. "Where were you?" Mort would ask her, staring at a magazine as if he didn't really care.

"No place in particular," she'd shrug.

Mort would be quiet for a while, then start up again, the game taking on its latest twist. "Were you drinking?" he would ask her. "Let me smell you!" He would approach her and she'd crouch down, yellow eyes, yellow hair, Jenna Pierce, curled up on the couch ready to spring up at him as he'd sniff around her, grinning like it was all in fun.

"I smell sex!" he'd proclaim triumphantly. "I win! You've been out having sex with someone, am I right? I win, so that means you lose."

Mort wanted to love this person, didn't he? Tried with all his heart. But where was his heart? When he put his hand against his chest, staring at Jenna Pierce, yellow eyes and caring not a thing for him, sprawled out on the gold-colored couch like some goddamn lazy cat! he felt only the automatic ticking of the timer, the bomb that was nestled somewhere against the insides of his skin, moving the minutes toward his destination. He knew it was there, had felt its threat before, and he was powerless to stop its advance. Was this all? He had only ever wanted to love.

Later, on this particular Thanksgiving night when Mort returned to his apartment and, as he had predicted, Jenna was somewhere else, he sunk down onto the shag carpet with a bottle of vodka and waited for her by the door, leaping upon her when she came in, grabbing onto her legs as she tried to move out the door back into the night. The degradation of this! Holding Jenna Pierce's legs as if he could trap whatever it was inside her that would make her leave him again and again. When he finally did let go of her she ran into the bedroom, slammed the door, then shrieked through the shut door, "You can't keep me caged up in this place!" Standing outside the bedroom, pressing the side of his face against the thin wood Mort could hear the rustling of her undressing; he imagined he could even hear her yank back the covers and climb into his bed, mumbling dark things.

When Jenna was finally asleep Mort thought about his mother. When he was in his greatest despair he liked to torment himself this way, by trying to imagine what his life would have been like if Elaine hadn't sent him away to his father, if Elaine hadn't sent him away, then died, before he ever had the chance to ask her…why? Why did she get so suddenly sick of it all? His mother was a smart woman though she was depressed, of course, he recognized this now. Mort was also smart and depressed and driven to his thirst by these things. He assumed smart people were depressed by nature, that maybe having too many thoughts and no one to talk them out to, no one intelligent enough to listen, got them to that place of desperation. The thoughts build up like a slow poison. After their Thanksgiving meal was finished and Mort's father shook his hand good-bye, he had felt the weight of this poison, all the things he would never say to his father, the things he could never ask, all the years of never being touched by his father other than a hand shake. It disgusted Mort that his own hand had grown into his father's hand, the very shape and feel of it—businessmen's hands never realizing anything more permanent than paper.

Elaine Salvitore had been a reader and Mort imagined talking about books with her. That was what he missed the most, he decided on this night, pouring himself another vodka, the talking about these things. He had read book after book at Maine Academy; when everyone else played sports, had friends, did things, Mort read. It's the talking he missed.

On the gold-colored couch Mort sat and imagined his mother beside him, talking about some book. She was beautiful and young still, the way he remembered her, as if the years had not disappeared. He grew angrier by the minute, slamming down his vodka and then gin when the vodka was gone, in the bleakness of the room. Jenna never bothered to put pictures on the walls though she always claimed she was going to, didn't she? The thin skin of beige paint bothered Mort greatly. There was no fragrance of turkey like there should be on Thanksgiving, instead the room smelled of something temporary and clinical, a day passing into another.

He thought about this woman Jenna Pierce, lazy as an old cat in the next room, and he rose up off the couch, lunging a little to one side in his drunkenness and staggered into the bedroom. He tugged the covers back to Jenna's waist then sat heavily on the bed beside her. She was wearing a sleeveless white shirt that had slipped below one shoulder, and the shell of Jenna's thin shoulder blade stuck up like a broken wing. For some reason the sight of this vulnerability infuriated Mort and he was tempted to hide it, but instead yanked the covers completely off her. His greater weight drove the mattress down, moving the smallness of her against him. Mort froze at the touch of her sleep-warmed skin, the long pale brown hairs of his arm standing on end. "Listen to me!" he shouted into Jenna's oblique, confused face. "You never read. People who don't read are ignorant!"

Jenna Pierce moaned and mumbled something, reached down and tried to pull the covers back up around her.

"I need you to read! I need something in my life besides drinking my self sick every night, don't you see? Don't you see why I do it? What else is there!"

Jenna fluttered open her yellow eyes and blinked up at him, moth-like. "Why in God's name are you doing this to me? Let me sleep if you won't let me out of here. You're not the only one who's had a lot to drink."

"Do you understand anything? Books are about characters who have the capacity to love, but the world, being the goddamn hopeless place it is, conspires against them. They're out of sync, do you get it? The people they could have loved don't come in time to save them."

"For crying out loud let me sleep!" Jenna Pierce commanded and Mort felt the violence in his blood, his darkness surge. He grabbed her around her white neck, bending her neck back against the pillow. The smell of her hammered up at him, the lemony lotion she smothered onto her skin along with the scent of someone else he was sure she was with earlier in the night, mingling into the breath of his drinking. "I insist you get this tragedy here! Only an ignorant person would miss it. I insist you not be ignorant! There's tragedy in literature, that's why you read, so you'll understand the world isn't a happy place. Here's a plot for you: A man who could love is destined to live his life knowing the object of this love is in a different place, she's found someone else who's totally wrong for her but that's how it goes, doesn't it? So he can't love, no matter how hard he wants to, he can't. It's a catastrophe, you idiot, a waste of a life, don't you get anything about anything? Christ, what a fate, stupid young woman, brainless as wood."

Jenna Pierce narrowed her yellow eyes at Mort, her head cocked crazily to one side like a bird with its neck broken, eyes rolling back into their sockets as if this was who she was, all she would ever be, fragile as a feather and as easily destroyed. "Let me go!" she whispered hoarsely, the pressure of his hand constricting her throat. He remembers the feel of her skin, pliable and warm, like rubber, like something not even alive.

• • •

Last night, fever raging, Mort had a dream that disturbed him. He saw a fat turkey on a huge plate, prison blue, made of a hard and scratched-up plastic. The turkey had its feathers still and its head was attached to its elongated and stringy neck. It was quite dead, he was sure of that; didn't move a bit as Mort bent over it, its head cocked to one side, yellow eyes peering up at him sightless and already clouded. But then the mouth opened slowly, he could see the curl of its strange black tongue and he shoved the .357 deep down inside its throat.

Mort remembers how on Thanksgiving visitors came to R.H.A.C. in the morning, several hours before the holiday meal. He pictures it now, this particular Thanksgiving a few years back, four? five? time has a different movement in prison; a tide of visitors surging through the visiting room door with their various escorts, making the room swell with foreign scents and an undercurrent of noise like the humming of electric wires, making the guards uneasy. Extra guards on duty today, over-time pay. Most every chair is filled.

He remembers inhaling a breath of the women's perfume, waiting for his own visitor, staring through the barred window to the ground below. Immediately outside the building guards stand at attention, rifles cradled against their shoulders like skinny brown babies. Mort knows how much the guards hate holidays at the joint. The inmates don't deserve them they think, and it makes Screws' jobs feel too much like work. A spray of black birds rises off the short yellow field to the left of the guards, drifting back down again like ashes. The guards don't look at the birds but gaze straight ahead at the building, as if the bricks themselves are the lives they must watch over and despise.

He grins out the window at the Screws prickling there in the thin November sunlight. A wind's picked up and he likes to think of it pressing against their exposed flesh, teasing their hairless wrists where black regulation gloves don't quite cover the raw skin, at the place where the uniform stops. He's sure their wrists are hairless. They aren't real men, just human contrivances, robots that bleed.

Henretta Harley is on her way up. Mort pictures her legs as they climb the metal stairs, the knots of her calve muscles contracting, releasing. He tries to imagine what she'll look like but can see only Eli. And Jenna Pierce. Today he will remember Jenna, a penance reserved for this holiday. "Salvitore!" a Screw's machine gun voice sputters out. Rat-tat-tat, if his name was a weapon he'd be shot. Mort turns around, away from the window. He smells her before he will look at her, standing beside the table. The guard motions to her, pointing at the chair opposite Mort. She shakes her head at first then shrugs, pulling the metal chair out with a scraping sound, all the while fixing her cold blue-eyed stare at Mort, slinking into the seat like ice.

"Christ!" Mort exclaims, returning her stare. Her eyes lock into his, face to face, close enough where it seems he could reach over the table and touch her cheek, the hollow under her cheekbone. She unsnaps her jacket with one firing tug; the snaps pop open and she yanks it off her shoulders, lets it drop to the floor.

"I asked you to come see me and here you are," he says to her. Remember this, he tells himself, you are in charge.

Henri leans forward, cool eyes passing over Mort's face, neck, the parts of him above the table. "You're sending letters to my sister. Eli's married and you are a killer. Who the fuck do you think you are, sending her letters?"

He nods his head in agreement. "I expected more from you, Mrs. Harley. Those are pretty pedestrian conclusions. Yes, I'm in here for murder. Yes, I'm sending Eli letters and I'm sending some to her husband too. If there's one thing I've got, it's time to write letters."

"You're preying on her! She's a broken woman and you're preying on her like you're a jackal or something. Why don't you pick on someone at your own subterranean level of humanity?"

Mort inhales deeply. (Oh, the breath of this memory! To be able to breathe freely again!) He smells the scent of the soap she uses, drugstore sweet. No bottled perfume. He imagines her in the shower, long limbed through the glass door, longer bones than Eli and a neck he could sink his teeth into, shaped like something expendable.

"Like me for instance," Henri continues. "You pick on me and I'd eat you alive!" She sits back, flips her mass of blond hair behind her shoulders, shoulder bones poking up under a tight knit shirt. "I'm a killer too. Her husband tell you that when he came here? I found out about Dallas visiting you. You're deluded if you actually think anyone gives a damn about you just because we come here."

"He's got it for you, do you know? Poor Dallas Hyde, like a school boy coming across his first *Playboy*. Or more like *Penthouse*. Raunchier, and he's shocked at himself but also pleased, and he's scared of all those stirred up things going on inside his brand new skin." Mort grins, studies her closely for her reaction.

Henri shrugs. "This is news?" She smiles suddenly, lopsided, a strip of teeth and one cheek puckering into a deep dimpled furrow. Her eyes appear uninterested in what her mouth is doing, though, still fixing Mort inside her stark cold gaze. "Is that why I'm here? So you can tell me Dallas likes me? What, are we in the fifth grade?"

"Maybe I just wanted to spend Thanksgiving with somebody. I don't have a family. Aren't holidays something we all have to get through, even us pariahs?"

Henri rolls her eyes at him, snaps her teeth together, a clicking sound. "My heart is breaking. Do I get to choose when I leave or do they choose for me?"

He laughs. "It isn't exactly a hotel here, sweetie. More like a bus station. Your guard will come around to take you back out, on schedule, at the end of this half hour." He looks through her shirt at the place where her breasts are. She's not wearing a bra but there's some skin of material between her own flesh and the knit fabric, a camisole maybe? That would be more Eli's style. Henri's probably wearing a tank top, thin and tight.

"Your mama never taught you it's not nice to stare at a lady's breasts?"

"You're no lady," Mort whispers, grinning his grin. He's got her program now. She likes to shock then move into a man where he's charred and still crackling.

"Ouch," Henri says, puckering a pair of full plain lips into a kiss-off shape. "I'm so wounded. You've got fifteen minutes left to tell me why I'm here before I become like your lunch and leave you with indigestion."

Mort shakes his head, runs his hand through his greying hair, smoothing it back off his forehead. He hadn't expected a cheap detective novel in Eli's sister. "Are you always so elegant in your communication or are you reserving this graciousness for me? I want to talk to you about something meaningful you can do for your own flesh and blood. I want to convince you to give your sister a baby," he says, the taste of his own blood dancing on his tongue. "It's the decent thing you can do for her."

"Would she settle for a fifteen-year old?" Henri asks, her eyes narrowing at Mort like peels of blue paint, "because I've got a daughter for sale."

She doesn't miss a beat, he thinks, nodding his head. Henri doesn't miss a beat. He could almost live with this one, though he'd need to strangle her every time she opened her mouth.

"What's your take in all this? Why are you sticking your nose in our family stuff? What the hell does it matter to you if Eli has a kid or not, and what makes you think she wants one so bad? Eli's got her art. It's Dallas who wants the kid."

Mort leans across the table toward Henri, his elbows resting on the cool formica surface. She doesn't pull away, but stands her ground. He breathes a breath full of her, her soap-scented skin, her anger. "What if I told you your sister married the wrong man?"

"And what if I told you we all marry wrong men and spend our lives trying to make them right or we get the hell out!" Henri stands up suddenly, banging the chair back with her foot, hands squeezing the slender curves of her hips in her tight black pants. The mumble of conversation throughout the room shrivels instantly. Mort feels the other inmates eyes leave the faces of their visitors and breeze over Henri, blond, pin-up gorgeous, someone to dream about later when they're alone in their cells, someone they can make into anything they want her to be, someone they will never have to know. "I realize what you're trying to do, don't think for a goddamn minute you can fool me," she says, bending over, snatching her jacket off the floor. Mort has this crazy idea he'd like to spank her, but could he stop with just that? Henretta Harley curved over his lap, yellow hair sweeping down to the floor like a broom, exposed neck white and quivering.

Underneath the table his hand works at his knee but from the neck up he's cool as death. "I don't have an ulterior motive, if that's what you're driving at. Eli's a broken woman, you said so yourself. She needs a child. Her art is not enough. Only a real baby can fill that gap. You're her sister, so genetically it would almost be right. You'd give her a kidney, wouldn't you?"

Henri shakes her head and laughs down at him, glint of white teeth. "You're suggesting I have a baby with my sister's husband and give it to Eli? Were you thinking fertility clinic egg-in-a-dish stuff, or the less expensive method behind a closed bedroom door? Are you criminally sick or just pathologically bored?"

Mort drives a fingernail into his knee, the thin layer of skin covering the patella, right through the fabric of his pants. Henri motions to a guard hanging bloated as a balloon around the door. She points at her watch. "I can't imagine what Eli would see in you," she says, slipping her arms back into her jacket, "that she hasn't reported your meddling to prison authorities. She begged me not to, but I'll have you know I'm not famous for keeping promises." He watches her breasts push out with her exertion then pull back again as she exhales. "You're an aging criminal who's lost his own life so you're trying to live again through manipulating somebody else's. Pathetic, if you ask me." Then Henri hesitates, blue eyes staring. A muscle around her mouth tenses and jumps a little. "So how did you do it?" Her voice is flat.

"Do what?" he answers, knowing Henri's next words before she opens her mouth, an exasperated whistling through her teeth.

"Kill the person you killed! A woman, I'll bet? Probably a woman. Men like you always kill women." She shakes her head, a shimmer of blond bangs sliding across eyebrows that are pale and fuzzy as caterpillars.

He lets his eyes linger on Henri's face for a minute. He can't read the expression there, something dark, muddied. "What if I told you I used a knife? Is that what you want to hear? They hunt boars with knives in Hawaii, did you know that? A coincidence how we all came here from Hawaii, isn't it? You, Dallas, Eli, myself, even our new prison chaplain. Is this the promised land, do you think? Anyhow, in Hawaii they tackle the boar down then plunge the blade into its heart. It's more personal that way, and it's a quick, clean death. Fair too, because the victim has a fighting chance. With a gun there's rarely a second chance, unless you're a terrible shot, of course."

Henri steels her eyes at Mort, twisting a hank of hair around her fingers. "Well, do you regret it? Do you hate yourself for it?"

He grins. "There's not a breath I take that I don't wish there had been some other choice. Some people are just put on this earth to drive others over the edge."

"When you cause someone's death it's like you died yourself. You have no soul. Only difference between you and death are functioning lungs. You're a dead person, Morton Salvitore. A breathing dead person. I know. I was the cause of my little sister's death. I've got something inside me that reminds me to breathe, in, out, in, out."

The Screw is standing beside her now. "Are you all set, Miss?" he asks, his eyes passing over Mort with a kind of bored loathing, dismissing him.

Henri nods, then leans forward, close to Mort's face. "Believe me. The only thing human left in us is our guilt."

• • •

But he has his Elinor. Mort sees her beside him, nights in his cell when the cold grey dark will fall around them both, her red hair the color of his hope. He howls his loneliness into her, follows the trail of his voice flowing inside her like her own blood. He lays Elinor down on his cot, 6 by 8 foot cell, not even enough room to breathe, really, but he breathes for her; in this vision he can breathe once more. They rise up over this life that was never enough anyway. She forgives him Jenna Pierce. She's the one who can forgive him, and then he won't have to try and know anymore. What the truth was. If there was a truth.

He feels the thick liquid rise inside like drowning from the inside out. He remembers the thirst that was in him that night and so many of his nights spent alone, cold, and yet that burning too the way he's burning up now, ashes in his throat as if finally his darkness is just falling away. He wanted her to lie on top of him, he remembers this much, the weight of her on top of him, pressing down on him as if to crush some sort of sense back into him, some sort of feeling beyond the blackness, the numbness, the waste. He needed to know that a life flowed through him, warm and true and real as blood. Mort needed Jenna Pierce to make him come alive.

JIMMY IN PRISON

THESE DAYS IT'S THE FACE JIMMY REMEMBERS BEST, comes back to him in his dreams and even when he's awake staring out of the bars that surround his cell—other inmates call these cages their "house" but Jimmy knows. The way its face was pressed against the window of their trailer, teddy bear face, wide and fleshy, tan muzzle, nose black and shiny as a checker piece, peering eyes, its paws like giant ragged hands shoved up against a pane that was already cracked. His mother's banging on the pots and pans, beating them together like she's playing the drums, Shoo! Shoo! And she's thundering, Where is your father? Where is that goddamn man when I need him! All the while the bear watches, kind of annoyed, like Jimmy's mother's giving it a headache the way she's pounding on those pots and pans. Would you please stop that racket? the bear is thinking, you're giving me a headache.

And Jimmy's sprawled on his bed that's squashed up against the opposite wall, stomach down, head popping and bobbing about like a puppet—his mother ordered him to lie straight and be still for once, goddamnit! Three rooms in their trailer, Jimmy's bed and his older brothers' beds line the walls like BBs or peas; Like we're vegetables, not even people at all, says his mother.

The bear had started coming around the trailer park the week before, first thaw of spring, air pink and finally warmer in a tangy sort of way. Jimmy could hear new birds and the light glowed in the sky like it meant to stay. Usually he liked to count the birds coming back from wherever they went. But this was the year of the bear. He remembers it that way, the year of the bear.

Jimmy's father and some of the other men want to shoot it. His father's so hungry to shoot it's like an itch gets into his eyes, the way the muscles around them twitch and hop, teasing his hand down the barrel of his shotgun, just thinking about it. His father's eyes are little like pellets, and grey as metal.

Mr. Barnard who manages the trailer park says no. They can't use firearms this close in, he says. It's against the rules, they'll have to trap it. Anyhow, says Mr. Barnard, It wouldn't be sporting. That bear's a beggar bear, he says, Long frozen up winter, no food, lost its natural fear.

Not even the kind of trap that'll maim the sonofabitch, says Jimmy's father bitterly, Something *Barnyard* got from a park ranger, a goddamn zoo cage with a sensitive door. Sensitive my ass! wails his father, This is a bear not a goddamn psychiatry patient.

Jimmy feels something about that bear, watching the bear's face in their window pushed up against the cracked glass. It's like this is his own face, empty of anything so intent as hostility, more curious, a face like a curled up fist flattened against the window, black meaty eyes reflecting what the bear can't know, what Jimmy can't know. Jimmy feels like he's a part of that bear, almost like he's the bear's son, not his father's, not his mother's; he feels the life of that bear as it moves inside him, his own blood sluggish, the texture of the gnarly fur against his own skin, scratchy, tangled, the pungent odor of its breath, the scent of the bear's blood that's the color of Jimmy's own blood, the bear's droppings that are Jimmy's too, claiming their little porch that his father never got around to fixing, anyway. His mother bellows, Now look at this, will you? That damn animal's gone and broke up my steps. I'll kill it myself! hisses his mother. Jimmy's mother suffers from dizzy spells and poor circulation. She gets icy fingers, purple toes, and not much humor about things.

She's beating the pots and pans again, Shoo! Go away! It's only a

Black Bear, she says to Jimmy, Not the fierce sonofabitch your father likes to think. Then she's throwing things at the window, clothes, dish rags, her kerchief that she yanks off her head, grey-yellow hair thin as pins around her neck, a newspaper, Jimmy's plastic squirt gun, a Monopoly board, things that go thud or whoosh. That animal knows we're not its territory, she's muttering, Knows damn well it don't belong. And as the bear bows down onto all fours again, turning lethargically away from the window, Jimmy feels its weightedness inside him like he can barely move, like he just wants to lie down and sleep. Through the broken glass Jimmy sees the shotgun, long and brown and black, he sees his father coming out of the woods and everything inside him rears up like his blood is on fire, rises up and roars, No!

The bear plods into the woods, a different path than the one Jimmy's father was on and his father throws open the tinny door to their trailer, hollers—I wasn't going to shoot it you idiot, I was just joking! That kid's the dumbest we've got, Jimmy's father says to his mother. Barnyard set up the goddamn trap already, don't you know? You can't miss the damn thing, like that beast is going to fall inside by accident or something? Some stupid, if you ask me.

The next day the bear gets into their trailer while Jimmy and his mother are in Rock Harbor. When they return the bear's disappeared and Jimmy's mother marches inside letting out a long groan and a Sonofabitch! at all the food stuff spread over the floor, pried open jar of peanut butter, half chewed up package of hot dog buns, wrapping and all, marshmallows.... The thing spit marshmallows the hell all over the wall, she whines to Jimmy, If it don't like them then it shouldn't eat them. On Jimmy's bed he sees the paw marks, the open window over his bed is where the bear came through, up and down his own blue blanket the bear walked. Jimmy traces a muddy mark with his hand, fits his hand inside of it, leans down and smells where the bear has been, breathes the smell of the bear like the bear is himself and he is the bear's own scent. I love that bear, he tells his mother.

Then it is trapped, lured into the cage by a hunk of steaming sausage, bang goes the sensitive door. All night Jimmy hears the

bear rattling the bars of the cage, crack, slap, clang, crash, bang.
Jimmy tries to cover his ears, hide from the sound of the bear's own
fear which is his fear too, his pillow over his head, the frantic clang-
ing and banging and roaring, exploding under Jimmy's own skin.
That beast is going to kill itself, throwing its whole damn weight
against that metal, Jimmy's father announces smugly. They'll have
to send for a road crew to hoist it out, instead of the goddamn park
ranger.

In the hour before dawn Jimmy creeps out of their trailer, behind
a tree near where the trap is, and he watches the huge form of the
bear rattling and rearing and crashing tirelessly against the bars,
shadowed in the half-moon's light falling onto its shape like dust.
Jimmy knows. What else matters? He knows this and little else, no
ideas, no solutions, no faith or even a will to hope, just this
ravenous need. Jimmy crouches down under the tree near the bear,
wraps his arms around his head, feels the wild longing and the rage
beating inside him like another heart; he lifts his face toward a sky
the color of milk, drops open his jaw and howls.

YOU'VE GOT TO BE CAREFUL

You've got to be careful what you say to her. You tell her good breakfast and she thinks you mean she should've been fixing you breakfast all along. You tell her her hair looks fine so she's sure it doesn't because you said it. She hates me for her grandma dying last year, blames me because I'm the one who's left. That's when Heather sort of folded up herself.

You've got to be especially careful these days, since what happened. I can hardly think it let alone speak it. That word they used over and over in the trial like it's some sort of a label, the language of a thing but not the thing itself, what destroyed my granddaughter. As if he's a word, not the person that did it. He's in The Rack so that's something. I remember that prison, back when I was a guard there. The darkness gets you first, the way concrete walls have of swallowing the light, sopping up fluorescent like sponges. Some inmates got together and demanded lamps. Can you think of it? As if Corrections going to allow outlets in their cells, a bit of wire smuggled out of the shop and poof, no need for the electric chair here. There's a new type of people in the world, think wanting a thing's good as getting it.

That's the way with Heather. Poof, she's a different girl. Like her own skin swallowed her up. She's my favorite, I could never tell her.

I was harder on her than her sister because I knew Heather could take it. That's how you become worthy of respect, a few knocks here and there, you discover the line to grab on to, to hold steady. One day their mother drops those girls off like she's delivering the goddamn mail and she doesn't come back. Just a visit now and then like we're some sort of hospital, like she can come and go and be free of it all, shake off those daughters like shedding her winter clothes. I could've choked that woman myself, my own daughter or not. Miranda was blubbering. But not Heather. Heather stood quiet as stone, those bony knees, that freckly kind of skin, watched her own mother walk away looking like, I don't know, something could break your heart. So of course I had to steel myself against that, what good for a child if she thinks you'd offer her goddamn Heaven? You got to be iron for this life. It's the next we can ease up in.

I like to remember her with those fireflies, summer nights and she's a kid again, chasing around our jungly back yard, lit up in those splinters of light. You can't know in those days what the world will do to them. You don't know who or what's going to ruin her. If I had known I would've shackled her to me, like it or not. You're given the job to protect them and then you can't do it. This goddamn world won't let you.

You've got to be careful what you say to her because she's not a little girl, anymore. She's a something else, not a woman, exactly, but trapped in between. I watch her study herself in the hall mirror, she doesn't know I can see her from where I sit in the living room. This room is so full of her grandmother Heather won't come in here anymore. Tight bowed lips, her mother's mouth, like some lily that refuses to open, eyes scrubbed empty as cups. What is she thinking gives her that look, not sorrow, a nothing sort of face? When she stares at me she sees old. I see her watch the way I can't move about so good anymore, the way I lower myself into a chair with my two hands because my knees, never the best, anyway—my father used to beat his cane against them to quiet us down when the Nazis started coming around—just quit. To fold them properly I have to take them in my hands, like bending down the joints of a jumbo baby doll. She sees me strangle on food sometimes, hears the wind whistle out of me, a cluttered edge of it sticking in my throat. These things are usual. I'm seventy. She thinks I'm going to die. Then she has nobody.

What do you do for a girl hurt this way? All I tried to teach her, respect God when even I had my doubts, nightmares and I'm back in my boyhood, green Polish hillside—only now it's grey, everything is, grey and ashy as the sky. "Why are they doing this, Father?" I ask him. "Hush!" My father's face a mask of what I know now, fear, helplessness, silent rage. Rounding up Jews like herds of something, not people we share the street with, our market, a good hot sun over our heads. Surely God will stop it. Faith in Him and my father is the same and unshakable then. Father says "Hush." He hits us with his cane. Why does he let this happen? My father shrinks down into the dream until he's nothing in the end, lit up like a match head, a small glowing then gone.

I taught her to respect her grandmother. Hate me if she must but mind me or else. The way we are brought up before the Nazis, fearing and right. What good did it do? I taught Heather those things when I should've been teaching her to kick a sonofabitch where he doesn't rise again. Some say the one who did it didn't know better. They say he is simple, struck dumb from living in a family too poor to pay attention.

He should've been strapped down and fried, is what I say.

You'll want to be careful, the doctor told me and Heather's mother (though what good talking to her mother, like telling the wind when to blow). He said to watch Heather for signs of not coping.

Coping? You bear things and push on, is all I know. He said Heather is "experiencing" her despair, that there's a darkness inside her. I see it sometimes, this place she covers with the frizzy, fuzzy little things of a life she thinks is not worth mentioning. Like her concern with her clothes, for instance, the way she checks herself out in the hall mirror, wheeling around and around then back yet again, searching for flaws. Means nothing, her doctor informed us, like covering a bald spot with fake hair.

Which brought to mind Toska's chemotherapy. One blessing is

that Heather didn't get back from California that summer to see her grandmother go through this hell, the drugs they pumped into her, like spraying enough poison on an ant colony to wipe it clean. For a while they managed to halt everything but Toska's beautiful long hair tufting out by the handfuls. Her hair was a gift from God. Why would He take it this way?

Heather's depression, the doctor said, is situational. She's had to "process" a lot, her father's drowning, the death of her grandmother, living in a non-nuclear setting (this he said without looking at Heather's mother, my own daughter, I'm ashamed to admit, who sat there chain smoking despite the THANK YOU FOR NOT SMOKING sign on the doctor's desk, who took Heather's sister back but not Heather). And now "this incident" he said.

The doctor calls what happened to Heather an incident. Does he think it was incidental? A mistake not meant to occur? If I were younger I think I would kill the person who did it. I can feel my hands around his neck, hands bigger than most, used to a day's work—doing God's work, what should've been done.

After the trial Heather didn't get out of her bed for days, eyes shut tight. Her friend, the pokey one with that sharp little nose for everyone else's business, came by. This time I welcomed her. "Come in, Cedra!" I announced boldly at the door, bowed legs, that cramp in my gut makes me bend over sometimes like I'm a little kid with a heaviness in his pants. I listened from the bottom of the stairs, Cedra at Heather, pulling at her, tugging her out of that bed. Then I heard nothing so I inched my way up the stairs, just outside my granddaughter's room. Heather, eyes closed, arms white as paper fallen back on the sheets too weighted to move. As if she was the one who drowned.

I don't understand something called depression. We press on. Toska gave birth to our other daughter, Little Megan I called her, Toska sweating, writhing in silence for what could've been days, months, stretched out on that hospital bed flat as a plank of wood. I thought she would die. I thought everything good in my life would disappear. The baby came out twisted, feet first, birth rope taut around her neck as if even her own cord tried to yank her out of there. Born a blue baby Megan's mind would never take on the things a mind must. They told us she couldn't live past four, and then seven. By the time she was the age Heather is now she came up no higher than my hip bones. Little Megan. A sweetness would break your heart, dead at seventeen. Her own heart just swelled up and quit. Too much love to pump through that damaged little body, I guess.

Toska didn't open her mouth for two weeks. Is that depression? She lay hour after hour on our couch, I served her tea on a TV tray, zwieback cookies, navel oranges from California that she loved. Everything left the living room the way I brought it there, painted kettle still warm at its sides. "God needed her more than us," I whispered to my wife. And I believed it.

Heather combs her hair in the hall mirror, hair that is the color of an old barn, a burnt stately red. I watch from my place in the living room, my brown recliner blending into this house like earth itself; she doesn't know how I watch. I think about when Heather dyed her hair a while ago, and how once she even shaved it, how mad I was. Doesn't mean a thing. I wish I could tell her this, that some of what seemed so important just isn't. I wish I could ask her to sit with me. But I never did before so why would she now? Toska was there, before.

"Where do you go?" I call out to Heather as she yanks her jacket from the hall closet. You've got to be careful what you ask, how you ask it. I try to sound casual. There's ice in my veins now each time she leaves the house.

"With a friend." She turns around at the door, staring into the living room, into me. I read the look, her You-are-old-so-you-can't-stop-me look. "His name's Bent Paul, if you have to know."

I frown, stern, I hope, I can still do stern even though what I feel is hopeless. "Mr. Paul will pick you up?"

She tosses her hair back, a short rope of red like a coil of lava. Tight sounds squeeze from her throat, her Nothing-is-funny-enough-to-laugh-at laugh. "If he does it's on a skate board. Bent's fourteen.

I thought I'd give the younger guys a shot. He still thinks pulling wings off of insects is a good time. Maybe he's on to something, what do you think?"

You've got to be careful about answering her, picking through the things she says that aren't questions at all, that she doesn't expect answers to. Because if you answer those kinds of things she won't talk to you for days. "No," I say, but Heather is already out the door.

So I sleep because, let's face it, there's not much left for me better than a good long nap. At least I think I sleep. How would I know, anymore? The way the minutes pull into hours, moments of sun burning into the living room, lighting up what used to be—Toska's things, the wreath she made of dried flowers yellowing on the wall, figurines on the coffee table, only graceful to me now since once she held them, dusted them, placed them back down gently as if these were her own heart, heart of her home—and then the night, blackness, the hours all rolling together, squeezed out like toothpaste, whatever time I have left.

Toska knew her death. Came to her in the night. Sitting beside her I lay my head down at the hard edge of her bed for just a moment and her hand slid across my forehead, fingers cool, light as snow. My eyes remained shut, so much of it drained out of me, whatever it was I could have said. I lifted my head and she was gone, that instant, her face a mere shell of skin over the thin high stretch of her cheekbones. Once I kissed those hollows underneath. I wish I said something to her, anything. "Do you sleep, Toska?" She never made a sound. So like my wife, endurance a sort of algae, choking the life right out of her.

I dream of revenge. I'm younger, young enough so he's no match. None of these kids are, their slippery ways, the way they think the world owes them a place in it. Bent Paul. Pulls the wings off of insects and they totter drunkenly up his arms, his skin bleached and rubbery as a baby's. He takes her to where they said it happened, the rented trailer just outside of town. Rock Harbor, Maine, winters are slow here, a dark and lingering sleep, frozen silence hard put to give way to any promise underneath. This time it's daylight. I follow

them, enough steps behind to be invisible as God. I hear in the distance birds, breathe the rotting vegetation and all over stink of that
place, never kept up, no pride blooming here the way spring must,
rich with hope, scent of everything that needs to be alive. Then the
humming of the insects, at first a low steady thrum like a throttle
being released, now the full maddening scream.

Bent Paul. The other one's name was Jimmy, Pretty Jimmy the
kids called him; what difference is a name in the end? They're
inside and I'm at the window, shotgun in my arms. Muscles, bones,
blood, surging and raw, as if even these aren't mine, as if I'm something born new. I've never been one for hunting, saw enough people
tossed into ditches like so many rocks or weeds, animal ripeness not
even precious enough to place back in the earth. This one's neither,
not human, not beast. A cellular mistake, life never realized. I aim
the barrel into the glass, pull back and release. The sound is the
whole world shattering, its wrongness falling apart in a spray sharp
and clean as the rain.

DRIVING IN THE DARK

CERTAINLY THERE ARE THINGS FOR HER TO THINK ABOUT during this late night drive, this endless road through the hills of Maine. Although in the darkness Jas can't see these hills, these sentinels rising, one after the other, cold and barren though the calendar says spring. She passes by little towns that appear suddenly out of the black, little hovels of houses perched so close to the road she wonders which came first, the road or the houses? Old houses, Jas assumes, though in this utter darkness everything appears ancient, deserted, lifeless, from some other time that she is not part of.

Another town rises out of the night, its cluster of buildings balled up like a fist on the arm of the hill; Jas's aging Escort chugs by like a dream. She prays her car will keep running, driving through this part of the state that seems to have shaken away its population like an old woman shakes out her sheets—rarely does she even see other cars. There is no wind, just cold, though it's April. Breathless, empty, the long road home.

But there are things to think about, and Jas concentrates on these to avoid listening too closely to the timid chunk-chunking of the Escort's engine (if it were to die out here, would they ever find her? Would they know to look?). One who might know is Caroll, who moved them to Maine from Ohio because he had a vision that life here would happen the way he wanted it to.

Jas, Jasmine, was originally just Janis. Caroll (formerly Harold) renamed her and fashioned her new "look," long hair like a shawl around her shoulders, the long skirts, blotches of colors like bad art, skinny spandex tops though her breasts are too big for them, he can't alter that. They live in a rented cottage in Rock Harbor, hunkered down at the base of a hill, sagging walls, slanted foundation, like it would just as soon become part of the hill. They light candles at night—"Pretend there's no such thing as electricity," Caroll admonished her—and incense, its smell pungent and sharp like the worst kind of memory of a time Jas never knew anyway.

"We'll go back to the simplicity of things," Harold had said. Shredding up the records of his former downtown life as a Columbus accountant Harold became Caroll, a potter, his brick kiln blazing beside their house at all hours like the jaws of hell. Janis had been a graduate student in Neoclassical Literature at Ohio State University but she couldn't say why. She couldn't say where she was going with that Master's degree, or what she would do when she got there. Harold was older, his purpose more jelled, and he was emphatic in his support of his decisions. Janis went along. Although she wouldn't get married, that was one decision Jas made, she wouldn't marry him. Whether he called her Janis, Jasmine or Jas, he would not call her his wife. Harold had been married before. His wife left him for his dog, he told Janis.

She got a job as a librarian's assistant at the Bangor Public Library, an hour and fifteen minutes from Rock Harbor. "You read," Caroll said, "why not?" The drive home, the land, the great, hunkering spaces in between towns was like commuting on another planet.

Jas winds the Escort around hairpin turns, it jumps like a horse over little bumps and starts of land, dark surprises loitering on the road like snakes. Then, of course, there's the baby to think about (though she's tried not to think about the baby, yet somehow, every day, almost every hour these thoughts slip up on her, like a fragrance borne on a sudden breeze, or a strange sound, moments of life that happen beyond one's control). The baby was to have been called

Margaret. That was another thing Jas insisted on, the baby would be named Margaret. A strong name, a dignified name, not "Unity" like Caroll wanted. Not a spineless tag defining something nebulous the child would be burdened to make truth for the rest of her life.

As it turned out she had no life; no breath, no small but perfect child body sleeping in the bassinet Jas had fashioned from a wicker laundry basket, no infant to rock in her arms, its tiny shape pressed against Jas's own chest, its little heart beating like the fluttering of a bird's wing against Jas's slower, older heart. In her dreams Jas listens for that breath of life the way she listens to the wind, rattling the branches of the white pine outside their house.

"Margaret" was nothing more than a mess of blood, Jas told herself, lying rigid in those antiseptic hospital sheets, those flat-faced hospital nurses that were not connected to Jas, the "Janis" Jas knew herself to be; they could have been French, African, Greek, Balinese, they didn't even speak her language, so locked into her own world was Jas, the world of her dying womb.

"We're from Ohio!" Jas shouted to the woman at the Pen Bay admitting desk when Caroll first brought her to the hospital. Jas was bundled up in a sheet that had been torn from their bed, the same sheet she bled so heavily on. Caroll tried desperately to imagine all sorts of other explanations before finally rushing her to the hospital, bearing her in his arms as though she were the child he would never hold. "No matter what you pretend, we're still from Ohio," Jas told him as they wheeled her away.

That was six months ago and this is now, thinks Jas, passing by little towns, instant towns with names like Brooks, Freedom, and the black empty stretches of Maine in between. She sighs and flips the radio button on, fuzz, static, a crackling of voices drifting in and out, she's still too far away from a signal to pick up anything substantial. Or maybe it's so late that most of the stations have gone to bed and she really is totally alone. Tonight she stayed at the library long past midnight, ordering books, taking inventory, taking stock of things, no hurry to go home.

Jas focuses for one moment on the glowing numbers of the useless radio, and when she looks up again at the road before her every-

189

thing seems to happen at once, yet slowly, like being captured in a slow motion film. She sees the animal frozen in her headlights the second before she hears that sickening thud, feels the Escort swerve, hears the wrenching squeal of its tires as desperately, hopelessly, she slams down on the brake, depresses the clutch, shifts down.

The deer crumples up and rolls slowly across the hood, or it seems that way; it seems as if Jas sees its eyes in passing, staring at her, its anguished gaze locked into hers through the glass that separates them.

For a minute or so Jas keeps driving, first gear, struggling to move forward like struggling to breathe. When she had the miscarriage, lying in that hospital bed doubled over with the pains that were like knives stabbing, slashing, as though it were those pains that were murdering the baby, Jas had pleaded, "Just let me go home!" She saw herself back in her childhood neighborhood, the white trellis fence neatly separating her parents' house from the others that looked just like it. How manicured their life was, Columbus spread out as flat, as simple, as predictable then as her future.

Jas inches the Escort over to the side of the road and shuts off the engine. The silence is immediate. A great dark gulf of it, like something that has its own place, vital and apart from the loneliness of the land it hovers over, land that is empty of everything but Jas and the animal. Opening the car's window she imagines she can hear it breathing, or crying, a hoarse, rasping, moaning sound.

But maybe it's OK? Could that be? Maybe it was a leg she hit, a hoof, causing it to lose its balance, yes, just lose its balance so that naturally it would fall across her hood, then hobble off into the night, hurt, but not dying. Please, not dying!

Jas climbs slowly out of the car, buttoning Caroll's old woolen pea coat tightly around her neck. The air is freezing, the moonless night is black as the road. How will she see if the deer is here? She imagines stumbling on it and shudders violently. She will have to turn the Escort around and shine its headlights in the place she suspects the deer would be, if it's still there.

Jas gets back in, turns the key in the ignition, listens to the familiar chunka-chunka rip through the quiet; again she thinks about

bolting. Her hand still clutching the key chain trembles. Who
would know if she just traveled on? A few months ago she had
found herself driving to Bangor Airport, a whim one night after
leaving work early. She could use her VISA, Jas had thought, the
one Caroll didn't know about, escaping his scissors, his shredding,
his remaking of their world. In just three hours she'd be back in
Columbus, and she'd call Caroll who would sound so annoyed, it
wouldn't have been part of The Plan.

Jas points the Escort out into the road then back again, reversing
its direction, aiming the headlights at the side. She sees the lump
instantly, the dark, still form lying there—and something else. "Oh,
God!"

Jas squeezes her eyes shut, presses her forehead down upon the
steering wheel. She lifts her head up again slowly, eyes opened;
maybe she imagined it?

But, no, the spindly legs are plainly visible in the white glow of
the headlights. A fawn, standing beside what Jas can only assume is
its mother. It's a punishment, she thinks, she knew there would be
punishments. A woman doesn't just "lose" her baby for no reason,
Caroll had pointed out. Jas was built for bearing babies, kettle
shaped, strong as a goat.

Jas knew the reason. Fact was, she didn't want a baby. Not that
she wouldn't love Margaret. Not that she didn't grieve, wasn't still
grieving the loss of something. But it was Caroll's decision to create
Margaret, and Jas had quietly agreed. Later, beside a snoring Caroll,
on the futon with the tie-dyed covers they called their bed, Jas
wept.

She knows she has to get out of the car again. She has to see if
that deer is alive. Maybe it's just stunned; injured, certainly, but not
mortally. People recover from car accidents, quite often they do. Jas
could go back to the nearest town, was that Morrill? Freedom? She
could call a vet and the vet will fix the doe. Meanwhile, maybe Jas
could take care of the fawn. Now there's a thought. As a child she
had nursed hurt creatures back to life, the dove with its wing broken, the baby finch fallen from its nest, an abandoned hamster, the
bullfrog that was missing part of its hind leg. She was a champion of

life then.

Jas climbs back out of the car, leaving it in neutral with the
engine idling so that the battery can feed the headlights. She
approaches the doe and its fawn slowly, her heart bumping hard in
her chest. She wonders if the fawn will suddenly take off, but it
stands rigid, if uncertain, mesmerized in the headlights. Perhaps it's
in shock, Jas thinks. It's very small. Maybe it doesn't know yet how
afraid it should be. Maybe it can't realize how terribly fragile life is.

Jas is close enough to the doe now to bend over and touch her,
but she hesitates and stands gazing at the fawn. She imagines she
hears a whimpering; is it the fawn? Or the labored breaths of its
mother? The doe is still alive. Jas knows this even before she finally
kneels down beside it. It's alive but in great pain—Jas gasps when
she sees one of its legs lying at an incredible angle, like a stick beside
the body it's attached to. She can tell even in the darkness the
deer's bleeding from her mouth, rivers of blood flowing out of her
mouth and nose. Jas can smell the blood, its rusty, thin scent. The
animal is breathing, sharp, tortured little breaths, each released like
a sigh.

"Oh, God," Jas whispers. Her hand hovers over the body—are
they really this big?—as if to stroke it, to comfort it. She cries, the
sound of her sobs in her own ears drowning out the deer's anguished
breaths. She is so immersed in her misery that Jas only partly hears
the Chevrolet Pickup as it slides up behind her Escort, the slam of
its door, the crunch of footsteps behind her. She sees but doesn't
comprehend how another pair of headlights has, for a moment, illuminated the scene before her even brighter, more brutal, more hor-
rible.

"Nailed her, did you? You hurt?"

Startled, Jas loses her balance and her hand grazes against the
deer's hind leg. Fumbling for a grasp on the pavement where she's
been squatting, Jas yanks her hand back; in the doe's fur she felt the
stiffening of death. She gazes up in panic at the figure of a woman in
the headlights.

"Well, you're lucky your motor's still purring. You got a little car.
Them things been known to take out a small car. Moose especially,

192

though. I seen a moose gallop away from a little car that hit it and the people in the car left for dead. Likely as not your hood's rumpled as an accordion, I'll bet."

"This deer's dying," Jas mumbles inanely, swiping at the tears in her eyes with the back of her wrist. She gazes over at the fawn who amazingly still stands in the same place beside its mother, its long skinny neck bent down low, its mouth nuzzling against the doe's head. Jas stifles back another sob.

"Sometimes they move about in herds, do you know? Come spring, the does and their young. Did you see any others?"

Jas shakes her head. "Can I do something?" She stares up at the woman who stands in a band of bright light from the Escort, her legs slightly apart, hands on her hips. She is wiry, youngish, dressed in jeans and a leather bomber jacket, her scant hair pulled back severely in a short ponytail. She is ordinary looking, and seemingly unconcerned.

"I'll get my brother's .357."

"What?" This time Jas loses her balance completely, toppling over, her rear-end smacking down onto the pavement.

The woman shrugs. "I got his truck on account of mine's dead. He packs a .22 Magnum during hunting season, though myself I like a .30-.30. But he's got a .357 stashed under the seat for other times, you never know. It's what we got."

"You're going to shoot it?"

"Well, what do you think? The thing's on its last leg, don't you know? You got to put it out of its misery. It's not like we're jackin' it or something."

The woman, her step light and quick, walks back to the pickup. Jas sits cross-legged at the side of the dark road, in her garish skirt, her ceramic jewelry, her incense-scented hair, stunned. She can hear the labored breaths of the dying deer, the licking sounds of its fawn, and whimpering, definitely whimpering, from one of them. She starts to cry again.

The woman reappears, standing a little behind where Jas sits. "Well, it weren't your fault," she says. "These things happen. The meat can be put away for next winter. Feed a whole family for a couple months, do you know? My brother's family for one. He's got four kids, two of them step-kids, you know how it is. Anyhow, he lost his job on account of the ship yard cutting back. You're not supposed to take hit deer without reporting it first, but, hell, I'd do it to feed kids. Wouldn't you?"

Jas turns a little and peers at the gun in the woman's hand, shining bold and silvery in the headlights. "What about the fawn?"

The woman kneels down beside Jas. Her knees pop as she settles herself into a squatting position. She stares at the fawn still patiently nuzzling the dying doe. "The thing is," she begins softly, "a little fellow like that can't live without a mother. Who'll take care of him? He can't survive out here. A fox or a coyote come, they'll run him down in a minute."

"What about me?"

"Take care of a fawn?" The woman shakes her head. "Honey, you ain't from around here, huh? A deer's a wild animal. It's got to be free, not kept in some house like a kitten." She reaches out over the doe's long body and places her hand on its neck; the fawn steps back warily, staring with big, illuminated eyes at Jas and the woman. "She ain't got much longer. We got to put her out of her pain."

"And the fawn?" Jas whispers. There's a bitter taste in her mouth. The scent of the doe's blood is making her sick. That smell surrounded her when she lost the baby. She had known it as the smell of dying, of complete loss of hope.

The woman, like some old friend, puts her hand on Jas's hand. The Escort engine suddenly quits, probably from idling too long and over-heating. For a moment there is only the deep silence of the night, and the sounds of the deer's last breaths. The woman sighs. "When I shoot the doe, her fawn's going to take off and run like there's no tomorrow from the noise. He can't survive out there, no way, and he's going to have some kind of slow, awful death. You know he'll have a terrible death."

"What about a wildlife rehab place, or a vet? Couldn't we take it to the Nature Conservancy, or Audubon, or somewhere?"

The woman leans closer and peers into Jas's face. Jas can smell the stale minty scent of gum on her breath, her jacket smells like cigarette smoke. "Like I told you, he's going to cut on out of here when I fire the .357. Even if we try to grab him first, he's going to run the minute we put our hands near. Maybe he don't know enough to be afraid of us when we're just sitting here, but he damn well knows we're not his mother. So here's the thing. We shoot him first."

Jas recoils from the woman's touch. "Kill the fawn? What kind of nightmare is this?"

"We'd be saving him from a nightmare, don't you know?"

Jas closes her eyes, rests her chin in her hands and presses her arms against her breasts, her breasts that will never nurse a baby, her breasts that lately have felt so strapped in and confined, imprisoned in the spandex tops that are too tight and she wonders for a crazy moment how she'd look in a leather bomber jacket with nothing underneath. Jas rocks herself back and forth in the darkness. "OK," she says finally, opening her eyes. Slowly she stands, her gaze fixed upon the fawn.

The woman stands up beside Jas. She reaches into the pocket of her jacket, pulls out a cigarette and a lighter, pops the cigarette into her mouth, flicks the flame from the lighter at it, sucks in, blows out. With her free hand she cocks the gun.

WAKING UP IN SACRED PLACES

AFTER OUR CAT CAME BACK FROM THE DEAD I decided it was time to go looking for Jesus. Here's how it went: Last June Alfred got bone cancer, a tumor bulging out one side of his eye, so at first we thought maybe it was another abscess from a late night fight. "That cat's more of a man than most of my men," said my mother. "Probably he's mooning the little Persian next door as we speak," she said. How does a cat moon? I wondered. Though I didn't ask. It's best not to ask my mother about these kinds of things since she'll just make up her own sense anyway. Recently Henri, she's my mother, decided she'd had about enough of the men in her life and she's a little cranky about it too. Said the last straw was Humor Peach who injected himself in his private part to get it up, Henri said, and then it wouldn't come down. "Like he was mainlining Stay Puff starch," she said. We've been talking this way since the day I turned eighteen, or at least Henri talks like this to me. I'm not all that gung ho on guys these days, except sometimes the boat boys in the summer, brown skin and sleek as cats, tending the tourist yachts that bump around in Rock Harbor's harbor like they own it. The boys slip up and down those decks, mopping them, polishing the wood like it's to eat off of instead of sailing to some faraway place; their bleached hair and teeth are as white as salt.

196

Henri loved our cat. I'm sure she loves us too, her daughters, but human love is a lot more complicated, she's always said. No doubt about it, Henri loved the cat. When the bulge beside Alfred's eye didn't go away and his eyes turned yellow as butter, kind of hollow and wispy and they rolled up into the backs of his eyelids as inch by inch he lowered himself on the tile floor for about the millionth nap of the day, she said, "That's it." And she took him to the vet.

For the rest of the summer Alfred withered away, slipping off pounds easy as removing a sweater. He wouldn't eat much though Henri'd get right down beside him on the floor, chunk of tuna on her finger, stroking the side of his mouth with it, cooing like he's a little bird. "Sweet baby," she said, "my poor sweet little baby." Alfred took to hiding in dark places, closets, under beds, behind the stove that never gets lit in the summer and sometimes not even in the winter until Henri makes a boyfriend chop us some wood. "He knows," my mother whispered, "Alfred knows."

And then Alfred died. And then he came back. It was the night after they cremated him, his box of ashes on the table beside my mother's bed. "For the time being," Henri said. "I've had worse here," she said, "Humor's penile injection kit for one." I thought my mother would never stop bawling. She's generally pretty tough about things, "Harder than a six-inch nail" my Aunt Eli once said. I guess not when it came to Alfred. I cried too, but to myself as I always do. "Everything I love quits on me," Henri wailed. Which is mostly true, except, as it turned out, for Alfred. We first heard his mewing from somewhere inside those dark places, the bathroom closet, under Henri's bed. I checked and double-checked looking for a live cat, maybe the little Persian he had those yellow eyes on got in somehow, there were so many possible explanations. And I tried to think of them, I did.

My mother hunkered down in the corner of the living room, bare wood floor, her knees pressed in against her chin, skinny arms curled so tightly around her legs she looked like a double helix, or a couple strands of pasta stuck together, strings of her long blond hair like wheat over her face. "Oh God," she whimpered, "It's my fault. What have I done?" We heard the mewing again, soft but an urgen-

197

cy too, Meow, Meeeoooow, like he needed in out of a long night, or a spot of tuna to get him by.

"Cedra!" Henri moaned, "I think it's because I prayed a threat prayer. My father warned us. You can't do that, he said. You can ask for things within reason, even bargain some, but never threaten. I just didn't think I could bear it. That's what I said, I said Jesus God if you make Alfred die I'll have nothing and I won't stand to live that way! After my sister died my father stopped believing. What's the difference? That's what he said."

The mewing came again, this time louder, plaintive, and then a sense of movement in the hall behind us where nothing changes in actuality, but every ion, every electron appears hyped, like that second before a jet breaks the sound barrier or the instant when thunder explodes.

"Oh God!" Henri cried. "My life's come to this, exactly nothing. Divorced, rented house in the middle of Maine, he barely sends enough money to keep his own daughters let alone you, one little sister dead, the other barren so she blames things on me, Jesus! Jesus! How can I take more? To think I had a man who plastered his gold albums on our bathroom walls. Like paint, Cedra. Do you remember? That was our life. He said I went too far, taking his kids 3,000 miles away. Well, I don't see him back here claiming them, do you? Don't I at least get to be forgiven?"

"Consider this," I said to my mother. "Maybe Alfred, if it is Alfred, just doesn't want to leave you, is all. Maybe this is a good thing. Maybe he just loves you too much." I was about to add that now she could have the benefits of a cat without cleaning the litter box, but thought better of it. I wasn't so sure about this whole thing either. It was asking me to believe in the unseen presence of things, fantasies I gave up on when I quit playing house, when I understood there could never be a Santa.

And Alfred or the ghost of Alfred, or some unique blend of wind, rain, tears and spirit, howled. "Jesus, Jesus!" My mother sunk her blond head between her knees and for the rest of the night I patted her like she was my pet, and the ghost cat or Alfred or whatever it was, entered our pores, our flesh, our bones, our hearts, like a wound, raw and begging to be healed.

Finding Jesus is not an easy thing for someone brought up without on-ramp access. Things I'd overheard through the years ran through my head in one luminous cliche: God is love, Jesus loves you yes he does, Onward Christian soldiers, The meek shall inherit the earth, Do unto others as they do you. My mother used to tell us church was the world on a good day. That from her better moods. Otherwise she'd say things like, "I'm not suggesting there isn't a God, but would He let Sunday School kids sell candy bars on his behalf? They're not even Milky Way, for chrissake, no Mars bars, nothing celestial here." Of course, that was before Henri needed to be forgiven. Yesterday she bought herself a rosary though she's hardly a Catholic, and last night when the wailing started from somewhere inside the walls of her bedroom she clutched onto it like the beads were her own mother's necklace, groaning and lamenting, "I believe, I believe, I believe!"

This morning I talked to my friend Scott Barker who's a prison guard and a new convert to some sort of godliness that takes up all of his Sundays. He told me that one day he had a long look around his workplace, and he saw as if for the first time the concrete, the hopelessness, the despair; the men whose chances, if they ever had any were mostly used up. Scott realized there wasn't much separating himself from all of that beyond the gun he was trained to carry. So he took up Jesus, and now it's Jesus who carries him. Scott said, "You should approach Him with a pure heart. Try to be clean as an empty plate. Maybe if you could forgive someone who's done something really bad." Which is how we came to think about Pretty Jimmy who raped my best friend Heather. "Jesus will listen," Scott said, "but you know it's not a small request, sending a cat to Heaven."

My mother's been inside Rock Harbor Adult Correctional before, threatening some murderer who was harassing her sister. (Aunt Eli taught art in the prison until she re-thought her marriage and flew back to Hawaii.) Henri told me what to expect. "You don't wear a skirt because they'll hang out under the metal stairs staring up. But even in pants they'll be watching you, like they're on the inside of your skin. If you think you'll find any answers in that place," Henri said, "don't count on it." Then her eyes got that wild look. "He's here!" she hissed. "Can you smell his wet fur smell?" No use pointing out that if Alfred's a ghost, then how is he wet?

In the R.H.A.C. visiting room I examine my outfit while waiting for Jimmy, baggy overalls, plain white tee shirt, not calling much attention to myself yet not some total freak costume either like a lawyer's get up. A suit of tweedy armor and Jimmy won't talk a word to me. I have no idea what I'm going to say to him. My heart is beating hard, little flashings, a lighthouse under my breast. I can't think of my heart without thinking of my breast, which then makes me conscious of being in a room full of men who all did things bad enough to be here. My face is hot. Nobody's looking at me though, at the people visiting them. It could be an airport without the sense of rush. Time feels stretched out. In the end only half of us get to leave.

When a guard leads him in, the round shells of his shoulders under the grey prison shirt, a lump like a chunk of dirt catches in my throat. I'd forgotten his looks. Usually when I think about Jimmy I picture him on top of Heather. I imagine this now and an open place inside me closes up. This isn't a good start, I think, getting to Jesus. But how do I forgive someone who did that to my best friend? I stare at the grey shirt, overwashed, faded; how many others, rapists, robbers, murderers, wore it before Jimmy? Jimmy, Jimmy, Jimmy. I breathe in and out, slowly.

"Why do you come here?" he says, sitting opposite me on a metal chair, diddling and twisting and popping his long hands in his lap, then on top of the formica table between us. Fingernails play a crisp tuneless song.

His speech sounds foreign, like somebody testing the language. I imagine I can hear the ticking of the big wall clock behind Jimmy, dragging the minutes forward. I look at the clock, not directly at him. "Are you all right? Do you need anything?" I ask, feeling dumb. I didn't even bring him cookies for chrissake, though Scott said they don't let much inside these walls that doesn't walk, bleed, and have a social security number.

Jimmy shrugs, green eyes intense. "I need a TV," he says. "Mom was supposed to bring me mine but it wasn't prison safe so they said I have to buy theirs. OK, I told them, but I don't have the money." He lowers his head and I gaze at those brown curls, shorter now, but not so short you couldn't reach out and ease one lightly around the tip of your finger, like a shaving of chocolate.

And then because I have no idea what else to say, I'm telling him about Alfred, rushing the story out like I'm expecting him to laugh at me, scoff, roll his eyes the way guys do at the unbelievable when it comes from the mouth of a girl. "I need to ask Jesus to take back the cat," I say. "Or else my mother's going to have some kind of a breakdown, and I can't exactly think it does my nerves any good to hear Alfred, who's supposed to be ashes in a box the size of a Big Mac, meowing somewhere in our house. You see, now I not only have to believe in Jesus but in ghosts too."

Jimmy nods his head solemnly, stunning eyes and the ridges of his cheek bones like little hills on the tan valley of his face. My God, I remind myself, what the man did to Heather! But I'm supposed to try and forgive him so I concentrate on this. It wasn't his fault anyway, not wholly; probably if I could get to Led Nash who belittled Jimmy into it and cheered him on, if I could forgive him I could bypass Jesus and go straight to God.

"I knew a fish that came back," Jimmy says. "It happens if you go fishing and you catch them but you don't put them in a bucket, you just let them flop around. My dad and my brothers did that off the dock on Mirror Lake, let the fish flop around. And then one of them stopped flopping so I picked him up. He was dead, eyes wide open, but when I put him in my brother's pail what do you think? He started swimming. At first a kind of a squiggle, then round and round the bucket he went, tail flashing like he was really mad."

I frown, remind myself he's a bit slow, always has been and probably prison isn't going to improve this. Twenty-two, the body of Brad Pitt and the brain drive of an eleven-year-old I figure, on a good day. "Well, Jimmy," I say patiently, "most likely the fish wasn't really dead. Probably it was in shock and the water revived it, is all."

"No," Jimmy shakes his head and a wayward curl slants across a perfectly arched eyebrow. "No, Cedra. I know dead. This fish was dead. And then he wasn't."

I leave after the allotted half hour, telling Jimmy I'll be back on his next visitors' day, at the end of the week. I have no idea why. Couldn't I just say I forgive him and ask Jesus to take away Alfred and let my mother have some peace? Would He really know I was lying? I'm not sure how to feel about Jimmy. Heather's never been the same since it happened. It's like either a piece of her is missing, or a chunk of someone else was added on. Because we don't connect anymore like we were meant to be best friends, like she's a plug and I'm the socket, that sort of thing. Instead we're lights switching on different rooms. She hangs out with a mostly younger crowd now, skaters, punks if you ask me. But if you look in her eyes there's an old person there, and none too pleased with the way things are. When I look at Jimmy a feeling inside me stirs up. I try not to let it, try to will it down, but there it is, a flopping of something in my gut. Like Jimmy's fish, and it's definitely not dead.

On Sunday Scott takes me to his church. He says he thinks this might be the more direct path, after all. I know church is a very religious place and I expect everyone to be cheerful and loud and maybe doing this in tongues, the language of the truly blessed, because Scott told me they finally have joy in their lives, accepting Jesus as their savior. I'd like Jesus to save my mother. It's more than just the Alfred thing; this is a woman not meant to have to question her own life. We haven't always gotten along, but after I turned eighteen and she told me to call her Henri, things were different. For one, I stopped pestering her about my father who died before I could know him. It's not like I can change any of that, though I'd still like to find out if he was at least smart and maybe tall, and if my mother loved him, just a little. And for another Henri knows I could leave her any time. She's not good about people leaving her. "I'm the one does the leaving," she says. And anyway, God knows where I'd go. Most folks who manage to move away from Maine come back again. It's like velcro here, stifling yet awful snug. I like Henri best when she's not going off on some guy, when she's acting sort of like a mother. Lately she's too busy chanting over her rosary to worry about penile injection kits, or who's going to chop her wood in the winter.

So I don't know what it was inside me made me do it, steal the plastic Jesus out of Scott Barker's church. I've never done anything like that before. I'm not saying here that I'm good. I've smoked marijuana to relax, inhaled a few beers to get high, done the boat boys occasionally. But I've never been a thief.

What I know is that earlier this morning, bright and hot and filled with what I imagined might be hope, I walked into that church with Scott, expecting to feel different. Holier, maybe, or at least safe. I visualized myself in a polished wooden pew even before we sat down on the unpainted bench, imagined sun light streaking through stain glass windows, blue and godly and significant as a rainbow. In fact the windows were smudged and plain, and flies coated them from the outside, maybe inside too. I thought I'd listen to the singing, the joy, the assurance of people who found themselves in Jesus, Scott said, the Spirit shining through them, becoming the grace and wisdom that eluded me. I figured I'd at least find some answers, if not Jesus Himself.

I waited. All through the minister's sermon, words droning around my ears like insects buzzing, trying to get inside my head but some invisible barrier, a brain cell mosquito net was knocking them out. The heat of the late August morning settled in the church, on people's necks, their breaths, hymns not graceful and uplifting, but a little out of tune, it sounded to me, and Scott too close, brushing against me when we knelt to pray so that I couldn't think of things holy, couldn't think of anything at all but his prickly black arm hairs on my naked elbow.

When Pastor Robin invited the "flock" to rise and come forward for the healing service I told Scott I had to go to the bathroom, figuring it would be a while, given the numbers of the afflicted sliding up to the front of the church. I contemplated for a moment if He could heal my thick thighs, but by then I was having trouble breathing and felt itchy and strange inside my skin that kept bumping against Scott's skin, pressed together as we were on that small bench. "Transcend thy body and bathe thy soul in the waters of Jesus's love!" Pastor Robin howled, uplifted hands and arms waving like fleshy white antennae from the dark depths of his frock.

He's a plastic Jesus, not very big, about six inches tall and the color of cream. He was perched upright on a table in the corridor that stretches through the parish to the bathrooms, beside some pamphlets called Spread The Word. Too light to be a paperweight for the pamphlets, he seemed to have no purpose other than simply to be. I lit in on his face, one of those perfect doll faces where all the features are symmetrical, peaceful as a cow's. His eyes won't blink shut but he's permanently pleasant looking, a kind, doughy-eyed sort of expression. I slipped Jesus into my pack, and then I left Scott's church because now I was a sinner. And if I know anything about church, I know it's not a place for sinners.

At home Henri's in her bedroom, her entire wardrobe strewn about. "What are you doing?" I ask, the plastic Jesus blazing hot as a barbecue tong against one side of my back, but I can't put my pack down, maybe never again.

Henri shrugs, "I guess we're moving. I have no idea where but I can't sleep anymore with Alfred meowing all the time, I can't live this way!"

"You won't leave Maine," I tell her. "It won't let you." I stare at my mother, she's skinnier than ever, a bruised look around her eyes. "I prayed for you, Henri," I tell her, because I don't know what else to say. That's what Scott said to me when I told him I was having a hard time forgiving Pretty Jimmy because I couldn't concentrate on it, those green eyes of his, that hard chin like he tried to swallow a rock and it got stuck there, that hair.

"You should be praying for Alfred," Henri says, "it's too late for me. I've done the rosary thing, I even meditated to Buddha but I suppose they know I'm not for real. My own father stopped believing. He got Alzheimer's so he's like a child now, about as close to God as you can get." She plops down on her bed in the middle of a pile of clothes. The TV drones from the next room, my little sister Maple hunkered down in front of it, pink thumb planted in her mouth. "It's strange, Cedra, I have all these clothes, this furniture, knickknacks that are mine, jewelry, all this stuff associated with me, and I don't have a clue. I used to stare at Jumper's gold albums on our bathroom wall, just sit on that toilet and look at them while he was who knows where. Is that love? Not a clue."

The next day I visit Pretty Jimmy with Jesus still in my pack. They search my pack at the guards' station as I walk through the metal detector, then they hand it back to me and I'm escorted to the visiting room. Apparently Jesus is not considered contraband. This is my third visit. Each time Jimmy rambles on about things that mean absolutely nothing but it's like he's crooning to me, special notes that make my skin sticky, turn the muscles on the insides of my thighs to jelly.

Again we sit at the formica table opposite each other and Jimmy says, "Do you like snakes? I'm going to have a snake farm when I get out. I can sell them to people like me who like snakes, and I'll treat those snakes right. I would," he says. "Some people are mean to snakes because they're afraid. People who believe The Bible blame the bad things in the world on that first snake. But he was just doing what he was put there to do. He was actually pretty smart. He didn't eat that apple, did he? He didn't have to because he already knew things. People are mean to what they're afraid of but I'm not afraid of snakes. Are you, Cedra?"

I shake my head and that's a lie. But at this point would it make any difference?

Jimmy says, "I've been thinking about your cat and here's what I come up with. I don't believe he's a ghost. Things alive have this kind of energy you see, some call it God, others say it's atoms or something like that. Whatever you name it, it can't just go away all at once. If you spill a bucket of sand you don't pick up every bit, right? When I was a little kid I dropped a pail of dirt in our trailer by mistake. I was making an ant farm and my dad got so mad when I couldn't get it all cleaned up he stuck the bucket on my head, said I had to wear it for the rest of the day. 'A dummy's cap,' he said. Well, I think it's the energy of Alfred that's left in your house. He's letting you know the rest of him went on to some place better."

I study Jimmy's mouth as he speaks, the way his words roll slowly out, hesitating at those full brown lips as if even his language is not sure how it wants to be in this world. I think about what his lips would feel like against mine, and then I know I'm a sinner because not only am I not working on forgiving Pretty Jimmy, making my heart clean as a plate, I'm deliberately forgetting what he did to Heather and picturing him with me.

"So why did you do it?" I ask him. "The thing you're in here for. Could you please tell me why the hell you would do something like that? And don't say it's because your so-called friend Led Nash made you."

Jimmy stares out through the barred window at the other end of the room and I follow his eyes, green like the fields we can barely see. A crow circles, drops, black shadow without voice. Jimmy, his own voice tender, almost a whisper says, "I had a garter snake that was my friend. His name was Jim Two. My mom wouldn't let me keep him. Said we had enough mouths, but snakes can last a long time without eating, did you know? And they feel good when you touch them, not slimy like people think. They feel like something you want to hold." His green eyes lock into my eyes. "Don't you worry about no ghosts, Cedra. Soon enough, all that's left of Alfred is just the part of you that loved him."

I look at the guard standing at the door, short, a half-in mustache, not much older than me. He doesn't seem too interested in Jimmy or the other inmates with their visitors either. He keeps gazing down at his watch even though the clock would tell him just as well. A wave of voices rises and falls through the room. I lean across the table, a little closer to Jimmy. "Do you want to touch Jesus?" I ask him.

I reach into my pack slowly, pulling a few things out onto the table along with Jesus, a hair brush, a pen, the portable pack of tissues Henri sticks in sometimes when she's thinking about being my mother. I want the guard to look over and see that these things are

OK, they've been checked out, no contraband here.

I think probably Jimmy will ask me about Jesus, ask me why I have him in my pack, and then I'll tell him the truth. I'll tell him I stole Jesus from a church, and we'll be even. It won't save my mother or help Alfred's energy get to where the rest of him is any sooner, but the sudden need to speak a truth burns inside me so strong I inhale a ragged, steamy breath like breathing dry ice.

Jimmy reaches out a long fingered hand and touches Jesus's head. "I can't wait to have those snakes," he says. "Snakes get a whole different skin, did you know that? Like being born somebody new. Course I'll have to sell some of those snakes to make my living, but while they're mine I would love them. I know I could. You believe I can love them, right, Cedra?"

"Well," I say slowly, nodding my head, and suddenly I'm smiling at him like I really mean it. "I believe you, Jimmy." I place my hand on top of his and his skin settles against mine like it's supposed to be there, like all these years my hand was hanging empty, just waiting for this fit. My fingers are warm and prickly, tingling with something I haven't felt before, as if maybe I've got some of that Spirit after all. Something promising. Something you might even call hope.

ABOUT THE AUTHOR

Originally from Hawaii, Jaimee Wriston Colbert now lives in
Rockport, Maine, teaching writing and communications at the
University of Maine, Augusta, and the Maine Photographic
Workshop's Rockport College. She also teaches creative writing
for Stonecoast Writing Conference, Maine Writers and
Publishers Alliance, and at the Maine State Prison. Her first
book, *Sex, Salvation, and the Automobile*, a collection of short
fiction, won the Zephyr Publishing Prize in Fiction and was
published in 1994. Her short stories have appeared in a variety
of literary journals, including *Pacific Coast Journal, Snake
Nation Review, Tampa Review, TriQuarterly, Potato Eyes, New
Letters*, and in the anthology *Ohio Short Fiction*, and have
been broadcast over Maine Public Radio's Audio Bookshelf.